"Rosen's deftly clued, noir-tinged ⟨...⟩ line between hope and heartbreak, ⟨...⟩ ploring the role of family in our lives. This fresh take on the classic private investigator begs to be brought to the big screen."
—*Library Journal* (starred review)

"*Lavender House* is a fabulous, genre-bending mystery-noir, told with wit, panache, and style. Lev Rosen is one of a kind and just gets better and better—his eye for characters is both acerbic and compassionate, and his storytelling is top-notch."
—Dan Chaon, *New York Times* bestselling author of *Sleepwalk*

"The best kind of noir novel—steeped in the tropes of the genre but unafraid to invert, modernize, and tweak them. Sharply written, loaded with characters you can't forget and a can't-miss San Francisco setting."
—Alex Segura, acclaimed author of *Secret Identity*

"Terrific . . . A brisk, entertaining novel . . . Rosen's novel is a winning homage to old-time crime fiction."
—*San Francisco Chronicle*

"Readers who love queer history, complicated family dynamics, flawed characters, and a good murder mystery will be eager for more. Perfect for fans of *Knives Out, Lavender House* is a queer, mid-century take on the family-centric murder mystery showcasing Lev AC Rosen's masterful character development."
—Shelf Awareness

"This book's real pleasure lies in the richly realized portrayal of its cast and their personal struggles. Rosen puts a welcome gay spin on the traditional country-house whodunit."
—*Publishers Weekly*

ALSO BY LEV AC ROSEN

Depth
All Men of Genius
The Bell in the Fog

FOR YOUNG ADULTS, AS L.C. ROSEN
Camp
Jack of Hearts (and Other Parts)

FOR CHILDREN

The Memory Wall
Woundabout (with Ellis Rosen)

LEV AC ROSEN

LAVENDER HOUSE

TOR PUBLISHING GROUP

NEW YORK

LAVENDER HOUSE

Copyright © 2022 by Lev AC Rosen

A Forge Book
Published by Tom Doherty Associates / Tor Publishing Group
120 Broadway
New York, NY 10271

www.tor-forge.com

Forge® is a registered trademark of Macmillan Publishing Group, LLC.

The Library of Congress has cataloged the hardcover edition as follows:

Names: Rosen, Lev AC, author.
Title: Lavender House / Lev AC Rosen.
Description: First edition. | New York : Forge, 2022. | "A Tom Doherty Associates book."
Identifiers: LCCN 2022019892 (print) | LCCN 2022019893 (ebook) | ISBN 9781250834225 (hardcover) | ISBN 9781250834232 (ebook)
Subjects: LCGFT: Novels.
Classification: LCC PS3618.O83149 L38 2022 (print) | LCC PS3618.O83149 (ebook) | DDC 813/.6—dc23/eng/20220425
LC record available at https://lccn.loc.gov/2022019892
LC ebook record available at https://lccn.loc.gov/2022019893

ISBN 978-1-250-83424-9 (trade paperback)

Our books may be purchased in bulk for promotional, educational, or business use. Please contact your local bookseller or the Macmillan Corporate and Premium Sales Department at 1-800-221-7945, extension 5442, or by email at MacmillanSpecialMarkets@macmillan.com.

First Forge Paperback Edition: 2023

Printed in the United States of America

0 9 8 7 6 5

For Aunt Goldy,

who could absolutely get away with murder.

Maybe she already has.

LAVENDER HOUSE

ONE

I thought I'd have the place all to myself, this early. Like church on a Tuesday—no one but you and God—or in my case, the bartender. But there's a guy and girl, high school kids or maybe just twenty, sitting at one of the booths in the back. They're trying to keep their voices low, but he's failing, getting angry. Something about wiener dogs. It's weird the things people fight over.

He pounds the table and she whimpers a little. I sigh, feel my body shifting to get up. I don't have to do this anymore. Hell, no one even wants me to. That's why I was fired. But some habits you can't break. So I down what's left of my martini, motion the bartender to pour another, and stand up and go to the back of the place, where he's holding her wrist, tight. Her arm is stretching like a shoelace as she tries to stand up, but he won't let go. On her other wrist, she's wearing a charm bracelet. Just a few charms: An eagle, that's a mascot for one of the local schools, with "1950" under it, so she graduated two years ago. A book, so she's a reader. A wiener dog, for her pet, I'm guessing, and the source of the argument. And an apple. Teacher's favorite, or she just really likes apples, maybe. Not enough life lived for many charms. Not enough to cover the bruise, either.

"I think the lady wants to go," I tell him. I've had enough to drink that I sound like a two-bit tough guy. Maybe I am a two-bit tough guy.

"Mind your own business, pal," he says. He talks like he's seen too many mobster movies. Or maybe he's just trying to match me.

"Miss, you want to leave?" I ask her, looking past him.

"Hey, hey, mister, don't ignore me," the kid says. I keep my eyes on the girl.

She nods, but doesn't say anything, so I reach out and I pull back his finger from her wrist, hard. He yelps in pain but she gets loose and runs out of the bar, the little bell on the door jingling as it closes behind her.

"It's too early for this, fellas," the bartender says, the words coming out of him in one long sigh.

"I was just helping the lady," I say, turning my back on the kid, walking back to the bar. I know he's going to come up behind me, so I wait till I feel him, then spin and catch the fist as it connects with my shoulder. Not that hard. Just enough I wheeze a little, which makes him smile, like he's won some-thing. I don't like that smile. Reminds me too much of the mirror. So I grab his wrist and yank his arm back.

"Hey, hey," the kid says, "fuck you."

He swings with his other fist, so I catch that one, too, and turn him around, holding his arms behind him.

"You can't do this!" the kid says. He looks over at the bar-tender, who keeps his eyes on the glasses in front of him. The kid stares as I march him to the door and then turns his head around to look at me. "You're drinking martinis? This early? That's cool, man. I can buy you one. We can talk this out."

I roll my eyes, kick the door open, and push him out of it, onto the ground. He goes face first, but I know he'll just have a scrape. I've done this enough—before. Sometimes it makes me feel better, helping, like I've done some good in the world. Not today, though. Probably for the best. Might make me reconsider my plans.

He stares at me, the sun beating down on him and the concrete, like he's waiting for me to say something.

"Don't be rude to women," I announce, loud enough someone across the street looks over. It's the best I've got. I hiccup. Then I grin, 'cause I'm pretty drunk and I still managed to toss him out. And because I have another martini waiting for me.

"Screw you," he says, getting back up, but it sounds weak and he knows it. I turn around and bounce off the glass door of the bar, which has closed behind me. There goes my heroic exit. The kid starts laughing, but I step back, rub my nose, and turn the handle, walking back in, the kid still cackling behind me.

I take my seat and drink the new martini in front of me in one swallow. The bartender looks at me like I'm the sorriest sight in San Francisco, and maybe he's right, but I try not to let it show. I lift my chin and order another, keeping my voice even, proud. I'm proud to be in this bar at 2 p.m. on a Monday. I'm proud to have thrown some kid out on the street, even though it's not my job anymore. Hell, I'm proud to be jobless, blacklisted. I'm proud to have just ordered my fifth drink. I'm probably not fooling anyone, but I can try. He mixes it for me turned away, and if he makes a face, I can't see it. And with the kids gone, no one else is around to judge. I tap my fingers slowly on the bar. I'm patient. I have all day—that's the plan: drink all day so when it's dark, and no one will notice, I'll be drunk enough to pitch myself into the bay.

I like the bay for it. It's how Jan Westman was found. I remember looking at her on the shore of Stinson Beach, when we still thought it was just a case of a drunk falling into the bay. She looked peaceful. She hadn't been in the water more than a night. Her skin was pale, a little blue, her eyes closed by the old man who found her and called in the local police, who called us after finding her ID. He'd folded her arms over her chest, too, and Lou said it was morbid, but I thought she looked relaxed, at ease with what had happened. I was actually surprised when her blood came back sober and we had to look at it as murder, and then when we caught the guy and found out what had been done to her. If a night in the water can wash away trauma, make a body like hers look serene, I think it can at least do it halfway for me.

When the door of the bar opens, it rattles me out of the memory, and I'm staring at my drink again, Patti Page singing "Tennessee Waltz" from the radio, her voice soft with static. I have the record of this one. I almost wonder what will happen to it, after, but then the martini slides that thought away.

I don't even bother glancing up to see who's come in until she sits down next to me. Her lips are painted bright red. She's wearing a yellow skirt that cuts at the calf and a matching jacket decorated with a circular black-stoned brooch. Perched on her short, dark (surely dyed at her age) hair is a small hat with a small pin in it of an overlapping "WAC"—the Women's Athletic Club. Her style is dated, but very high society. I've seen plenty of women like her, their money protecting them from the change they fear so badly, like a suit made of gold foil.

She lights her cigarette, perched in a holder, and asks the bartender for a Manhattan. She has a deep, sharp voice, and it cuts through the fog of drunkenness in my mind. She's right out of a movie—she could ask me to kill her husband any second now. She swivels on the stool next to mine, and I have half a mind to tell her she's barking up the wrong tree—why not? But when I look up, she's not making eyes at me. Not like that, anyway. She looks at me like she feels sorry for me, a baby bird fallen from the nest. Well, screw her. I might be over, as far as lives go, but I'm nothing to feel sorry for. I'm doing this on my terms.

I smile at her, hoping she'll stop looking at me like that. That works sometimes—I'm a good-looking guy and a smile makes people feel at ease. But since the day before yesterday my smiles haven't fit right, and this one is no different. She's not impressed by it. But I can tell that's not my fault. She's not impressed by much, this woman. So I turn away, prepared to ignore her outright. But then.

"Evander Mills?" she asks as the bartender puts her Manhattan down in front of her. She says it like it's a question she already knows the answer to. I get the impression that's the only kind she asks.

"How do you know my name?" I try not to let the alcohol slur my words.

She sips her drink, then takes the cherry out and sets it on the bar, staring at it like it owes her money and isn't the one bit of sweetness in her drink.

"I know why you were fired from the police force," she says, eyes still on the cherry.

And just like that, whatever traces of the martinis that were left in me vanish in a shiver of ice and the acrid smell of her cigarette smoke. I stand up, because otherwise I'd fall off my stool. I don't look at her. I fumble in my coat for my wallet and take it out, ready to settle, but she rests a gloved hand on my arm and squeezes.

"Relax," she says. "It's a selling point with me."

I stop fumbling and stare at her hand on my arm. She drops it, but lifts her chin and now she's smiling at me. Her smile fits. It's like the ones I get and give in the Black Cat sometimes. Not the smile that's an invitation, but the one that says, "I know you, we're safe here, we're home." Even if they never worked on me, not like they were supposed to, I know those smiles.

"Oh," I say.

Her eyes are shot with strands of red, not the kind from exhaustion or reefer. The kind from crying for days. She's wearing concealer, but nothing can hide eyes like that except sunglasses.

She glances at the bartender, who, having nothing else to do, is watching us, seeing how this will play out. Then she turns to me and takes a money clip out of the black purse she's put on the bar and throws down enough cash for both of us.

"Let's go sit over there," she says, grabbing her drink and motioning with her chin at the booth farthest from the bar. I pick up my drink and follow her as she walks over, then sit down opposite her. The cheap leather squeaks under me. This is the same booth the kids were in. It still smells like the girl's perfume, too sweet.

"I know you need work. I might have a job for you." She says it softly, so the bartender can't hear—that sort of job. The booth we're in is in the corner and light from the big windows shines in, making me squint. It's hard to read her with her back to the light like that.

"What kind?" I sip my drink.

"The kind like you used to do for the police. The inspector kind." She takes a long drag of her cigarette. "You were good, right?"

"Yeah," I say. My chest gets warm with pride or arrogance or alcohol, I'm not sure which, then it gets cold again real fast, when I remember that that part of my life is over. "But look, I don't want people to think that I—" That I'm queer, I almost say. Though, of course, I am. And everyone knows it now. Or at least, everyone on the police force, which is enough.

"No one will think anything," she says briskly. "No one will say anything. That's the whole point of a private detective, isn't it? Privacy. And besides, I'm not someone people would know in that sense."

I sip again. I've never worked freelance before, but this could be good. This could be something worth hanging around for. Money. Go out with a bang—a few more nights at the Black Cat, or maybe even the Oak Room or the Ruby, fanning out cash and boys flocking around me before I'm back to waiting for sundown and a dark part of the bay to wash myself off the world. I suddenly realize I want that so bad I can taste it, smell it—lips, breath on my neck, tinged with whisky. One more night. A kiss goodbye.

A chance to help someone again, too. I don't think about that part, though. I just open my mouth.

"All right, so what's the case?"

She swirls the last of her drink in the glass. "What made you good at it? Being an inspector?"

"I like helping people."

She raises an eyebrow. "That wouldn't make you good at it."

I smile, but I can feel it looks sad, so I take it off. "Crimes are about secrets," I tell her. "And I have enough experience keeping secrets I'm very good at finding them." I pause. A bitter laugh spits out of me. "At least, I thought I was."

She nods. "How did you end up getting caught, then?" she asks. "If you were so good at it."

I look down at the table. Formica winks back up. Lou was out sick. He usually told me what club they were hitting—not 'cause he knew about me, but because I asked every couple of weeks, and he thought it was just us chatting like partners do. "I had a system," I tell her. "It was flawed." Flawed 'cause I asked Jim instead, forgetting he was an idiot, trusting him not to get it wrong. Since the judge ruled that gay people could gather and be served, the bars weren't illegal, not exactly. But if you found "immoral" goings-on, that was enough to shut them down. Immoral like kissing, like touching, like—"And I really wanted . . ." I stop. She reaches out and puts her hand over mine.

"I know," she says. "We all make mistakes when we want something."

"Still. I wish it had been a different kind of mistake." I remember Jim kicking open the door to the bathroom, chuckling, saying loudly he needed to check it was clean. Making everyone feel uncomfortable—that was the goal. When the door opened I was on my knees, already trying to scramble up. We were paraded out in cuffs before we could zip up our flies. The bartender claiming he had no idea, the female impersonator on stage sighing loudly, the other patrons shooting us looks—pity, anger, amusement. The bar got fined, but not shut down, at least.

"Did you tell everyone else?" she asks.

I feel a cold drop of ice in my blood. "About what?" I look back up at her.

"The police, when they were coming. Your system. Did you warn people?"

I wait too long, long enough it may as well be an answer, so I move on. "You said you had a case?" I ask her.

She pulls her hand away. There's a moment where we look at each other, so quiet we can hear each other breathing. I know what she's thinking, but I don't answer the question she doesn't ask: Why not? Because the answers are selfish, arrogant: I was too worried about myself to think of anyone else. Their own fault for not looking out for themselves. Other queers aren't my responsibility anyway. I wouldn't tell her the truth: that we're all alone in this world, and it never occurred to me to pretend like we weren't.

"Murder," she says suddenly, in the same hard tone she used to order her drink, which she now lifts and finishes in one swallow. "You've solved those before, right?"

"Sure," I say. "Plenty. This is someone close to you? The one you've been crying over?"

She frowns and touches at the corner of her eye with her thumb, pulling at the skin a little. "I thought I'd hid it," she says.

I shake my head. "Sorry for your loss."

"Thank you. It was my . . ." She glances up again, looks behind me. I turn to see—the bartender is still watching us. "Maybe we should drive. You're interested in the job?"

"Yeah," I say, licking the inside of my mouth. "Interested. But I don't even know your name."

She smiles, and then throws back her head in a loud laugh. "I haven't said it, have I?" She extends her hand. "I'm Pearl Velez."

Her grip is as hard as her voice. She smirks as we shake.

"And you were about to say—the victim?"

"Irene . . ." she says. Then glances at the bartender again.

She stands up, tossing her cigarette into the glass. "But let's talk more about that on the way."

I down what's left of my drink and follow her outside to where one of those new Packard Mayfair convertibles is waiting. It's dark red with black leather interior and the top is down. She opens her door and slips in and when I stare, she reaches over and pops open the passenger door for me. I get in and before I even close the door, she's burning rubber, reaching into the glove compartment for a pair of sunglasses with her eyes still on the road. The radio is already on, Rosemary Clooney singing "Mixed Emotions." Pearl drives fast, confident, wild. She swerves around anyone obeying the speed limit and throttles the gears to climb over the hills, heading west, zipping over the Golden Gate Bridge. Some mist still lingers over the water, but the sun is bright enough I squint and slump in my seat, holding on to the door handle so I don't fly away. Once we're over the bridge, she really lets it out, moving so fast I can feel the wind pressing itself into my mouth and nose, like water blasting through my brain to clean the drunkenness out.

"So where are we going, Pearl?" I have to shout to be heard over the wind in our faces.

"We're going to our home. Irene's home. Her full name was Irene Lamontaine, and she was my wife."

The wind is loud, so for a moment I think I didn't hear her right.

"Your what?" I ask.

She smiles without looking at me, and I can't quite read her expression behind the sunglasses, but I think it's amused, like this is the sort of thing she has to repeat a lot. "My wife."

I lean back. Even in the clubs and bars, no woman calls another woman her wife, at least not as loudly as Pearl is. They whisper it, or say it as a joke, or defensively, trying to start a fight. No one says it like Pearl just did, like it's the most normal thing in the world.

"Come on, Mr. Mills," she says, still smiling. "Surely my loving a woman isn't enough to shock you."

"Only that you'd say it out loud like that." I try to keep my voice casual.

"Where we're going, we say everything out loud," she responds, her voice a growl imitating the engine.

"Then why do you need me?" I ask.

She doesn't answer—I'm not sure if she heard me. The wind pulls through her hair, makes it flutter, and she speeds the car up just a bit. Around us, San Francisco has faded away into a stretch of the 101. The water is to our right, past some open fields. The light is cold and yellow.

"So everyone there . . . ?" I let the question hang.

"Yes," she says. "We're all queer. It's why we don't want the police around."

I lean back in the seat. Sure, I've been around queers in groups before. The Black Cat, the Beige Room, Mona's, plenty of places in the city, and I've been to most of them. But those are for the night. Those are for lingering looks and meetings in the bathroom, dancing sometimes, flirting, and always looking out for the cops, for a blackmailer, for something that would force you back out onto the street, into the real world, where no one would look at you the same if they knew. You'd be unemployable, except at some low-wage bar gig back in one of those clubs. Friendless, aside from the others like you. A whole other life you didn't choose—or the other option. My option, before Pearl sat down next to me.

But shacking up? Friends? Family? We don't get to do that,

unless we're very careful, or have nothing left in the real world, are already cast out. Not someone like Pearl.

"You're smiling," she says. I realize she's right. "Why?"

"I guess, it's just, two days ago, I would have told you to turn the car around."

"And now?" she asks.

"Now . . ." I laugh. None of the guys I'd worked with for the past ten years, guys I'd called friends, who I thought would have taken a bullet for me—none of them would even look at me as they led me from lockup to the chief's office. Even he wouldn't meet my eye as he told me I was done. Conduct unbecoming, perversion, lewd acts. They said they wouldn't lock me up, though. That was their one token for my years of service. They'd just let everyone know what I was and what they'd found me doing and my life in the real world would be over.

"Now," I say, "what do I have to lose?"

TWO

The fields become trees after we leave the highway, still heading west, redwoods shooting up like prison bars all around us, becoming so dark and thick the sun is blocked out and I don't even see the turnoff before she takes it. We screech to a sudden halt in front of a pair of modern-looking gates.

"Would you mind?" Pearl asks, nodding at the gates. "Just push them open and closed. I'll send someone to lock them up later."

I step out of the car and walk up to the gate, my legs still a little wobbly under me from the booze. We haven't spoken much since the bridge, the wind was so loud I didn't want to bother asking questions I'd have to repeat. Instead I pictured what kind of place we might be headed to. I thought maybe some farm, or a little apartment in one of the towns up here. Pearl smelled like money, but I underestimated her, because this is not what I expected. The gates are at least twice as tall as me, wrought iron, a big gilded "L" on the front that looks familiar. They look heavy, but swing open easily.

The air has a smell, I realize. Not just the trees. More than that, something herbal and floral, but not just some wildflow-ers or a planter of tulips. Beyond the gate are more trees and a hill, so I can't see much. Pearl drives through and I close the gate behind her then step back into the car.

"What's that smell?" I ask.

"The flowers," she says. "Irene always liked having all the flowers around to pick new scents. Lavender was her favorite, though, so we grow that everywhere. That's why we call this place Lavender House." She pulls the car forward and laughs, deep and throaty. "Well, and for the other reason."

We crest the hill and the trees stop suddenly, showing the estate—a huge swath of land, entirely walled in, and redwoods all around the walls, lined up like soldiers. Completely sealed off, hidden. Standing in the center of it all is a large art deco house with a domed roof in the middle, and two wings curv-ing around a white gravel roundabout, which itself is curved around a fountain. Spreading out from the mansion are fields of flowers. Pink, white, pale blue, yellow, green, but lavender is the one I see the most of, lining pathways and racing like veins through the other plants. All the blossoms stand tall and sway a little, soft and pale, and they almost seem to ripple, like rivers spreading out from the main house.

"Scents," I say. "Lamontaine—like the soap?"

"Exactly," Pearl says.

I let out a low whistle. That's big money, then. A family company, they call themselves in the radio ads. Probably would ruin them if anyone knew what kind of family.

We drive forward and she pulls the car up in the round-about behind three other cars of different makes and colors. On either side of the house are a few narrow trees that burst into large pink blossoms at the top. The fountain in the center of the roundabout, I notice, is scorched at the top, black, but still functioning, water pouring over the dark spot like a wavering shadow.

I look up at the house, closer now. The brick is white, but the metal is pale purple. It's three stories, plus the domed roof, with huge curved windows that remind me a little of flowers. At the top of the west wing, I see a curtain pull aside and a shadow stare down at us. I wonder how expected I am—if Pearl brought me here on her own, or by committee.

"I guess Elsie's not here," Pearl says, looking at the cars. She shuts off the motor and gets out, stretching her arms above her head. "You'll have to talk to her later."

She moves for the house but stops after a few steps, and turns slowly, looking at me, where I still sit in the passenger seat. "Coming?"

"I have a few questions first," I say, slowly opening the door and stepping out. She puts her hands on her hips and gives me one quick nod. She's impatient but needs me. "So, Irene Lamontaine is dead, and you're her wife?"

"I told you that already."

"When did she die?"

"About three weeks ago," Pearl says. She looks at one of the windows on the ground floor. The curtain there moves a little. Bringing me here was definitely *just* Pearl's idea.

"And you only hired me now?" I ask.

"You weren't available until the day before last, and I didn't hear about that until this morning," Pearl says, crossing her arms. "Before that, I was looking for someone we could trust to let in. You're someone we can trust."

I nod. "All right. But before we go in, you need to explain the situation. Who lives here?"

She turns and walks toward the front door, and I follow. "Myself and Irene. Our son—Irene's, technically, though we raised him together—Henry. We're lucky enough that he also turned out to be less traditional in his wants."

"Lucky?" I ask. The word feels like a slap. "That's not what I'd call it."

Pearl nods, frowning a little. "Perhaps it was selfish, but we were happy. He has a longtime companion, Cliff, who lives here and poses as his social secretary when required. When Henry took over managing the soap company, Irene insisted he marry, for appearances. Lamontaine Soap is a family company. We sell to happy housewives and the like—and bachelors make housewives nervous. So we found him a wife—Margo. She has girlfriends, but appreciates the importance of maintaining appearances. Right now she's seeing a girl named Elsie. Everyone, of course, is very discreet outside the house." She frowns a little. "Oh, and Margo's mother lives with us too. Alice. She's the only one who isn't . . . like us."

We reach the door just as Pearl finishes talking, and she glances up, quickly, at the third-floor window where I'd seen someone watching us.

"But she knows," I say.

"Of course," Pearl says, turning the knob and opening the door. "That's the point of our home. No secrets."

I try not to laugh at that. "What about the help?" I ask.

"Yes. Three." She lingers, not walking inside yet.

"How do you keep them from gossiping if there are no secrets?"

"The staff are very well paid—they wouldn't risk their jobs for a quick payday to some gossip rag."

"That's quite an assumption. Lamontaine is a big business."

"Most of them are happy to have a place to be themselves, as well. Our gardener, Judy, shares a room with our cook, Dot. Our butler, Mr. Kelly, was the one who told me about you—he enjoys visiting the clubs on his nights off. We're very careful about who we let in through the gate."

I nod, and Pearl goes inside, me following. We're standing in a foyer: white marble floor, dark purple carpeted stairs that lead up to a landing, then split, twisting back up above us in both directions. A huge portrait of a woman hangs at the landing, and standing under it feels like being in the shadow of a mountain, like it takes up the entire horizon.

The woman in the portrait is about fifty, with flaming red hair falling to her shoulders in gentle curls. You can tell from her expression that the painter wanted to make her seem sweet, but she wouldn't let him. Instead, they reached a compromise: she looks severe, but amused. Superior, deigning to look you in the eye as long you know to look away immediately. Her black satin dress exposes her collarbones before rising higher at the shoulders with pleated, bat-like wings. Going down, it hugs her torso, then hangs straight. Her ears gleam with diamonds that match her ring and bracelet. From all that, she's not the kind of woman I think of as surrounding herself with flowers, but as if to contradict me, around her, in the background, otherwise black, are baskets of flowers—roses, lavender, violets, sunflowers, and others I don't know the names of, all cut and laid out as if in some Victorian stall.

"That's Irene," Pearl says, a slight tremor in her voice.

"Looks like a witch there, doesn't she?" asks a young man sitting just below the portrait on the landing. I hadn't noticed him before—the painting dominated everything—but I take him in now: in his twenties, with wide shoulders, a trim waist, and thick legs. He's wearing a peach-colored shirt with no tie or jacket, and his dark hair is parted down the side, but that doesn't tame the curls. He's handsome, and when he smirks at me, I feel a familiar tug. I can tell he sees me feeling it, because he smiles now, the kind of smile I know. He rises, slowly, eyes on me. Then I realize what he just said, and glance over at Pearl, expecting some anger, but she just stares down at her hands as she tugs her gloves off.

"Don't talk about her that way, Cliff, please," Pearl says, the conversation already exhausting her, they've had it so many times. Cliff turns away from me at her voice, his smile falling back into a look of boredom.

"I'm not trying to be mean," Cliff says, standing and walking slowly down the stairs. "I just mean the painting. She looks like she's making a potion, not selling soap." He reaches the bottom of the landing and walks close to me, so close I can feel his warm breath on my face and smell the gin on it. "So you're the private dick?"

"Evander Mills," I say, extending my hand, trying to ignore the innuendo. He smiles and takes it, his fingers circling the inside of my palm as we shake. It's like being back in one of the bars. The flirting, the gin. Like he's brought the feeling of the Black Cat into this mansion in the woods. It's comforting, that feeling, and arousing. Or maybe that's just him.

"Cliff Carbury," he says, turning away. "I'm the . . ." He pauses.

"He's Henry's boyfriend. Our son-in-law, nearly," Pearl says.

"*Nearly*," Cliff repeats, sneering slightly. If Pearl notices, she doesn't act like it.

On either side of the foyer are large doors, one of which Cliff pushes open. Beyond it is what looks to be a sitting room, in a modern style, done almost entirely in white. Pearl follows him, and I follow her. The sitting room is bright, with a glass table in the center and pale gray sofas and armchairs arranged in a group on the white carpet. A black vase of lavender sits in the center of the table. Against the wall is a large standing record player and radio. An Admiral, can't be more than a year or two old. High-end one, the kind I'd love to have but could never afford. Across the room, with a few chairs around it, is a new television set. The room feels like a museum, but without any art on display, like something is missing, or waiting.

To one side of the television, a blond woman, maybe in her early thirties, sits in a small chair, talking into a phone, an issue of *Vogue* open facedown in her lap.

"Yes," she says in a near whisper. "I'm telling you, she's done it. He's here. You'd better hurry back." She pauses. "No." She pauses again and sighs. "Fine. Before dinner."

As she speaks, Cliff sits down on one of the sofas and tilts his head back to look at the ceiling. He fishes a cigarette case out of his pants pocket, takes out a cigarette, and puts it between his lips, then snaps the case shut and looks at me. "You don't have a light, do you?" he asks, his voice slightly muffled from keeping his lips clamped around the cigarette.

The blonde hangs up the phone, stands, and puts the magazine down on the table, smiling at us in a way so practiced she may as well be posing for photos. She probably does, for the society pages. I think I've even seen a few. Her dress is white but patterned with pink and yellow flowers and cut very fashionably, with exposed shoulders, tight waist, and skirt that ends below the knee. She wears one of those wide belts that all the rich ladies are wearing now, in pale pink. Her hair ends just below her jaw and has been curled to look effortlessly sweet, but has started to straighten out from the slight pull she gives it as she tucks it behind her ears, as she does now.

"You have matches in your cigarette case, Cliff," she says without looking at him. "Hello. I'm Margo Lamontaine," she says, extending her hand. "And you are?"

"Evander Mills," I say, shaking.

"I've asked Evander to investigate Irene's murder," Pearl says.

Margo nods, her mouth pursed. "Pearl, I know this is hard for you—"

"Don't start," Pearl interrupts. "I've hired him, and I've already told him everything."

From the sofa, Cliff barks a laugh. Margo's expression shifts from welcoming to examining, an eyebrow raising, her green eyes going sharp.

"Everything?" she asks. Her voice sounds ready to run, or maybe fight.

"Don't worry, dear," Pearl says, placing a hand on Margo's arm. "He's one of us."

"I could've told you that," Cliff says. He's fished out his own matches and strikes one, lighting his cigarette. The faint floral smell I'd grown so used to I'd stopped noticing it becomes pronounced again as it mingles with the tobacco.

"One of us doesn't mean he won't march right to the papers for a payday anyway," Margo says, dropping her pleasant smile and attempt at a welcoming demeanor. Without the veneer, her picture of the perfect wife and hostess, already frayed at the edges, comes undone, and she suddenly looks strange in that dress, with that hair, a costume she's trying to shrug off after a long night on stage. I get the impression this Margo, the real Margo, would never be caught dead wearing flowers. She marches over to Cliff, extending a hand. Sighing, he hands her his cigarette and then takes out another and lights it. Margo inhales deeply and then blows smoke out her nose, her eyes closed. I grin at the juxtaposition—perfect society wife gone bad—but try not to show it. "Really, Pearl, we talked this over and thought it was a bad idea."

"*You* did!" Pearl says. "*You* thought it was a bad idea! But Irene was . . ." Pearl takes off her hat and stares down into it, circling the hat in her hands. "I know she was sometimes a dragon to you. But she was my wife, Margo. She was my everything. You understand that, don't you?"

"Not really," Margo says. "I have a *husband*." She practically hisses the last word. That's two of them upset about the arranged marriage now. Strange, if it's just for show.

"Only technically," Pearl says. "Imagine if Elsie was pushed over a railing and left to die. Wouldn't you want her killer brought to justice?"

Margo's eyes flick to my face at the mention of the name Elsie, then back to Pearl. "So you really told him everything, didn't you?" She inhales again, then holds the cigarette away from her mouth and looks me over. Her free arm she crosses over her chest. She seems unimpressed by everything around her, the sort who thought they were climbing to a pile of gold and then looked around one day and realized it was trash.

"So, Evander Mills," she asks, blowing smoke, "what's your résumé? Or did Pearl just pick out the least drunk-looking fairy from the docks?"

"I was an inspector for the SFPD until two days ago," I say, lifting my chin up. I'm proud of that. Was proud of it.

She tilts her head, looking slightly impressed. "What happened two days ago?"

"I was caught in the bathroom of the Black Cat," I say.

"Caught?" Cliff asks, smiling at me. "Doing what?"

"Things men do in the bathroom of the Black Cat," I say. He grins, like he's about to ask for more detail, but Margo speaks first and I tear my eyes away from his lips.

"You should have gone to the Ruby," Margo says. "No police there."

"I'll remember that for next time."

"And how long have you been an inspector?" she asks, looking me up and down. "You can't be older than thirty."

"Thirty-two. I've been an inspector three years. I was a beat cop three years before that." I keep my tone neutral. It's a job interview.

"Since forty-five. So you came right out of the military?" she asks.

"Navy. I was stationed here, on a minesweeper escorting ships to and from Pearl Harbor."

"I bet you looked good in the uniform," Cliff says.

"Enlisted or drafted?" Margo asks, ignoring him.

"Enlisted."

"And before that?"

"I worked for my dad in L.A."

"Doing?" She taps her cigarette over the ashtray.

"He was an insurance investigator."

"Why not go back to work for him?"

"He's dead. And I liked it here."

"Because of the thriving nightlife?" Cliff asks.

"Something like that." More the variety of it—more clubs meant if I went to a different one each night, the chances of me getting caught in a raid were slimmer.

"I wasn't here during the war," Cliff says, "but I'll bet it was a delight. The army everywhere was practically an orgy every night. Throw in all the civilians in town . . ." He grins. "I was USO myself. A dancer in the shows." He kicks high from where he's sitting.

"Honestly, you're like a cat in heat," Margo says.

"I haven't left the house in weeks," Cliff responds quickly. "Let a girl have some fun."

"Will that do?" Pearl asks, putting her hands up to stop them. "Does he meet your standards, Margo?"

Margo leans back, sitting on the arm of the sofa, and inhales on her cigarette, then blows the smoke out in a perfect circle at me, framing her face like a locket. "Tell me this, Inspector Mills—they moved the body. Pearl has kept the crime scene locked up, untouched since the police left, but the body is gone. We buried her two weeks ago. Are you going to dig her up to inspect her?"

"Of course not," Pearl says. "He'll get the coroner's report from the police."

"Ahhh." Margo waves her cigarette. "Is that what you'll do, Inspector?"

I look down at my feet. "I can ask them," I say.

"And they'll talk to you? After catching you . . . doing the things men do in the bathroom of the Black Cat?"

Pearl turns to me, and I can feel the job being pulled out from under my feet. "I have a few friends who might help me out," I lie.

"But they know who you are," Margo says, inhaling again. "They know *what* you are, and they'll know you're working our case, and then they might just wonder. Why would *they* hire someone like *him*?" She inhales on her cigarette again, blows another smoke ring, this time at Pearl. The way she drew out the "like him" makes me shiver, but I manage to hide it. "You see the trouble?"

"Oh, that's no trouble," Pearl says. "I'll say he's a friend of the family—we're giving him charity, that sort of thing. What's your mother's name, Evander?"

"Mary," I say. Cliff snorts a laugh from the couch.

"Fine, then Mary and I were old friends. From L.A., you said? So, pen pals, then. Met during a trip. I told her I'd keep an eye out for you when you moved up here. You were drunk, drugged maybe—you know how those people are."

"Us people, you mean," Cliff says.

"And it's such a shame what happened," Pearl continues, ignoring him. She tilts her head and her expression locks into place—she's telling a story to someone now, covering up. She's practiced in this, I can tell—she probably does it a lot. "Maybe I can even get you your job back."

I rub the back of my neck. I don't know if it'll work, but being here, among these people, a last night out before I throw myself in the water, the way Cliff looks at me—I want all that. I don't want it to end, not just yet. "I guess it could work," I say.

"See, Margo?" Pearl says, chin out, triumphant. "You only see problems. I see solutions."

Margo gives Pearl a smile nastier than most glares. "Whatever you say, Pearl." She stands and leaves the room.

Pearl turns to me. "She's just a little anxious about being discovered, you know. We all are. But I know we can trust you, can't we, Evander?"

"Of course." I'm not sure what else I can say.

"Cliff, can you ask Mr. Kelly to set up the guest room for Evander? I'm going to show him the library."

"Sure," Cliff says, not moving.

"I don't know if I need to stay the night," I say. If it was murder, then spending the night in the same house as the murderer I'm trying to catch seems like a good way to end up the next victim.

"You do," Pearl says, already walking across the sitting room. I follow her. "Henry won't be home until after work, and who knows when Elsie will turn up."

"Still—" I say, feeling like I should protest.

"Where will you go, Evander?" Pearl asks with an embarrassed chuckle, like I've put her on the spot making her ask me. "I tried your apartment first when I went looking for you. Your landlord kicked you out after your old colleagues told him about you. You're staying where? A hotel?"

I nod, feeling my skin grow warmer.

"It's nothing to be ashamed of," she says. "But we're cheaper than a hotel, and it'll help you with the case. Don't fuss. Besides, I drove you, and I won't be driving you back until tomorrow. If you even want me to then." She pauses, looks at the floor then back up at me. "I try to help our kind when I can. Maybe, when this is all done, I really can find you some work. We might need someone to oversee security on the estate . . . but let's worry about that later."

She smiles as she opens the door at the far side of the room. Beyond it is another marble-tiled hallway. I follow her, trying to figure out where we must be. The west wing, I think, though after a few turns, I'm not sure. We go down a narrow staircase, and she takes a key out of her pocket and unlocks the door at the bottom. "They took the body away," she says without opening it. "I've kept everything else as it was." She pulls the door open, then steps aside. "I don't want to go in. I hope you understand. The lights are just on your right."

"Sure," I say. I stop in the doorway and look at her. She looks nervous.

"You know, for a widow, this isn't what I'd expect."

"Excuse me?" she asks, without looking up. Her voice wavers.

"I mean, you've been calm and collected this whole time, cheerful even. You've been crying, sure, but . . . were you fighting with her, Pearl? How was your"—I pause, letting the word settle on my tongue before speaking it—"marriage?" It's pushing it, I know, asking her up front like this, especially when she just hired me. But this is how I started most cases on the force—test the loved ones.

She breathes in through her nose loudly enough for me to hear it and then looks up at me. The light is dim, but her eyes flash. Her spine has gone straight.

"It was a marriage. It had its ups and downs. But I loved her."

I let that hang there, seeing if she'll say more. She takes a step closer.

"I have lived like this for three weeks not knowing what's happened," she says, her voice a whisper. "I dealt with police who didn't care and didn't think I had any rights when it came to her . . ." She looks up, her hands move to her hips. "I'm furious. I'm so angry it makes me want to cry. To take to bed and put myself under the sheets and scream until I have no voice. But I can't. You of all people should know I can't. If I tell anyone what she means to me . . . meant to me . . . no, means." She makes a fist and slams it against the wall. "I've never been able to tell anyone what we are to each other. And I can't now that she's gone. Because then people will wonder about our relationship, about the way Henry was raised, and then about Henry . . ." She sighs. I realize she's using her fist on the wall to prop herself up. "I am not calm. I am angry, and sad . . . but

I am doing what I always do—pretending. It's muscle memory. It's all I have . . . Call me cold if it makes you feel superior, Mr. Mills. But it's the last thing I am."

I nod. If that was a performance, it was a good one—I believe she's really hurt. Really angry, too. "It's just something I had to ask," I say. "See your reaction."

She leans back against the wall, rolls her eyes, then wipes at the edges of them with her thumb. "Just part of the routine?" she asks, dryly. "Wonderful. We all have our own muscle memories, I suppose."

"I'm going to follow the clues wherever they go," I tell her. "If it was a murder." On the force, that's what I would have done. Just followed the clues, found the killer, brought them to justice. Here, I realize, I'm supposed to bring them to Pearl.

She pauses, I think realizing the same thing. I wonder where her rage will go if it is a murder, if I do find out who did it—if it's one of her family.

"Fine." She crosses her arms. "That's what I'm paying you for."

"If I don't think this was murder, though, I can't help you. I'm not going to take your money if I don't think there's a case."

"Very noble of you."

"Look, you want me to do this job, I'm going to do it right," I tell her.

We lock eyes, then she nods.

"What kind of library is downstairs, anyway?" I ask, walking in and feeling for a light. It's chilly inside.

"Soap," Pearl says from outside. "I'm sorry, I really have to . . ." I hear footsteps clicking away, back up the stairs, and the door swings shut behind me, leaving me alone in the dark.

THREE

I find the light after a few breathless seconds. It clicks on with a buzz, and suddenly the whole room—the library, they'd called it—is laid out in front of me. I'm standing on a dark wooden balcony with a wrought iron railing. There's a spiral staircase on the other side of the balcony, leading down to the lower level, which I can survey from up here, like a sailor in the crow's nest. Dark wood floors, walls papered in purple and gold. No windows, because we're underground. That's why it's cold, too. Like a wine cellar. And everywhere are shelves, but instead of books, there are stacks of small rectangles, wrapped in paper. Six colors repeating themselves: lavender, pink, yellow, baby blue, mint green, and white. The room smells heavily of flowers and lye.

I try the door first, and it opens easily, so I haven't been locked in. Then I walk over to one of the shelves. Each row of wrapped rectangles is labeled with a date. April 1952, just last month, is the closest, so I choose a pink rectangle and unwrap it. The paper is waxed, and underneath is a bar of soap with rounded edges and stamped with the same "L" I saw on the front gates, encircled by a wreath of different flowers. The soap itself is pink, like the paper it was wrapped in, and dotted with darker spots. It's large enough my fingers are still far from meeting when I wrap my hand around it. I try to remember the Lamontaine Soap ads I've seen in magazines. "You'll Be Fresh as Flowers!" Actual flower petals in the soap. Different flowers for each of their six signature scents. I put the soap to my nose and inhale. Rose, mostly, but other florals too. It's feminine, but sharper than most rose perfumes I've smelled. I wrap it back up and unwrap another pink bar from January 1951. Smells the same to me. The whole room kind of blends, though. Smells so strongly of perfume and lye it makes me wince. That could just be that I'm not drunk anymore, though. I've moved on to a hangover.

Along the back wall of the balcony are shelves with bottles, about thirty ounces each. I look at them and they're all labeled with different flowers. I unscrew one and sniff—lily, like it says on the label. Scented oils, maybe? Or perfume? However they mix the scent into the soap, it doesn't just come from flower petals.

In the center of the balcony, not outlined so I almost step on it, is a bottle, shattered. I bend down and try to sniff at the spot, but I don't smell anything. The label says lavender. Next I go down the spiral staircase, and that's where her body must have been. There's a crack of splinters in the center of the floor, just below the balcony, and a dark red stain. She would have fallen from the balcony, and landed—maybe head first. I walk around the stain, trying to figure out how her body would have hit the ground. If she did land on her head, maybe she was unconscious and bled out. Or maybe the fall snapped her neck, if she fell just right. It's not a long enough drop to kill otherwise, but it's a long enough drop to break a skull, scrape her open so she bled, maybe to death. She might have been able to wake up, call for help before that, though. She probably wouldn't have died if someone had managed to hear her, or found her, so a sharp shove over the railing wouldn't have been a reliable way to kill unless whoever did it knew no one would come looking—or they just did it to incapacitate her before suffocation or something else.

If there was a push, maybe it wasn't meant to be murder, just a moment of anger, but then she was on the floor and bleeding and they panicked. I walk around the stain. It's smaller than it should be—more contained. I kneel down, and sniff the blood, but it's old and the smell of the soaps is overwhelming. Wedged between the floorboards, something catches my eye. I take a pen out of my pocket, and push it out. White, like bone, but the texture is wrong—a tooth. Well, part of a tooth. Between the floorboards.

I shake my head. That doesn't make sense. People don't land that way—even when pushed. I need a coroner's report.

I walk the room again, staring at the soaps. They go back as far as 1931. Against the back of the wall are larger shelves, these with tubs of lye and oils, dried flowers in jars labeled by year, and bottles of dye. There are also a few molds, but everything is clean, unused. She wasn't making anything that night. I'm not even sure she could make it here, without a stove. I need to ask more about the process of making soap, too. Surely she didn't hand-make every bar they sold here in the basement. They sell in almost every high-end store up and down the coast and as far east as Chicago—it would be millions of bars. Even with the flowers in them, they must be factory made.

I go back to the bloodstain and try to imagine the distance the body might have been from the railing, trying to determine if a push would have sent her farther out, but without a photo of how her body was, I can't know that, either. The only entrance is the one I came in, and there are no windows. The cold would have lowered her body temperature fast. I wonder how long it was before they found her. On the way out, I stop and look at the broken bottle again, the pattern of the glass, which bursts out from the center—dropped, not thrown, then. No heated arguments here. Just a drop, a shatter, and then another drop and another shatter. No proof it was murder. But no proof it wasn't.

I shut off the lights and walk outside, and there, leaning against the wall, is Cliff. He looks up and smiles at me. "Pearl asked if I could show you your room," he says in a low voice, one hand on his hip. "It's right down the hall from mine."

He moves his feet carefully, with precision, one in front of the other, a sort of innate elegance to his motions.

"Yeah?" I ask, smiling at him. "And where's your husband's room?"

"Ours adjoin—just like a real married couple. Except we're not. Henry doesn't call me husband the way Pearl and Irene called each other wife. Says it's too confusing since he actually has a wife—though her room is in a different wing."

He starts walking up the stairs and I follow. He glances back once to make sure I'm watching him carefully.

"So what's it like?" I ask. "Living so openly?"

"Not *so* openly," he says. "When I moved in, I thought I had it made. Handsome man, rich too. And I was somewhere really safe. Somewhere I could be free, like it was during the war." He pauses, shrugs. "But Henry is too careful. He can't be seen out at places we could be free—me neither, now. Irene always made that clear: Here was the only safe place. Here was the only place we could be a couple. Sometimes it feels more like a prison than paradise." He stops at the top of the stairs, turns to me with a worried expression, like he's said too much. "Not that I'm unhappy. But it's just not as freeing as you might think, having this *one* house where I can hold my boyfriend's hand, or wake up in bed with him and not have to run when I hear the maid come in. Though sometimes we do go out to the movies, sit next to each other in the back, and when it's dark, and if there's no one in our row, we hold hands. Drop them if someone gets close, of course, but I like that. That's the closest we get to bringing 'in here' out there. Saw *All About Eve* three times last year. Henry can do that line, the—" He pauses, clears his throat, then says in a low rough tone, "Fasten your seat belts, it's going to be a bumpy night." He shrugs and starts walking again. "He can do it much better."

He leads me to another staircase, then up it. Upstairs, the hallways are dark wood, and the walls are closer, darker. It's not the modern white of downstairs. It even smells mustier, but in a pleasant way. Or maybe that's Cliff. "So what if we can only hold hands outside if we're careful? We can do it as much as we want in here. Why would I ever want to leave, right?" He shrugs, and I can tell he does want to leave, but I don't feel sorry for him—he has a better life than I ever would have. Still, I understand what he's trying not to say: he wants more, and feels bad for wanting it.

"Honestly, it's more about who I share the place with," Cliff says in a low voice. "If it were just Henry, it would be one thing. But you saw Pearl and Margo. Worse than a couple of showgirls."

"They're always like that?" I ask.

"It was like this before Irene died, too. Both wanting to do more to help the company. Or at least have more power. Irene was the boss, Henry was her number two, but their positions were always unclear. With her gone, they're both vying for the top of the marquee."

"I thought it was pretty entertaining," I confess. "I wouldn't mind seeing the second act."

"You say that now, but wait until the matinee performance tomorrow," Cliff says. "It gets old fast. Trust me."

"How does Henry feel about all of it?"

"Oh, he barely notices. He runs the company, does what he always does. He's . . . steady. They don't get to him." I notice the pause as he describes his boyfriend—the one he lives with—and wonder about the way he looked at me, too. Some guys just look at other men that way—I see it at the clubs all the time. Men with long eyelashes, like Cliff, who walk the bar like a stalking cat before settling in on their prey. Some of them are with a different man every night, but some just *seem* like they're with a different man every night. Usually I can read those boys pretty well, same as I can read anybody—but with Cliff, I'm not sure. And I know I'm hoping he likes a little variety, which can't be good for my professionalism.

"So how about you?" he asks as we walk down the hall.

"How about me?"

"What was it like being a gay cop?"

"Oh. It was . . . what it was." I shiver a little, but hide it.

"Did you fit in? Get along with the other cops?"

"We worked together well enough. I solved a lot of crimes."

"But not friends, right?"

"Friendly . . ." I start. I'd like to think me and the guys were allies, at least, soldiers. That they would have had my back in a shoot-out. And maybe they would have. Before. But we didn't talk about much beyond work. I never went out for drinks with them. They thought I was a teetotaler. Made fun of me for it. Which I was fine with—it was better than them knowing the truth. "No, not friends."

"Of course not." He pauses, turns to look at me. "You knew what you were during the war, right? Why even be a cop?"

"It made sense, after the war. With experience working as an insurance investigator."

"Really?" he asks, clearly not believing. I did want to be a cop. I wanted to make the city safer.

"It was a good way to keep tabs on what bars they were going to hit, harass, so I could be far away from them." It's not why I became a cop, but it's why I stayed one, I think. That and I couldn't imagine what another life would look like.

"Looking out for number one," Cliff says. "I understand that. It's why I enlisted as soon as I could."

"Wanted to get out into the world, meet interesting men?"

Cliff laughs. "Something like that."

He stops in front of a door, then leans against the wall, looking at me. His shirt is unbuttoned enough that I can see the shine of his collarbone. I try to look away and my eyes find his mouth, and then his eyes, too. All of it no good to focus on. He's a suspect, after all. Clearly not Irene's biggest fan. And his flirting could be to distract me from that.

"So," he says. "Evander. Kind of a mouthful. What do the boys in the bathroom say when they call out your name?"

I smile. There's flirting and then there's this, which is practically an invitation. "Andy," I say. "Most people call me Andy."

"Well, Andy, here's your room. I'm just down there." He points down the hall. "This door doesn't lock from outside, I should warn you." He opens the door to my room and turns the lock on the inside. The deadbolt thrusts out, and then back in as he turns it back. "We lost the key a while back. Most of the doors here are like that."

"Oh," I say. I think again about sleeping under the same roof as a murderer. At least I can lock it once I'm in bed.

"Worried someone is going to slip into your bed in the middle of the night?" He grins.

"Should I be?"

"You're the detective," he says with a shrug. "And if you don't like the soap, just ask anyone for another one. I picked the one with the wrapping that matches your eyes."

He smirks at me, then turns and walks down the hall to his room, his hips swaying slightly.

I go into my room and close the door. It's empty white walls, with windows that overlook the front roundabout, with the fountain. The sun is already low on the horizon, the sky darkening. In the bathroom, three bars of soap have been stacked up like bricks, all wrapped in pale blue. I unwrap one and inhale—hyacinth, I think, but other things too, to keep it from being too sweet. Lemon. Cinnamon. I trace the "L" on the bar with my finger and then put it back down.

There's a knock on the door and before I'm even out of the bathroom, it's opened, and Pearl is there. The gloves and hat are gone, but otherwise she's the same. Either already comfortable in what she was wearing, or not comfortable enough to change in her own home when I'm in it, like when a suspect won't take off his hat.

"So?" she asks. "It was murder, wasn't it?"

I swallow and take a step toward her. "Did you see the body?"

"I did," she says carefully. "I found her. It was horrible. The blood."

"She was facedown?" I ask.

"Yes. Does that mean it was murder?"

"I'm not sure," I tell her, keeping my face as neutral as I can. "Without examining the body, or seeing where it was . . ."

She frowns and leans against the doorframe, like I've knocked the wind out of her.

"Sorry," I tell her. "I just can't be sure. But it looks . . . suspicious. I'll know more if the coroner will talk to me."

Pearl nods, her face softening for a moment, and I see how tired she is. She walks over to the bed and sits down on it. "I just thought it would be easy. Ridiculous to think, I know. But I thought I'd bring you in here, you'd take a look, and say it was murder and point out the guilty party, and then . . . and then . . ." She looks like she's about to cry so I fish in my jacket pocket for a handkerchief but she takes a deep breath and holds perfectly still, just for a second. She goes back to being Pearl.

"Sorry," she says. "Of course. You'll have to actually investigate. The coroner will talk to you, won't he?"

"I hope so," I say.

"You'll use the line about my knowing your mother?"

"About me being drugged?" I put on a grin but it feels nasty and I shove it away. "Sure, I'll try it. Not sure they'll bite. But I have other ways of getting them to work with me if I need them."

"Good." She stands up and wipes her skirt like there's dust on it. "I'm sorry I was . . . momentarily overcome. Tomorrow you can speak to the coroner. Tonight you'll stay here, meet the rest of the family." She points at the wardrobe in the corner. "There are shirts, pants, socks, and other things in the drawers and wardrobe, in a variety of sizes—all clean, of course.

We kept extras for when Henry was single and brought home *friends*. Some of them left things here, too."

"He brought men home a lot? Wasn't that dangerous?"

Pearl tilts her head. "Well, we told him not to bring any-one home, of course—told him to use a fake name, go back to their place, or a hotel—even a club bathroom, as long as it was locked, and to try to avoid the known queer clubs, or at least keep his head down in them. Being in one of those at all was too conspicuous."

"Sure." All the precautions I took. Most of the time. He probably wouldn't ever have gone to the Cat.

"But Henry never liked clubs. Found them too seedy. No offense."

"None taken." Maybe they're seedy. But they're also safe. A meetup in a bathroom means they're not going to try to roll you when you bring them home, rob you, kill you, leave your naked body tied to the bed. I've worked at least a dozen of those—and the murderers get off claiming the dead guy made an indecent advance. That's why I don't go looking outside the clubs, either. Fairy-bashers know all the spots and sometimes pretend to be looking for fun just to draw you out for a beating. Or blackmail.

"We didn't love him bringing the men home, but they were all harmless in that exposing us exposed them, and Henry has always been a bit of a romantic. Tried to show these men he met the life he could give them. They were all too afraid, though."

"Of being found out?" I ask. "Seems like you have a system for that."

"Well, you can't exactly explain to your parents or friends

that you've gone to live with a rich family in the woods without them asking questions. Even the ones who lived more openly—there were a few of those—found the situation stifling. They couldn't tell their friends who their new boyfriend was, they couldn't go out in public because then they'd figure it out . . ."

"And then Cliff came along?"

"Yes. We were so happy when he found Cliff. No family, and he was touring with a theater company, so no real roots—until we grew some for him. That's what our little home is for, I think. Putting down roots." She turns to walk out and then stops in the doorway. "And just so you know, Cliff is a flirt. It's not like you haven't seen that by now. But he doesn't mean anything by it. He and Henry are very happy."

"Yeah," I say, smiling automatically to hide the flutter of disappointment in my chest. "I know the type." I should be relieved, I know, but something about Cliff, the flirting, the walk, leaves me hoping Pearl's read on him isn't quite right.

"Good. Dinner is at six, in an hour, but I believe Elsie is here, if you want to meet her." She glances to her side, hoping I'll say yes and follow her.

"She was here when Irene died?"

"Yes."

"Then yeah, I want to meet her."

Pearl nods as if pleased, and I follow her out into the hall. I pause to lock my door behind me, then remember I can't. We go down the stairs, turning around a few more times before we're back in the sitting room. Margo is sitting on the love seat, whispering quickly to another woman—Elsie, I assume. She's in her thirties, with a severe black bob and dressed in a slightly oversized man's suit, without the tie. She has huge

dangling diamond earrings and a large ring on her finger—
enough that a cop in a bad mood wouldn't hassle her about
cross-dressing laws, but just barely. It's smart. I remember
guys from the force going out looking for women in pants just
to "show them what a real man is." I always ignored that, let
the guys walk out the door without stopping them. It makes
me flinch to think of it.

Elsie glances over and grins when she sees me. Margo tugs
on her sleeve but she ignores it and stands, extending her hand.
I shake it. Her grip is strong.

"You must be the inspector," she says, sounding amused.
"This is so exciting. I've never been part of a murder investigation before." She has a New York accent that gets fainter or
stronger on certain letters, making her words dance more than
I'm used to hearing.

"I'm not sure it's murder yet," I say.

"Still," she says, sitting back down. "I've been wrapped up in
lots of scandals, of course. Fights at the Ruby, famous people
caught there, that sort of thing. But *murder*? This is a novel
experience. I don't mean to be disrespectful," she adds quickly,
her eyes darting to Pearl, who says nothing.

"The Ruby." I nod, putting it together. "You're Elsie Gold.
The owner."

She spreads her arms out and grins. "That's me."

"And you're Margo's . . . ?"

"Paramour," she says, sitting back down next to Margo and
putting her hand on Margo's thigh. "I've always loved that term.
Exotic. Romantic." She turns to Margo and smiles, Margo tries
not to smile back, but can't help herself. "Special."

"I thought you lived in the city, above the club."

"I have an apartment there, but I like spending time here, too."

I turn to Margo. "And you're not worried that regularly having over someone so . . . notorious will bring undue attention?"

"We're out of the way, invisible," Margo says. "So no one really knows how often she's here. But plenty of well-to-do families are known for their friendships with . . . eccentrics."

"Eccentric?" Elsie cocks her head. "I prefer notorious."

"And you were here the night Irene died?" I ask, sitting down opposite them. Pearl takes an armchair beside me.

"Sure," Elsie says. "We all were. Do you really think it was a murder? Looked to me like she just took a slip and had an unhappy landing." She doesn't say it with much malice, but I glance over at Pearl anyway. She doesn't react. Just the way Elsie talks, then.

"I'm not sure yet," I say.

"So it might have just been an accident," Margo says, smiling at Pearl triumphantly.

"And it might not," Pearl interrupts, staring at her. "He's not sure."

"I think it's time someone tells me what happened that night," I say. "That will help me figure things out."

They all look at each other, silent, willing the others to speak first, or maybe trying to get their story straight with their eyes, I'm not sure. In cases where all the suspects are together, there's usually a silence like this, each of them willing the other in front of the firing squad first. I've never understood why. If you tell the story first, it's your story. Everyone else has to prove you're wrong. But no one ever wants to start.

"It was a normal night," Pearl says, finally, leaning forward. "A Thursday. We had dinner, we all watched Burns and Allen, and then Irene and I worked on a puzzle in the study."

"We were playing charades with the boys in here," Elsie

says. "Alice, Margo's mother, went to bed right after dinner, of course."

"And after a few hours, Irene said she wanted to go to the library, and I went to bed," Pearl says.

"She normally go down there that late?" I ask.

"All the time," Pearl says, sighing slightly. "She would be thinking about the right blend of scents. She was always fine-tuning. Trying to perfect each type of soap."

"She cared deeply about the company," Margo says. "She had to be the one making every decision."

"And you went to bed after Pearl?" I ask.

"Yes," Margo says. "Elsie and I went to bed about an hour later."

"The boys too," Elsie adds, standing and going to the bar cart by the window. "No one waited up for Irene. We know better."

"What time was that?" I ask.

"Probably just before midnight," Margo says. "It had started raining at ten."

"Yeah," Elsie says, smiling as she pours herself a drink. "It was quite a storm. Thunder so loud it rattled the windows. Lightning struck the fountain. It was wild."

So no one could have heard her call out. Maybe she wouldn't even have heard the door open, if the storm was loud enough to hear in the basement library. Easy to sneak in, give her a shove.

"The thunder probably just startled Irene, and she fell over the bannister," Margo says calmly, her eyes flickering to Pearl, who frowns. "It's terribly tragic, but not murder. Who would even want to kill her?" She looks away when she asks it, and Elsie suddenly turns to look out the window. Pearl, though, stares right at the two of them, her eyes hard as bullets.

"People kill people for a lot of reasons," I offer. "Love, hate, power, money."

"Well, Pearl inherited everything," Margo says, turning back to me with a smug grin. "Fifty-one percent of the company, the house, everything. And we all knew she would. So it doesn't make sense for any of *us* to have killed Irene." Her voice is sharp enough to slice a finger off, but she's trying to cover it up with a smile.

I look over at Pearl, who turns to me and nods, folding her arms over her chest. "That's true. Henry got forty-nine percent of the company. That's it. Everything else went to me. But money isn't the only reason. You said hate works, too." Pearl doesn't bother with a smile.

"And love," Margo adds quickly, sneering.

"All right," I say, standing and walking between them, worried they might physically attack each other. Elsie looks like she thinks the same, but she's leaned back against the wall, hands in her pockets, as if waiting for a show to get exciting. I don't blame her, it would probably be fun to watch, but we don't need any more blood spilled. "I don't know if it was even murder yet. Let's hold off on the accusations and let me do what you hired me to do—investigate. So, who has access to the library?"

"Everyone," Pearl says. "We don't keep it locked, normally. Just since . . ." She stares at the floor. No one speaks.

There's the sound of tires on the gravel outside, and Elsie turns and pulls the shade aside to look out. "Henry is home," she says, swirling her drink in her hand. "This should be fun."

FOUR

The front door opens in the hall and Pearl walks out to greet the man entering—I assume Henry. He's tall and broad with muscles that are visible even under his brown tweed suit. His red hair is parted sharply on one side, his chin scruffy with rusty stubble. He wears a pair of horn-rimmed glasses that almost match his hair and make him seem more severe. He leans down to kiss Pearl on the cheek, dropping his briefcase on the floor.

"Hello, Mo—" He stops, noticing me standing in the doorway. "Pearl. Ah, who's this?"

"This is Evander Mills. I've hired him to look into your mother's murder."

He leans back, taking me in, and I do the same to him. He's handsome, but his eyes have coldness in them. He looks me up and down, not with aggression, but as though I were numbers on a worksheet he has to complete. A problem to be solved, but not one he has any emotional investment in. Beside me, Margo and Elsie crowd into the doorway.

"Oh, don't worry," Margo says. "Pearl told him *all* about us."

"You told him everything?" he asks, turning on Pearl, his tone still even, unemotional.

"Relax, darling," Pearl says. "He's one of us."

This seems to be a new important factor in his calculations, and he turns back to me, reevaluating. When he's done, he nods, as though he's solved it. Then his face relaxes into a smile—but his eyes stay stony.

"Well, then," he says, extending a hand. His tone changes slightly too, back to how it was when he first came in—warmer. "Hello. Welcome. I hope you'll keep our little family secret. Though I daresay my mother here is being dramatic. There was no murder. It was a tragic accident."

"Everyone keeps telling me that," I say, shaking his hand. His grip is tight. His expression unreadable. He doesn't seem the type to do a mean Bette Davis impression, though he has a low, rich voice.

"He says he's not sure," Margo says. "Isn't that a surprise?"

"Well, we'll just have to give him, ah, what he needs to be sure. And then, Mother," he says, turning to Pearl and placing his hands on both of her shoulders, "you'll have to let it rest. I know you miss her. I do too, terribly. But all this . . . morbidity won't bring her back."

Pearl sighs. "Fine. *If* he decides it was an accident."

"Good," Henry says, letting her go. "Now, I would like a drink before dinner, and I have to go over a few work things."

"Actually, I need to talk to you," Elsie says. "Let me walk you to your office."

Henry nods, and I watch as Margo narrows her eyes at them as they walk off. Pearl walks back into the sitting room and falls into one of the chairs, staring at the ground.

"You understand, of course," Margo says, "that it's an unusual time here. We're not at our best." She glances up at the portrait of Irene, hovering over the landing, and for a moment looks angry, before her eyes dart back to me, cool, impossible to read.

"Sure," I say.

"I simply mean we normally seem happier."

"Seem?"

"Are." She smiles tightly and walks back into the sitting room, going over to the bar cart and pouring herself a hand of gin.

"So, your mother lives here?" I ask, following.

Her hand slips slightly, splashing the gin. "She does. She would be out on the street, otherwise. She's had some problems. Debt, finding work. My father died before I was born, so it wasn't an easy life for her. I'm trying to give her one now." It's clearly a rehearsed speech, and she doesn't put much effort into it.

"I see. It's kind of you to take her in."

Margo turns to me and drinks from her glass, then smiles first at me and then at Pearl. "It's what family does, right?"

"And she's . . . part of the family?"

"If you're asking if she's a lesbian, the answer is no. But she's grateful for the shelter we provide."

"So she doesn't approve?" I ask, reading between the lines.

"I don't know what goes on in my mother's head, Inspector. But as long as it stays in her head, I don't give a damn."

Pearl shifts in her chair at Margo's language, looking up at us. "Alice doesn't approve, no," she says. "We all know that. But we also all know without us she'd be destitute. Margo likes holding that over her."

"I do not, Pearl," Margo says, her face tightening into a ball. "We're all a family here. We all work together." She downs nearly half of the remaining gin in one swallow. "I'm going to go see what they're preparing for dinner." She walks from the room, taking her glass with her.

I sit back down in silence, and watch the garden out the window. Outside, I can hear insects buzzing, birds calling, the rush of water from the fountain. I stand, pour myself a finger of gin, and sit back down. I sip slowly. The drink tastes more expensive than the ones I was downing this morning, but it still burns.

"We must be quite a picture," Pearl says after a while.

"Like Margo said, you're all very emotional now." I sit down in the chair next to Pearl's. She looks over at me sadly. "It's funny." I cross my legs. "You'd think a place like this . . . a place where we could be ourselves and not worry about the police, and have a family . . . I used to dream about a place like this. I used to lie awake in bed and think to myself, 'If the world were perfect, either I'd be different, or everyone else would.' Mostly I tried to figure out how to change me. But sometimes I'd imagine if everyone else were different. It would be like this, maybe, I thought."

"Is it everything you dreamed?" She looks amused, but pleased, too. Under different circumstances, I think I would have just made her day.

"It's a little more real than that. People are people, I guess. And letting our hair down doesn't mean all our troubles disappear."

"Irene and I really wanted to create a home. A special home. But . . . the outside world doesn't go away. It's not that much different than your clubs. You have to leave sometime."

I nod, and take out my cigarette case and offer one to Pearl. She shakes her head. I light one and watch the light in the windows turn yellow.

"Still," I say. "It's a lot better than what I'd had planned for tonight."

"And what was that?" Pearl asks.

I let the silence hang too long as I remember what I'd wanted to do, just hours ago, and now it's gone. Or at least, faded. Here is better. Not perfect, of course, but better than out there. And maybe it could be even better than it is. They just need a little help. I feel a smile start to play at the corners of my mouth as I think of it. There's that feeling—the one I didn't get from kicking the kid out of the bar this morning. That feeling like I'm useful. Good at this. Can help—and here, especially. A place like this is worth trying to help. Maybe to make up for all the times I didn't help, didn't warn anyone.

"Evander? What did you have planned?" I turn back to Pearl, and she's looking at me like she's starting to have second thoughts. I don't blame her. I let my mouth fall back down, try not to look like I'm losing it.

"Just a bath," I say.

She raises an eyebrow at me. "Well, you can still have one of those. We have plenty of soap, too, to choose from."

I laugh. "I meant to ask—the stuff in the library. Did she make soap here?"

"Only occasionally. To perfect the formulas. Test bars. Then she'd tell the factories the right amount of scent and petals and all that."

I nod. "She really was a perfectionist."

"She was." Pearl smiles. "She loved making sure the product was just so. Took a lot of pride in it. Before her husband died there was just one type of bland white soap. She made it a brand."

"Fresh as flowers."

"Exactly. All her idea. Henry has run the day-to-day forever, he's so good with numbers, and he understands the machines, but Irene was the artist."

"I'll say," Elsie says, reappearing in the doorway. "That woman was obsessed with her scents. Smelling the flowers every day. Inhaling those bottles of scent like a dopehead hitting the hop."

"Elsie, please," Pearl says, standing up.

"I'm not saying it like it's a bad thing." Elsie shrugs. "Like you said, she was an artist. And she was devoted to her art. I can still hear the sound of her sniffing." She inhales deeply through her nose to demonstrate. I manage not to laugh, but I crack a smile, which Elsie sees. "Sounds creepy, I know, but you got used to it. Kinda miss it, even," she says sadly.

"She had a sensitive nose," Pearl says. "And you shouldn't speak of the dead that way."

"The dead don't mind," Elsie says. She still has the martini she made herself earlier and sips from it.

"What did you want with Henry, anyway?" Pearl asks.

"Just a little business. Nothing to worry about."

"It's my business. I'm the majority shareholder."

"Not that business," Elsie says with a wave of her hand. "But I want to know more about our guest. Caught performing 'lewd acts' at a *respectable* establishment, hm?" She grins.

"Yes," I say, smirking.

"Why not go to the Ruby? I'm trying to expand my clientele."

"A little out of my price range."

Elsie shrugs, sips her drink. "Well, next time you stop by, drinks are on the house."

"Thanks."

"Dinner," Margo says, appearing in the doorway. "Let's go eat."

I stand, and they all take turns glancing at me when they think the others aren't looking, like I'm the shadow out of the corner of all their eyes. We follow Margo across the entry hall into the room opposite the sitting room, a dining room with a long table and dark wood floors covered by a thick red rug. The wallpaper is green, printed with vines and different colored flowers bursting off them. An art deco chandelier hangs over everything, green to match the wallpaper. Below that, on the table, is a low crystal vase filled with flowers from the garden: roses, lilies, lavender. The light coming in through the windows is violet and red now and makes the outside world look bloody.

Almost ritualistically, everyone takes their seats. Pearl sits on the right side of the head of the table, Elsie next to her, and then Margo next to her. Henry comes in behind me and sits opposite Pearl, Cliff following and sitting beside him. Finally, a new woman walks in. Alice. I can tell she's Margo's mother, not just from the family resemblance, but from how she's everything Margo models her wife role on. Her hair is naturally loose with a slight wave, her dress is a pale blue that flows down past her knees. Her pearl necklace suits her. When she sees me, she smiles, and it's welcoming and bright, not forced. She looks closer to seventy than sixty, and though her hair has been colored blond, everything about her seems natural, easy. She sits next to Margo. The head of the table remains empty, but I sit at the opposite end, Alice on my left, an empty chair on my right. When I sit, everyone lets out a breath.

"You must be the guest," Alice says, smiling at me. "Everyone is making a fuss over you. A real-life inspector."

"He's like us, Mother," Margo says. "Don't get too excited."

Alice rolls her eyes and lays a hand over my wrist. "I'm excited to meet someone new is all." She withdraws her hand with a smile. "And an inspector. You must have such fun stories."

"I don't know if I'd call them fun," I say.

"Oh, of course," she says. "I didn't mean . . . I admit. I do like a good mystery novel. But I suppose it's different with you. Real people. I'm sorry. I was imagining it all as a story."

"Irene was a real person," Pearl says, her voice cool.

"I know that," Alice says sharply, looking down at the table. The tablecloth is layered—white lace in a pattern like snow-flakes over dark green linen. Alice pinches at the scalloped edge of the lace where it hangs by her legs. The lace there is loose from her doing that.

A butler suddenly emerges from a door on the far wall and begins setting down plates in front of each of us. The china looks expensive, with a ring of gold at the border of each piece and a painted flower in the center of the plate. Not lavender, but purple—an orchid.

"Crab cakes," Alice announces. "I oversee a lot of the house-hold work," she says to me. "Menus, overseeing cleaning up—a real woman's work." She smiles at me while her daughter glares at her. "I helped Mrs. Lamontaine, too, before the accident. Just minor secretarial work. I earn my keep here. In case any-one has told you otherwise."

"They haven't," I say as a crab cake is set down in front of me. I look up at the man setting it down and suddenly realize I know him. He's a regular at the Black Cat. The butler who told Pearl about me, probably. He doesn't seem to register my rec-ognition, though, and sets another plate down in front of Cliff, who is stroking Henry's arm. Henry looks down at his plate and slices methodically into the crab cake, his jaw clenched like he's angry.

I look back up at the butler, who is now pouring the wine. He's older, somewhere in his fifties I think, but with most of his hair left, silver and swept back, and an attractive face. He wears a plain black suit. Sensing me look at him he looks up, and then quickly glances around to make sure no one else is looking. Then he looks back at me, smiles, and winks, all while perfectly pouring Henry's glass. I don't remember ever talking to him at the Black Cat, but the wink makes me grin, makes me feel like I'm on somewhat more familiar territory than I've been up until now.

"These are lovely," Pearl says, taking a bite of the crab cake.

"I'll tell Dot you said so," Alice responds. There's a moment of quiet as knives scrape against plates and forks against teeth. They're not falling into easy conversation, but I'm not sure if that's because of me, or just how they are. I pick up my knife and fork—they're heavy, real silver. I've eaten out at nice places a few times before, but there's something awkward about being around a family table with a family I'm not part of. I wish I could go eat with the butler, the other staff. But up here at least I can learn more.

"How was work?" Pearl asks Henry.

"Fine," Henry says quickly. "The same as always."

"The company is adjusting to Irene's absence?"

"Yes, Mother," Henry says. "We've decided to just use the most recent formulas for now. We can reevaluate new mixes later."

"Well, Irene always changed it, every year. It was an event. People would run out and buy one of each in the new formulas to see how they'd changed and what they liked."

"I know. But we'll reevaluate in a few months. Maybe release a new bar a year after her death. One fellow in design said we should change the stamp on the bars, make it Mother's face. That might be sweet." He gestures with his fork while he talks.

"You should make it a new label, not the stamp," Margo says. "I don't think most people would want Irene staring at them from their soap dish, much less having to rub her all over themselves in the shower."

"Margo, really?" Alice asks with a sigh.

"I didn't mind it," Pearl says, though I'm not sure if she's challenging Margo, Alice, or both of them.

"Let's try to be less dramatic tonight," Alice says. "We have a guest." She turns back to me. "Tell me, Inspector, what was your biggest case?"

"I'm not an inspector anymore." It feels odd to say it out loud. Tastes bitter, and a little salty, like the ocean. "You can just call me Andy. And I've worked a lot of cases, but nothing you've heard of, I'm sure."

"Oh, come on," Alice says. "Tell me. I'm sure there's something."

"It's really not very glamorous. Gang murders, mostly. Last one I worked that was in the papers was Jan Westman. You read about that one?"

"Was she the one they found washed up?"

I nod, cutting a bit off my crab cake and taking a bite. It has the flavor of expensive ingredients. Rich people food.

"They thought she was drunk and had just drowned, but it turned out to be a murder," Alice tells the rest of the table. "Very hard case."

I nod.

"Tell us about it," Cliff says, grinning.

Henry slices into his crab cake again. "It would be good to have some idea of your methods, if you'll be, ah, working in our home."

"All right." I nod, slicing into my crab cake. "As Alice said, Jan

Westman's body was found washed up on Stinson Beach. She had a driver's license on her for the city, that's why they called us in. We thought she'd gotten drunk, fallen in the bay, floated up here. I've been called out to a lot of those. But usually, if that's what happened, their eyes are bloodshot. Not hers. So I asked the doctors at the morgue to check her blood—came back sober, and not as much water in her lungs as they'd expect. Said she was probably dead before she went in."

Alice gasps, putting her hand to her chest. I take the opportunity to eat a little.

"They can tell all that from the body?" Henry asks. I can't tell if he's worried or just surprised.

I shrug. "We've been able to test blood alcohol levels for decades. But they only did it in this case because I noticed the eyes."

Alice nods. "Oh, yes, he's very good."

"So, we knew it was murder. The body wasn't beaten or anything, though, no strangulation marks, and suffocation comes with red eyes too, so that was out. I worked with the doctors, examining her body—we found a small puncture mark—so they checked her blood for everything else. Came back full of morphine."

"So she was a junkie?" Henry asks, leaning forward. No, I realize, he's not worried—he's excited. He's liking this story, just trying not to show it.

"No," I say. "No other puncture marks, none of the usual signs of that—teeth, hair. She was a normal, healthy young girl that someone had shot up with enough morphine to kill, and then they'd thrown her in the water when they were done."

"So it was rape?" Elsie asks.

"Elsie," Pearl says. "Don't say that."

"We're already talking murder, Pearl."

"That was my first thought too," I say to Elsie, finishing off my crab cake. The butler swoops around the table, removing our plates and putting down new ones. I look up at him, but he doesn't look back this time. I was hoping for another wink. Like a life preserver.

"Celery soup," Alice says. "Please, Inspector, go on. This is thrilling." Henry starts to nod in agreement, but stops himself.

"Well, then it became the real detective work: finding out about her life, people who wanted to hurt her. She was a secretary at an architecture firm. She'd recently ended it with her boyfriend, one of the architects there, so he was suspect number one. She also had received flowers at the office from a mystery man, suspect number two, and then there was her boss, suspect three, and his wife, suspect four."

"Why those two?" Henry asks.

"Why do you think?" Elsie says. "She was sleeping with the boss, right?"

"I don't think so. But from my initial interview with him, I got the sense he wanted to be. So that put him on the list, and his wife, too."

"Got the sense how?" Cliff asks.

"The way he talked about her. Called her 'such a pretty young girl' more than once, and when I asked him about her, how long she'd worked there, why he'd hired her—got his mind thinking about her—he licked his lips."

"Something minor as that?" Henry asks.

"Everyone has little things they try to hide and can't," I say. The table is quiet, and I can see them all thinking about what they'd said and done in front of me. I take a spoonful of soup.

"Was it her boss, though?" Margo asks.

"No. We traced the flowers back to a new beau. He worked at a restaurant owned by Anthony Lima."

"The crime boss," Alice says, excited, as though she hasn't read all this already.

"Right. So we brought the kid in, and asked him about it. He tried to stay cool, but anyone could tell something was up—he was sweating, eyes all over the place." I grin as Henry's eyes go wider at these details. I've told a few stories before, at the policeman's ball and other fundraisers, and that's the look I usually get from the rich old ladies.

"After he left," I continue, "we tailed him to a warehouse in Oceanview full of sets, costumes—not the kind that covered much."

"Oh," Elsie says with a grin, "so the secretary was a pinup model?"

"That's not illegal," Cliff says.

"It is if it's against her will," I say. "And if she's been drugged to comply. And if it's not just her in the photos."

The table goes silent again, Cliff and Elsie looking ashamed of themselves for the first time today.

"So it was rape," Elsie says.

I nod. "On camera. I wasn't sure at the time, but I thought maybe. My partner, meanwhile, has tailed the beau back to his restaurant. He gives me a call and goes into the restaurant to watch him. The beau sees him, knows he's watching. I show up and go around back, talk to the chefs there. They don't want trouble. I tell them if the beau tries to burn anything, they fish it out, give it to me. And that's exactly what happened. It was film. Of the beau and Jan, doing . . . well, what you'd expect. We had a pretty good picture of what happened by then.

Brought the beau in again, showed him the photos we got, he squirmed." I grin a little, remembering it. I liked it when they knew we'd caught them. I liked watching them try to lie their way out. Bad lies always made me feel so much better about my good ones.

I look around the room, everyone is staring, waiting for the end. "Says he gave her the morphine to calm her down, but he left before she died. The photographer was the last one there. So we ask him who the photographer is, look him up. We go to the photographer's house, but he's gone. Hasn't been seen since last night. But if he's on the run, he needs the cash for it. We call up some of those nudie magazines, see if anyone has heard of this guy trying to sell some photos. They have, and they work with us to set up a sting. We meet the guy, catch him, he cries almost immediately, case closed."

"But what about Anthony Lima?" Elsie asks. "Clearly they all worked for him."

"No one flips on Lima," I say.

The room is silent as the soup is taken away, and the main course put down.

"Lamb chops," Alice says. "With mint jelly."

"Clearly you know your stuff," Henry says, slicing into his food. "But I daresay you won't find anything quite so scandalous here."

"Well," Cliff says, grinning at his boyfriend, "we hope he won't."

Henry smiles a little at that, but Margo rolls her eyes.

"So, what is your plan?" Margo asks. "You saw the library, you've spoken to us. Can you just . . . figure it out? How can you not know if it's a murder?"

"I'm going to talk to the local coroner tomorrow," I say, cutting my own lamb chop to avoid making eye contact with her. There's a chance everything will go exactly like Margo guessed it would, with the police refusing to help me. "But tonight I was hoping to explore the house, see if anyone remembers anything else, and . . . I'd like someone to tell me about making soap."

Elsie laughs. "Is that part of the case?"

"It seems to have been a key part of Irene's life," I say. "And while I saw the library, I didn't understand everything I was seeing."

"Well, we all know a bit about making soap at this point," Pearl says. "Family business. What would you like to know?"

"How does it work?"

"Ah," Henry says, taking a sip of wine and leaning back, comfortable to be talking about this, more than anything else. "In the factories it's about making sure everything is identical. To achieve that, we use the continuous process, splitting fat into acids and glycerin using a hydrolyzer, which uses high-pressure hot water to split the fat. We purify the fatty acids, mix that with alkali, and whip it up, to get some air in it before it cools down and we feed it into the mills to add the flower petals, perfumes, and generally knead it so it's soft before we put it in molds. We have two different sizes now, the large bath size, which are six by four inches, and the smaller personal size, which are four and a half by two and a half. Both are two inches thick. Once it's hardened in the molds, we wrap it up and ship it off."

I nod, taking that all in. It's a lot of words I don't know, but I get the gist, I think. "So how did your mother replicate that in the library?" I ask.

"Well, she used the old-fashioned way," Henry says. "Made life hard, let me tell you. She measured out how much perfume and flower petals to add per bar, but when you're making a hundred bars at a time, you have to multiply that by a hundred and distribute it as evenly as possible. She was always saying it wasn't quite right, because the flower petals weren't the exact same bar to bar. I told her that was impossible but . . ." He swirls his wine in his glass. "Well, she kept trying."

"At home," Pearl says, "she used the stovetop, bringing the fat and lye to the right temperature, mixing it, letting it cool to trace before adding the perfume and petals. The state that the soap was in was different from the factory because they weren't made the same way. She was trying to understand how to best translate her single-bar formulas to the factories. Always."

"Trace?" I ask.

"When it looks like pudding," Alice says.

"So those bottles in the library are perfumes?"

"And essential oils," Alice says. "Arranged by scent and maker."

"Which means oils that have been mixed with a perfume base, which changes the way they smell and develop on the skin," Henry says. "They have alcohol in them, which can also change the texture of the soap."

"Do oils evaporate?" I ask.

Henry frowns at me, confused. "From the bottles?"

"If they're spilled."

"Oh." He shrugs. "Depends on the oil, but they usually leave some stickiness behind if it's not cleaned. Why?"

"I was just curious about why they developed differently on the skin," I say. No one seems to have thought about the dropped bottle of lavender, and I'm not going to remind them. "Alcohol evaporates, right?"

"Ah." Henry smiles. "You're quick. Yes. Oils cling to the skin more, so in soap they make the scent last longer after washing up. Mother generally preferred them because of that, though usually she would mix both in her formulas, to get just the right smell and texture."

"When she changed the formula every year," Pearl says, leaning back in her chair and looking at the chandelier. She hugs herself, like she's cold. "It didn't just make the formulas different, it made her better at making them, seeing exactly what changed."

"And she always threw a party for the new soap," Cliff adds. "I loved that part. The New Rose! As if you could change a rose. But people loved it."

"That's true," Margo says. "The papers came and did a photo-shoot every year. They always wanted to know which of the batch was my favorite, but I could never tell you what had changed. I just asked Irene, and she told me what to say. She knew what made the soap special."

The table goes quiet and I look around at them all. They seem to be locked in their own memories of her. Henry looks wistful, Pearl sad, and surprisingly, Margo seems sad too.

There's a sudden shock of metal on ceramic as Alice slices through her lamb chop. "It's a fascinating art," she says.

"It's a pity you won't be keeping up with the new scents," Pearl says to Henry.

"We will, eventually. We need to . . . adjust to Mother's death is all. There are a lot of things that need to be changed without her. It's going to take time."

"That's why the consistency of the new bars—" Pearl starts.

"Do you have a new formula, Mother?" Henry interrupts. "Do

you know for sure which ones haven't been used? We can't just go back to the one from 1949, can we? Someone needs to come up with a new formula, and they need to come up with one that doesn't cost much."

"Doesn't cost much?" Pearl shakes her head. "That doesn't matter. We can just go through her notebooks."

"We will, Mother," Henry says, his voice now pleading. "Just . . . not now. All right? Not this time."

Pearl taps her fork on her empty plate and then puts it down, frowning slightly. "Fine."

The rest of us finish eating and Mr. Kelly takes the plates away, one by one, before bringing out new bowls that smell of brandy, caramel, and bananas.

"Bananas Foster!" Alice announces, clapping her hands. It makes me chuckle, her acting so young, but the rest of the room has gone silent, staring at her as Mr. Kelly sets the bowls down. It's a silence with an edge—eyes sharpen and point at Alice like knives.

"Really, Mother?" Margo sighs.

"You didn't wait very long," Pearl says, looking like she can't decide if she wants to cry or stab Alice with a dessert spoon.

"It's been three weeks, Pearl," Alice responds, digging into her dessert, taking a spoonful, and then closing her eyes and leaning back in joy. "It's so good. Just eat it."

Pearl stands and tosses her napkin down on the table. "I'm not hungry. I'll be in my study." She marches off and I look around the table, confused.

Alice sighs.

"You could have checked with her first," Margo says.

"You went to check on the menu," Cliff says. "Didn't you know it was coming?"

"It was too late to stop it by then," Margo says, pulling her hair behind her ear and then taking a spoonful of dessert.

"But you could have warned her too," Cliff says, then throws me a look. "Top of the marquee," he says.

I shake my head at him, not understanding.

"Oh, right," Cliff says. "Irene never allowed bananas in the house. Said the stench interfered with her ability to smell the perfumes for the soaps."

"It sticks to everything," Elsie says in a gravelly voice, apparently an impersonation of Irene. "It's a scent that you can't wash out for days." She turns up her nose and makes her eyes wide.

"I really didn't think it would offend her so much," Alice says, still happily eating. "It's been weeks."

"I understand you felt it was fine to do," Henry says to Alice, "and you certainly have the right, as you do so much of the menu planning. But I wish you would have told Mother beforehand. It would have been kind."

Alice frowns and puts down her spoon. "You're right. I thought it would be a nice surprise, but you're right. I'll go apologize." She stands up.

"Finish your dessert first, Mother," Margo says, spooning some of the desert into her own mouth with a smile. "Enjoy the thing you caused the drama over."

"It wasn't intentional, Margo," Alice says, her tone making it clear that she thinks that should make her blameless. But she sits back down and continues enjoying the bananas Foster without defending herself further. They all eat in silence, Pearl's bowl quickly removed by Mr. Kelly. As they finish, Mr. Kelly takes each of their bowls away and they stand, each walking almost aimlessly out of the room as they fish cigarettes out of their pockets, I assume to go smoke in the sitting room. That seems to be its main purpose. Cliff and Henry walk out together, and then Elsie, followed quickly by Margo. Mr. Kelly brings out a notebook, which he puts in front of Alice, who takes out a pair of glasses and reads over the notebook before nodding.

"Cancel the bananas, though," she says, putting away the glasses. "I don't want to be accused of causing a scene again."

Mr. Kelly nods and heads back into the kitchen.

"Well, today must have been quite an introduction for you, Andy," she says, smiling at me.

"It's good to get to know everyone."

"And do you think any of us could be a murderer?" She turns her whole body toward me, crossing her legs.

"I think anyone could be a murderer, given the right motive and opportunity," I say.

"I think like that too," she says, leaning forward. "I think it could be any of them."

"So you believe it was murder?" I ask. "Everyone but Pearl keeps trying to tell me it's not."

"I think it could be." She shrugs. "Irene was a difficult woman at times. It wouldn't surprise me."

"Difficult how?"

She shrugs. "She was a woman who liked things a certain way and was used to getting them. She was particular. Or maybe selfish, if I were speaking bluntly." She looks a little ashamed of saying it.

"What do you think happened that night?" I ask.

"Oh, I don't know," Alice says, standing up. "I was reading in my bedroom. I'm not much for company after dinner, so I go take a bath and read in my bedroom. It's quiet and cozy, and I remember that night it was raining so hard it was like I was the only person in the world." She smiles at me, tucking her hair behind her ear—like her daughter does, but gentler. "In fact, I'm going to go take a bath and read now, if you don't mind."

"Not at all," I say, standing. "Though I was hoping someone could give me a tour, help me get a sense of the place."

"Mr. Kelly!" Alice calls. The butler emerges, smiling. He has a pointed face that doesn't hide mischief well. "Mr. Kelly, will you please give Andy here a tour of the place? Show him whatever he wants."

"Of course," Mr. Kelly says. He turns to me. "What would you like to see first?"

"I've seen the library, but I don't quite understand how it connects to the rest of the house."

"I'll leave you, then, Andy," Alice says. "Good night." She bows her head a little and walks slowly from the room.

"Good night," I say to her. When she's gone I turn back to Mr. Kelly, whose posture has loosened somewhat, as has his smile.

"So, the library?"

"You mean the underground one, right?" he asks. His voice is less stiff with Alice gone, too. Smoother.

"Yeah. I want to understand how people could have gotten to it that night. And it would be good to talk to the rest of the staff."

"Well, aside from me, there's just Dot and Judy. They're having dinner in the kitchen now, if you want to meet them."

"Sure," I say.

"All right." He nods. "Follow me, then."

He leads me through the door he's been coming out of all night. There's a short flight of steps down and then a large kitchen, with fancy new gear like a dishwasher and a laundry washing machine so shiny that they could have been won off a game show. The tiles are dark brown and you can see the night out the windows at the top of the walls. In one corner is a small table with three chairs. Two of them are occupied. In one sits a woman in an apron. She's about forty, with black hair in a bob and a slight smile. Next to her is a pale woman, tall and lean, with red hair cut short as a man's. She wears dungarees and a men's white undershirt. They're eating, but they glance over at me when we come in. The cook raises her eyebrow.

"This is Andy," Mr. Kelly says. "The investigator. Andy, this is Dot, the chef, and Judy, the gardener."

"I help with laundry and odd jobs, too," Judy, in the dungarees, says.

"We're an efficient little household," Dot says.

"I can see," I say. I look over the kitchen. It's already cleaned up. "So, any of you know if someone murdered Irene?"

"Oh, getting right to it," Dot says with a snort.

"No," Judy says. "I'm outside most of the day. I don't bother with the drama inside the house."

"And I stick to the kitchen," Dot says. "If you want the gossip, Pat's your man."

I turn to Mr. Kelly, who grins. "I know this and that."

"All right," I say. "But before I get to that, everyone here has an alibi, right?"

"Well, we do," Dot says, taking Judy's hand. "We share a room and a bed."

"The staff aren't your suspects," Mr. Kelly says, shaking his head. "We all liked Irene well enough. She was secretive, valued our secrecy, so she was very careful hiring, but once she trusted us, she left us alone. Didn't scold if you messed up, either, just told you to do better."

"Honestly, it felt like we were just tools to her," Dot says. "To keep the house running. She didn't care about us, but I don't think we expected that from her. The money is good, and we get to live as ourselves. Sure we have to work, but we'd have to do that anywhere. This is the best we could ever hope for. None of us would risk ruining that."

I nod. It's possible they have motives, strong ones, worth the risk, but they're not just going to write them down and slide them to me like a note in school.

"Well, if you think of anything—people acting odd that night, something you heard—let me know. But, Mr. Kelly, if you could show me around the house a bit more, and tell me some of that gossip you mentioned, I'd appreciate it. Nice meeting you both."

I nod at the women, who don't say anything, just turn back to their meal.

"This way," Mr. Kelly says, taking me back up the stairs, through the dining room, and into a hallway.

"Thank you, Mr. Kelly," I say, following him. "I understand I have you to thank for this job, too."

"Oh, no need for thanks, honey. And call me Pat. You're staff, same as me. Even if they have you in one of the nicer bedrooms."

"I think Cliff did that just to flirt with me," I say.

"Oh, he definitely did it to flirt with you," Pat laughs. He stops in the middle of a hallway, all dark wood walls and floor, no windows. "So now we're right behind that nifty painting of Irene you saw when you first came in. Go that way"—he points—"and you're in the west wing. Up to your room and the boys' rooms, down to the library. The east wing"—he points again—"is the girls' rooms. Margo is on the third floor, but Pearl and Irene were on the second, next to the offices. And Alice is on the top floor. Dot, Jean, and I are back in the west wing, third floor. I think I'm right on top of you, in fact," he says, winking.

I grin, and he takes it as an invitation to step closer.

"So how many ways are there from the various bedrooms to the library?" I ask.

"This place is filled with hallways. They all could have left their rooms at the same time and gone to the library and back without seeing each other, aside from those leaving from the same room, I suppose. Main stairs, and through the lounge, staff stairs, back stairs, west stairs . . . they all would have had to cross at the stairs going down to the library, though. But from there . . ." He holds up both his hands and wiggles his fingers. "They could go anywhere."

I sigh. "So, really, no one has an alibi aside from they were all in bed."

Pat raises an eyebrow. "Is that what they said?"

I smile at him. "You're just dying to tell me everything you know, aren't you?"

"I was always terrible at poker," he says with a grin. "But you know what they say, unlucky at cards . . ." He takes another step closer. "But not here, where voices can echo. Would you like to join me in my room?" He raises his eyebrows, and I nod, and follow him as he turns and walks down the hall to the west wing. He walks quickly but quietly.

His room does seem to be above mine, from my understanding of the house. The ceiling is a little lower, but otherwise the lay-out is the same, except that his room is crowded—overflowing with books. I glance at the spines: Truman Capote, Gore Vidal, and many others. They're piled up next to his bed, and stacked two deep on the shelves that line the walls, and stacked on a desk in the corner. It gives the place a more closed-in, cozy feeling, but doesn't leave room for much of anything else.

Pat tosses himself on his bed, landing on his back, half sitting up, smiling at me, his legs wide.

"If you want, we could have a little fun, you know. They wouldn't mind here. I'm not supposed to bring anyone home, but then *I* didn't bring you."

I smile. It's tempting. He's good-looking, and I've never minded an older man. But there's something different about this place. Outside, back before, going to the clubs had been a hunger. It had been those moments of sighs, my body against another man's, his tongue between my teeth, him inside me, that had made the world go away. Those were moments I'd felt most like myself. But here, it's different.

"If I'm not your type, I won't be offended," Pat says, closing his legs, and sitting more upright.

"No, it's not that, it's just . . . I'm working."

"Business first. I get you."

He nods at his one chair, which is by the desk, and I pull it out and sit down. "So, what did you see the night Irene died? Is it like they told me?"

"What did they tell you?"

"It was raining, but otherwise a normal night: Alice to bed after dinner, Irene and Pearl doing a puzzle in the study, the rest of them in the lounge playing charades. Irene went to the library a few hours after dinner, I'm guessing around ten? Pearl went to bed, and then an hour later, the rest of them went off to bed. No one stirred again until morning."

"Well." Pat tilts his head. "That all happened. But some more happened after it."

"Like what? Arguments?"

"Nothing that wild, I'm afraid. No easy suspects. I know Elsie and her car were gone before sunrise, but I didn't hear her leave, so it must have been early. That's normal for her. But as I went around preparing things that night, after they'd all gone to bed, I saw Cliff alone in the sitting room. He was drinking. I'd replaced the brandy after they went to bed, but it was half-empty again by the time Cliff was gone. Maybe he had trouble sleeping?"

"Maybe." I nod.

"And I saw Margo in Irene's office when I was double-checking all the windows were closed. I'd closed them all when it started raining, but the office has some papers and I wanted to double-check before I turned in."

"What was she doing?"

"It looked like she was reading something at Irene's desk. Couldn't say what, though. She might just have been looking for a good book."

"Did either of them see you?"

He barks a laugh. "They don't see staff, Andy. No one here sees staff." I nod. I've heard this from the help before on other cases, and I guess everyone being queer doesn't change it.

"That everything?" he asks. "Because if work is over . . ." He leans back, his legs opening again.

I laugh. "You don't seem to have a lack of men in your life when I see you at the Cat," I say. "I didn't expect this much seduction from you."

"Oh, I love the boys at the Cat," he says. "And they love me. But I don't get to bring them back to my bedroom."

"So it's not about me."

"Sorry, honey, no, but you'll do the job well enough, I'm sure."

I laugh again. I realize I've never laughed this much talking to anyone. I almost want to join him on the bed. At the clubs, meeting someone in the bathroom is like coming up for air. But I'm breathing steadily right now. And the fact that I don't need to the way I do in the bathrooms of the clubs keeps me in the chair.

He grins at me in silence. "You're feeling it, aren't you? That's why you're not hopping into bed with me."

"Feeling what?"

"The . . ." He sits up, spreads his arms wide and wiggles his fingers again. "Freedom. Well, near freedom. Out there, you only find yourself *as* yourself when you're pressed against a man, tiles on your back. But here . . . you find yourself in the mirror."

"I . . . maybe," I say, nodding.

He hops up and goes to one of his shelves and takes down a book. "There is no homosexual problem aside from that created by a heterosexual society," he quotes, then hands me the book. I take it from him and read the title. *The Homosexual in America*. "Have you read it? It just came out. Really provocative and inspiring, but sad, too. But he's right! All our problems are because of heterosexuals. Having to hide, persecution, hating ourselves? There's no place for us to be happy in a society that doesn't want us. But here . . ." He opens his arms wide again. I wonder if he used to be a magician. "There is no heterosexual society." He falls back onto the bed. "I mean, sure, it's clawing at the walls, and you have to go back into it every time you leave. But while you're here. In this little glass bubble. It's heavenly. And that's what you're feeling."

I turn the book over in my hands and study it. It's a simple cover, just the title in large letters, a border around them. I'd be afraid to be seen with it in public, the word "homosexual" printed across it in bold. I almost want to drop it right there.

"So you don't want to break in my bed," Pat says. "Because for once you don't need sex to feel like yourself."

"That . . ." I nod. "That sounds right, maybe. Or at least, I'm feeling like someone else."

"Well, when it wears off, I'm right above you."

"I'll keep that in mind." I put the book on his desk and turn to look at him. The light is dim and buttery and he grins at me, all mischief and freedom, and I wonder if I could ever smile like that. "How did you know?" I ask him. "That I was a cop? You told Pearl a cop had just gotten busted at the Cat, so . . . how did you know? I never told anyone there I was an inspector."

"Oh, Andy . . . everybody knew." He looks at me sadly. "Doris Wachman spotted you out on patrol five years ago, and told everybody. That woman can't keep her mouth shut. At first we thought you were undercover, trying to catch us with our pants down, so to speak." He winks. "But then some of the boys said you were . . . quite the French lover."

I blush and look away.

"But no one got ratted out," he continues. "So we figured it out—you really were one of us. And one of them."

I nod. I was. Either one or the other, switching back and forth. It's funny to think they all knew when I went to such pains to hide it. The whole time, they just let me in, let me drink with them, touch them, and they didn't mind that when I left, I was the enemy.

"Is that why you never made any friends?" Pat asks. "Why you always did your business in the bathroom and never took anyone home or went home with anybody? I tried being friendly with you once. I don't know if you remember. Told you my name, said I saw you around and you looked sad, and asked if I could tell you a joke."

"What did I say?" I ask, shaking my head. "I don't remember."

"You ignored me. Did what you normally did: drank, looked sad, and tried to lock eyes with people to see if they were up for meeting you in the bathroom."

I sigh. "I'm sorry. I was afraid of getting too close. Getting blackmailed."

Pat shakes his head. "No one at the Cat would have done that. Except maybe to get out of a parking ticket," he laughs. "There's a whole world of people in San Francisco living relatively happily, Andy. You never seemed to want to do anything but dip your toes in."

"A double life makes that hard."

"Plenty of people lead double lives," Pat says, pointing at the book I put on the desk. "Read that. But you never seemed to live one. You weren't a cop during the day and queer when your hair was down. You were just a cop who needed something from us. And you're pretty enough some of us were happy to give it. Most of us, honestly. But it must have been lonely."

I look down at my feet and Pat stands and goes over to one of the bookshelves and pokes around until he finds what he was looking for and comes back with two cigarettes and a lighter. He offers me one and he lights it while it's in my mouth. Then he lights his own and lies back down. I think about asking him if he's ever been caught in a raid. If he's been locked up or beaten by the people I used to call my comrades in arms.

"Do you think Irene was an accident?" I ask him instead.

He shrugs. "Seems the most likely. The people in this house

love their dramatics, but it's hard to picture any of them push-ing a lady over a balcony."

"Maybe," I say.

"You're the inspector. You'll know. And . . . I'm glad you took the job, Andy."

"Thanks," I say. I stand up, still smoking, and walk to the door. "And thanks for the cigarette."

"Take the book, too," he says, getting up and fetching the book from the desk and handing it to me. "Read it."

"All right," I say, taking it. "Good night."

"Night, Andy."

I turn to go, but halfway out the door, I turn around and look back at him. "What was the joke?"

"What?"

"That you tried to tell me at the Cat. What was the joke?"

He grins. "Oh, I don't remember. But I got plenty. Here's one: Why do so many fairies still attend church even when we're told God hates us?"

I shake my head. "Why?"

"We all love watching someone play with a big organ."

I snort a laugh, shaking my head.

"No? I got more."

"Maybe tomorrow. Good night, Pat."

"Good night, Andy."

I walk away, wondering if I can find my way through the house yet. I go downstairs, to see if anyone else is still awake to say good night to, but the public rooms all seem to be empty. The dining room is dark, and suddenly feels much older than it did before, and the sitting room, without the lights on, is gray, a photo from a magazine on modern living, the kind that feels lifeless. The whole house feels colder, but calmer. And standing over the stairs, the portrait of Irene is presiding over an empty court. This was her house, and now she can't do anything more than glare. Her voice is gone, and it's either silent, everyone waiting for her to speak again, or they're all trying to speak over each other. I stare at her a minute before I go back to my room. There's light coming from under the door of either Henry's or Cliff's room, I'm not sure which, so I walk quietly down the hall and listen to see if they're awake.

"You can come with me," I hear Henry saying. "You're my social secretary. You can always come with me."

"No . . . no," Cliff says, sounding petulant. "It's fine. It's fine. Good night."

"Good night."

The light goes out and I walk back to my own room, locking the door behind me. I pull at the handle, to make sure it really is locked, and it rattles the frame, loud enough someone in the hall could hear it. I let go, and then strip, and get into bed. The sheets are softer than any I've ever slept in, and my skin feels cool against them. I'm asleep before I have time to wonder if being here is a terrible idea.

FIVE

When I wake up, I don't know where I am. I open my eyes and the ceiling isn't the gray-and-tan patched one above my bed. I feel all my nerves seize up. Was I knocked out by someone I was chasing? Did I stumble on something and now I'm about to be interrogated by some mob goon? And then I take a deep breath and remember: it's worse than that.

But today, when my nerves relax, I don't feel so sad. I don't want to immediately find a bar and drink. I look around the room. Light is streaming in and the smell of flowers is still everywhere. My clothes are in a heap on a chair, but Pearl said there were fresh clothes in the wardrobe I could borrow. I go into the bathroom, grabbing one of the larger blue bars of soap and remembering how Cliff had said it matched my eyes. It's a surprisingly modern bathroom, and I shower and shave quickly, the smell of the soap lingering on my skin in a way I've only noticed before when it was the smell of a man and I wanted to wash it off as quickly as possible.

In the wardrobe, I find an unopened box of Jockeys and an array of shirts and suits in a rainbow of colors. I've only ever worn white shirts with black, gray, or navy suits, and truth be told, I'm horrified at the thought of slipping into these. They're garish compared to my usual getup. My old clothes were inspector standard—plainclothes taken literally. When you get the promotion out of the blues, they tell you to dress to fade into the background, but I'd been dressing like that for years off-duty. Best to be forgettable, unnoticed. But my own clothes are wrinkled and smell like alcohol, so I go through the clothes carefully, searching for something that doesn't feel too outrageous.

There's a shirt the same color as the soap I used and a brown herringbone suit that goes nicely with it, both in my size, and a navy tie that doesn't feel like too much over the shirt. I change, and look at myself in the mirror, and for a moment, I'm shocked again, like when I just woke up. I look different while not looking different. Maybe it's the light, but whenever I've caught myself in a mirror before I thought I looked fine. Good enough. But compared to how I look now, I used to look like faded newspaper. Now I'm vibrant. I thought it was Cliff being flirty, but the shirt the color of the soap really does match my eyes. My hair, normally a color between blond and brown, now has a golden touch to it. Maybe it's the country air.

I turn around, done admiring myself, and head downstairs, wondering how they do breakfast. If it'll be the same ritualized event as last night and I'll be expected to show off again, like a trick pony. At least now I'll look good doing it.

I pause on the stairs, realizing what I just thought. In less than twenty minutes I've gone from thinking it might be too much color to thinking I look better than I have before. This place is doing something to me. I'm smiling, and for the first time in what feels like forever, I can tell it fits.

In the dining room, Pearl, Henry, and Alice are eating breakfast.

"Good morning, Andy," Pearl says when she sees me. "Please, come in. How do you like your eggs?"

Henry and Alice are dressed, but Pearl is in a black housecoat with a pattern of roses over it. Henry is reading the newspaper, some headline about McCarthy on it again, and the women are quiet and not making eye contact.

"Over easy," I say, sitting down. Pat, who I didn't even notice standing in the corner, nods and goes into the kitchen, and comes back out with water and a small bowl of fruit, which he puts down in front of me. I thank him, but he just nods. He's a different man around the family.

"Did you sleep well?" Pearl asks.

"Very," I say. "Thank you. And thank you for the clothing, as well."

"You look very good in it," Pearl says.

"Though less like a police officer," Henry adds.

"I had Mr. Kelly check you out of the hotel and retrieve your car and belongings. I'll have them brought to your room so you can change if you feel uncomfortable."

"Actually, I kinda like looking less like a police officer," I say. "If you don't mind."

"Not at all." Pearl smiles. "I'm glad the clothes could find a new home."

Pat appears again, putting a plate of eggs and toast down in front of me. "Coffee or tea?" he asks.

"Coffee, thank you," I say.

He nods and a moment later is pouring me a cup of coffee

so heady that I almost feel drunk smelling it. I take a sip and it tastes better than it smells, not the cheap bitter stuff from the station, but something full and smooth. I cut into my eggs and the yolks run free. I take a bite and it's done perfectly. Dot knows her stuff. Maybe I should think more about Pearl's offer to be full-time security. I can scramble some eggs, but most nights I just grabbed a burger or sandwich somewhere. Much better eating here.

After a few minutes of me enjoying the finer things, Margo appears in a plain navy dressing gown. Her hair is pinned back and her face is bare of any makeup, making her look older than she did last night, and harder, too, like wiping the cake off a knife and seeing the edge glint.

"No Elsie?" Pearl asks.

"Left early to do something at the club, she'll be back by lunch, I think."

Henry makes a soft noise, maybe a cough, and turns the page of the newspaper.

Margo sits down and within moments Pat has poured her a cup of coffee, which she downs in a single swallow. Pat immediately refills it, then leaves for the kitchen.

"You're dressed from the old tricks cabinet," Margo says, looking me over. "I thought you'd thrown all that away, Pearl."

"I wouldn't throw away perfectly good clothes," Pearl says.

This time Alice makes a slight noise, like a snort, and then quickly sips her tea.

"Right, you never know when you'll need to ask a detective to spend the night," Margo says, raising an eyebrow at me. "Where did you go after dinner, last night, Mr. Mills?"

"I spoke with some of the staff," I say, dipping my toast into the runny yolk of my egg and eating it.

"They tell you anything good?" Margo asks.

I smile as I finish chewing. "I'm going to go see the coroner today."

Margo laughs. "Good luck with that."

"What do you think they'll tell you?" Alice asks.

"I have some theories," I say, sipping my coffee.

"If they give you trouble, use what I said," Pearl says. "Your mother and I are old friends."

"I . . . hope I won't have to," I say. No one responds.

Cliff appears, his hair a mess, rubbing his eye. He's wearing a gold dressing gown, only loosely belted so I can see that under it he's wearing matching boxer shorts and nothing else. He looks at me confused. "You're in my seat," he says.

"Sorry," I say, getting up to move, but he waves me back down and goes to sit on the other side of Henry, who puts his hand on the table as soon as Cliff sits down. Cliff takes it as Pat puts down coffee in front of him. Cliff takes a sip then puts his head on Henry's shoulder. Henry turns and kisses him on the forehead. And everyone acts like it's the most natural thing in the world. No one even seems to notice it happen. I've seen affection like that in the clubs before, sure. But here, in morning light, at a breakfast table, it's like they're so bright it makes my eyes hurt.

I turn away from them, eyes almost watering, squinting until I'm facing shadows again.

"Do you have anything today?" Henry asks. I turn to see who he's talking to. Cliff shakes his head, downing his coffee.

"I need to go into the city to pick up my dress from I. Magnin," Margo says. "I have that luncheon tomorrow, the fundraiser with the mayor's wife?" Pat reappears and puts a plate of fried eggs down in front of Margo.

"Ah, right." Henry smiles at her. "Who's going to be there?"

"Samson from the *Chronicle* and Margaret from *Ladies' Home Journal*," Margo says, cutting into her eggs. "I'll make sure to get to her, of course, and I'll try to tell them both that the delay over the new scents is just so we can do something special in Irene's memory. Then I'll remind them that her favorite scent was the lavender, which she thought she'd perfected this year." She cuts off a piece of egg and brings it to her mouth. "That sound about right?" She bites down with a smile. She likes this, likes being invaluable to the business. And judging from the way Henry is beaming at her, she's good at it.

"Better than anything I could have come up with," Henry says. "You are brilliant, and we'd be lost without you."

"Very true," Margo says, pleased with the compliment. "Have you thought about what I suggested, with new wrapping instead of a whole new image stamped into the soap? It would be cheaper."

"Would it? The design alone is so much more intricate, plus printing."

"Palmolive put out their new wrappers and Barb says it was very cheap. If she's there tomorrow I'll try to find out the name of the printer they used, but even if I don't, I think it's the less-expensive move in the long run."

Henry nods. "Let me run the numbers, but you're probably right. That sound good to you, Pearl?"

"Oh." Pearl smiles, genuinely happy to be consulted. "You know the business better than I do. I just don't want you to forget what Irene did. People have expectations. And it would be nice to honor her somehow. That's all I meant with the new scents."

"I know," Henry says, looking across the table at Margo,

who nods, dabbing at the corners of her mouth. "We just have to figure out the best way to honor her and what she did while moving forward. Unless you want to start remixing the scents every year, Margo?"

Margo tilts her head. "I can try, if you want. But I don't have Irene's nose."

"Who does?" Pearl asks, frowning.

Cliff sniffs loudly, and Henry chuckles, kissing him on the forehead again.

"Stop that," Pearl says, but she's smiling.

I brush the toast crumbs from my palms and stand up. "I should get going. Thank you for breakfast."

"Good luck, Inspector," Margo says in a voice that makes it clear she thinks I won't find anything. After seeing them all at breakfast, so different from last night, I almost hope she's right. They seem happy. But if one of them is a murderer, it's all just another lie.

"Any rules about the gate?" I ask Pearl.

"I had Mr. Kelly put a key for the gate on your car key ring. Please lock up when you leave."

"Sure thing," I say. "I'll be back later."

"Good luck," Pearl says.

Outside, the sun is almost blinding and the flowers' scent potent enough it becomes unnatural, like a fantasy of perfume instead of actual plants in the dirt. My car is parked behind a few others. It's a decade-old black Buick sedan in need of a good wash. I get in, the keys are in the ignition, a fancy-looking new gate key hanging off them. I look around, and everything else looks about how I left it. It's odd, someone else having been in my car without me, like the feeling someone is watching you, but you can't see them.

I start the car and head off the estate, locking the gate behind me. The trees are dense and all look the same, like prison bars, so it takes me a few wrong turns before I find my way back to the highway, but once I'm there, I coast along it to San Rafael. I've been here a handful of times, enough to remember how to get here. I hope enough that they remember me, too, but not enough that anyone from SFPD called to let them know how and why I'm not on the force anymore.

San Rafael is a cute little town, the kind with a main street lined in signs that have musical notes on them, and big names cascading down the sides of small buildings. Outside the main town, it's mostly suburbs, ranging from middle to high class, and farther out than that are the private estates, like Lavender House. There are palm trees and a few careful-looking white churches that stand like chess pieces at the ends of streets. I cruise through town until I come to the coroner's office, which is in a building filled with other small medical practices: dentists, optometrists. The listing of the businesses on the front door is littered with body parts showing off their specialties. There's no morgue in Marin County, they just rent space in funeral parlors when they need it. But the coroner has an office where all the records are. And that's what I need.

I park and head up a few flights and then walk into the office. It's a cramped space, with a lazy ceiling fan offering the only hint of air. There's a desk, a few chairs that look like they were found washed up on a beach, a door leading to the offices, and more important, the files. The woman behind the desk looks bored, her head resting on one hand. She can't have been here more than an hour or two, but she looks like she's at the end of a long day.

"Hi," I say, walking in. I can't remember her name, and

when she looks up, I can tell she can't remember mine, either. She's older than me, maybe pushing sixty, with a full face and a nice smile. She hasn't colored her hair, and she's wearing an old-fashioned plaid dress with white buttons down the front like my dad's assistant at the insurance office used to wear. Secretaries are usually easy. A kind look and some appreciation for the work they do and they'll help you out. She doesn't look much different.

"You're the SFPD inspector," she says.

"Yeah. Was. Now I work private cases, and I'm hoping you can get me a file, if it's not trouble for you, I mean."

She lifts her head up and smiles.

"Sure," she says. "If it's not a sealed file, I don't mind show-ing you. What's the name?"

"Irene Lamontaine, like the soap. She had a bad fall about three weeks back?"

The woman nods. "I remember, very sad. You think they'll be changing up the soap formula again this year without her?"

"I think they're going to wait awhile."

She smiles. "That's good. I like how the iris one smells now." She tilts her head again. "Not that I'm happy for the reason."

"I know what you mean," I say. "I'm getting paid to see if she died naturally or not."

She nods. "All right, let me go check the records. You can't take anything out of here, you know, so I hope you brought a notebook."

"Always do," I say.

She vanishes into the back room with the keys, leaving me alone in the room. There's not much to do, so I look out the window at the street for a while, then stare at the bulletin board they have by the door. It's covered in wanted posters and photos of missing children, but one missing poster catches my eye. It's a sketch, with dark eyes looking out, in a familiar, welcoming expression. I study it for a moment more, before it hits me: it looks a lot like Cliff. *Clive Thorpe, age twenty-seven, missing, reward.* The rest of it is buried under some other missing posters. It's been there awhile. Maybe it's not him. Who would be looking for a grown man, after all, unless he's a criminal? And the poster isn't police. It's a missing poster. It's possible Cliff had some other life before—maybe married, wife, kids— that he just walked out on. You hear about that kind of thing. But Cliff didn't seem like the type. He didn't seem like he'd ever tried to hide anything, ever did anything that wouldn't make him happy. It's hard to imagine anyone looking for him. It could just be a similar face. It happens. On the force, I'd been called to more than one case of mistaken identity.

I'm about to pull it down, just in case, when the door opens again. I look up. It's not the woman. It's a man, the actual coroner. We've only met once before, but I recognize him. He stares at me awhile, trying to place me, then glares.

"What do you want?" he asks.

"Your girl is helping me," I say. "Just need a file for a case."

"You're not an inspector anymore . . ." He sticks his chin up and his hands go to his sides. He's bald with a big mustache, and it almost looks like it's quivering. "You pervert." He spits the word. I look down at my feet.

I've always been so good at hiding it. Always kept it out of sight, that part of me invisible, so no one thought to call me anything. Except when they caught me. But that was in the back of a police car, handcuffed. Here, I thought maybe I could get away with it. But, now, suddenly, hearing that word, it's like my whole body is retreating into itself. My hands and face are hot, my eyes water like I've been slapped. I want a hat to hide behind. I want to run out the door, even though I know I could knock this guy out with one punch. I want to vanish. I haven't felt like this since my grandpa was alive. He used to drink and yell, and when he did, I would crawl under my bed and hide there until he was asleep. I'd forgotten that, and it all comes back now. The smell of the cheap beer. The soft fur of the teddy bear I held under the bed, and how it smelled there, like socks and dust.

I don't say anything. I don't look up.

The door opens again and I hear the woman's feet as she steps out.

"I have the file," she says, then stops. I look up, and she's looking at the coroner, and then at me.

"Don't give him anything," the coroner hisses. "He was fired from the force for being a faggot."

I turn and leave. I don't even think about it. My feet take over and run away for me, like a rabbit when a wolf looks in its direction.

I get downstairs and back outside fast, practically running down the stairs and bursting out of the door like I was drowning. Outside I bend over, trying to catch my breath. I'm winded the way I've only been from being punched in the stomach before. My hands are shaking a little, but I manage to get into my car, open the glove compartment, and light up a cigarette after a few minutes and only a little fumbling. I suck the smoke down and it calms me a little.

I've never been called that. I've never seen the look in a man's eyes when he spat the word at me. When the guys at the station brought in other queers and tossed the word around, it was never at me, or if it was, it was so I could catch it like a ball and throw it back at them, like a game I was part of. Once they knew, they didn't even look at me, no one said a word as I was marched out. But now the ball has been thrown directly at my chest, and it's hit, hard. I have to remember how to breathe.

Without meaning to, or wanting to, I think of other people calling me that: Guys on the force I had beers with. Guys I served with. My best friend from high school. My mother. I imagine each one of them, knowing right away if they'd shout it or hiss it, or whisper it in horror once they knew. Because they could know now. It's something out there, spreading like a disease, and I don't know who's going to find out next. Who's going to say that word at me next. And if it'll be the last word they ever say to me.

Cigarette smoke is filling the car, but I don't roll down the windows. I like that it's covering my face, making me anonymous again.

My mother would say the word in shock, I think. She'd turn away and cry if we were in person. But we haven't seen each other in a while. She'd probably call. She'd cradle the receiver in both hands and say it into the wire, and I wouldn't say anything back, and then she'd hang up. All I'd have left of a family would be the empty sound of a dial tone.

I smoke the cigarette about halfway down, still sitting in my car, as my nerves settle. I wipe my eyes with the heels of my hands. They smell like smoke.

I survived that. So that's something. Surviving is good. Means I can keep living if I want. Keep surviving. That's all that's left, I think. But I don't know what to do next on the case. I can tell them what happened, explain about the tooth and why it could be murder, but I know it won't be enough for Margo or the others, and it'll just upset Pearl more. Make the family implode. I need to figure out a way to get the report. Maybe I can bribe him. Money from a faggot is still money, right? There's got to be some way, or else what am I even pretending for? Pretending I could be some kind of queer PI for a week instead of just throwing myself in the bay like I told myself I would. Better that than a dial tone.

I almost jump when there's a tap on the car window. The cigarette comes loose in my hand and falls to the floor. I stomp it out before it sets the cheap rubber mat on fire, then bend down and pick it up before looking out the window. It's the secretary from upstairs. She's frowning.

I roll down the window. "I was just about to leave. I'm not trying to cause trouble."

"I have the file," she says, her voice low.

"What?"

"I'm going for a smoke break in that alley over there." She nods across the block. "It's out of the sun, so it's cooler." I watch her go to the crosswalk and look both ways before walking across the street, fishing in her purse for a pack of cigarettes as she does so. Part of me wonders if this is a trap. If she called up some local boys and I'm going to walk into that alley and into a beating. But I need that report to confirm my suspicions, so I try to tell myself she's a nice old lady, and she wouldn't do anything like that, and the lie works long enough that I'm halfway there before I drop it.

Because anyone could do something like that.

I ball my hands into fists and try to keep my eyes sharp as I walk into the alley in case it is a trap. It smells like smoke and faintly of urine. There's a faint breeze, and it brings the sound of a soft sigh as I turn the corner. Maybe this will be it, I think. I survived some nasty words, so maybe I can survive some nasty kicks to the head, if those are what's waiting for me. Or maybe I don't. If it is a trap, some way to lure the queer to his beating, and I die on hot pavement, staring at the shadows of palm trees, then I hope they throw me in the water after.

But there's no one there but the secretary, leaning against the side of a brick building and blowing smoke out of her mouth like an arrow. She looks out the opposite end of the alley, the slant of sunlight on the wall not quite reaching her.

"Miss . . ."

She turns around, still smoking, and smiles at me, a kind of small, pitying smile that makes my stomach shrivel up inside me.

"I'm Gertie," she says. She holds her cigarette in her mouth as she fishes in her large bag and pulls out a big green file and holds it out to me. I step forward and take it, flipping it open. It's Irene's file.

"I can only give you a few minutes with it," she says. "Dr. Levinstein will get suspicious if I'm gone too long."

"Thank you," I say, riffling through the pages. I want to ask why she's helping, but I need to learn what I can first. There are a few photos and some notes. Not a very thorough autopsy: they didn't suspect murder. But she was on her stomach when they found her, very unusual. If it were my case, I would have asked about it. The coroner notes that maybe she'd flipped herself in her last moments. No mention of the chipped tooth, aside from a photo marked with "earlier accident?" He also says that she died from an acute pulmonary edema, not from bleeding out or hitting her head. But pulmonary edema are words I only have a passing knowledge of. "Any chance you can help me translate the doctor speak?" I ask.

She doesn't move, but her eyes coast over to the file. "I was a nurse in the war, so I can try."

"Pulmonary edema. From a fall. That sound right?"

"Unusual. Maybe if it was a long fall and crushed her. Was she healthy?"

I think of the stairs she was climbing over and over every day and nod.

"Then I'd say she was dead before she hit the ground, looking at this. I guess she could have turned herself over, if she didn't die when she hit the ground. But if she was so old she had the edema from hitting the ground, I doubt she could do that. She'd be gasping for breath, dying. Why would she flip herself over?"

I nod. "That's what I thought." Dead before she hit the ground. No live person falls like that. "What could do that?" I ask. "Cause an acute pulmonary edema?"

"Oh . . . plenty of stuff. Heart condition, crush injury, drowning, pneumonia, some fumes, some poisons."

"Poisons?"

"Cyanide, mostly. You find it in certain dyes, some household poisons like for wasps and other bugs, though they don't sell those as much since the war."

"Thanks," I say, and hand her back the folder. I should search around the house for old poisons, then. I look up at her. For a moment, I'd felt like I was on a case, a real case, like I was back on the force. But then the alley comes back to me, the sun hits the top of my head, and I remember I'm no cop. I thought I was going to die walking in here. Something else I survived. "Why'd you help me out, anyway?" I ask her.

She drops her cigarette and stubs it out with her toe. "I was a nurse in the war, like I said. I was a nurse before that, too, but I joined up to help the boys, worked on the base. My granddaughter, too, even though she was new at it. She was a good girl, real smart, resilient, too. Her mom got sick and died when she was little and her dad died overseas while the war was going on, so I was all she had. She met another nurse, and the two of them . . . I thought they were just best friends. The way girls can be. But then they ran off together. She sent me a letter, asking for forgiveness for . . . What a thing, to ask for forgiveness for falling in love. I was a little shocked at first. Maybe a little disgusted, the way we are with things we don't understand. But after a year or so of missing her, I decided it didn't much matter, as long as she was happy. I wrote back. Got the letter back, though—addressee unknown. Haven't heard from her since. It's been almost four years."

She looks down at her crushed cigarette and I realize she's doing it to hide the tears, and offer my handkerchief, but she waves it away, and looks up at me. "Her name was Prudence. Prudence Carsen. You . . . don't know her, do you? From a club, or something? I just want to see her again."

This might be worse than the beating I was expecting. "No," I mumble. "I'm sorry . . ." I don't really know anyone, I want to say, and San Francisco is a big city, if she's even still here. She's probably in the wind, maybe with a new name. The one queer who has family that loves her, and she disappeared anyway, because . . . that's what you do. You disappear. It's the safest thing.

"Oh." She sniffs, and looks up, her eyes are huge and pale blue. "That's all right. I knew it was a long shot. But . . . if you meet her can you tell her about me? Tell her Grandma still loves her and wants to see her again?"

"Sure," I say, and it's my turn to look at my feet, because I can't look her in the eye—she'll know I'm never going to find her granddaughter. And I don't want to know what it looks like—someone like them loving someone like us. I don't want to imagine her expression on my mother's face and dare to hope. "I can do that."

"Thanks," she says, and takes a deep breath. "You're a good boy." She pats me on the cheek and I look up at her and she's smiling, composed again. "Now wait a few minutes before you leave the alley after me. Dr. Levinstein sometimes watches me out the window, tapping his watch, the old scrooge."

I nod, and she walks out of the alley the way she came in, her heels clacking on the pavement as she goes. I lean back against the wall and wait. I think about her granddaughter, and then I think about my own grandmother. I try to remember how she looked—she died just before the war. Soft eyes, blue, like mine, gray hair always pinned back. I imagine her calling me the name the coroner called me, but it doesn't fit. It feels silly, somehow.

I shake that out of my head, and lean my cheek against the cool brick. Irene was dead before she fell. She took down the lavender, she inhaled, and she died. That's where it happened, not the fall. She was dying when she staggered to the edge, and maybe just fell over as she died. She was gone before she started falling. And something poisonous doesn't end up in a jar marked lavender by accident. It was murder, and now I have proof.

SIX

I drive back to Lavender House feeling up and down like the waves on the shore. At least I accomplished something. I can tell Pearl with certainty that she's not wrong, that it was murder. I just need to figure out who would have done it. I should probably start with looking for poisons, and who had access to them. I bite my tongue as I pull up the small drive to the house. I don't love murders at all, but this one stings. Each of them could be a killer, and while we haven't all become bosom buddies, they're the first queer people I've gotten to know since the war. The first place I've been myself, or something like it. I hate to think I've been showing that to a killer.

I arrive at the gate and step out of the car to unlock it, but it's already unlatched. I push it open—it doesn't make a sound—and I get back in the car and drive through. I get out again to lock the gate behind me. I stare down the road on the other side of it, the one I just came down. It's narrow, and winding, trees shadowing it so dark it could be evening already.

Pearl said to keep it locked, but it was open when she drove me here, too. How often does the staff leave, I wonder? Are there delivery men? Do I need to look outside the house for the murderer? That would certainly be easier on Pearl. And on me, maybe.

I drive down through the flowers toward the fountain and pink trees, but screech to a stop when a figure materializes in the middle of the road, one hand on their hip, the other holding a rifle like a cane, down to the ground.

There's a cloud that obscures the figure's face, but it passes and I see it's Elsie, looking straight at me. The gun makes me flinch for a moment, an old instinct to reach for my own weapon, but nothing about her reads as wanting to start something. She's wearing a men's tweed hunting suit, with tall leather boots and a brown women's hat with a large turkey feather in it. Once she's made eye contact with me, she steps out of the way so I can park. When I get out, she's standing in front of me.

"You know how to shoot, right?" she asks.

"Yes."

"You've killed before?"

"Why are you asking?" I close the car door. I flex my feet in my shoes, the gravel under them poking through the thin leather. They're the only thing I'm wearing that's mine, I realize. All the clothes are someone else's, but the shoes, at least, are familiar.

"We have a vermin problem, and I could use an extra marksman."

"Vermin?" I ask. I'm fairly sure she's using that word hoping I'll think she means a person.

She arches an eyebrow and smiles a little. "Rabbits. Tearing up the garden. The cook needs that garden. So, while you're helping out around here, I thought I'd enlist you for some hunting. No one else around here has the stomach for it."

"All right," I say. "Lead the way."

I can tell Pearl about it being murder later. I can tell them all later, after I get a better read on them. Elsie included. Especially if she's got the killer instinct she's asking me about.

She walks me around the side of the house, following a narrow stone path.

"So, you left early this morning," I say.

"Is that a detective observation?" she asks, looking back at me to smirk. "Am I supposed to say I was off doing something suspicious?"

"Just making conversation."

"I needed to pay for some deliveries at the club. They come early. Got up, drove out, signed, paid, made sure they hadn't stiffed me, and then came back."

Behind the house is a large greenhouse, standing far enough away to be out of the main house's shadow, but just barely. Beyond that is a large fenced-in garden, but Elsie leads me to the greenhouse first.

"Must be a busy life, there and back all the time." I don't ask why one of her employees couldn't have signed for her. Maybe she's just one of those women who need to do everything themselves to know it was done right.

"I don't mind it," she says, pushing open the greenhouse door. "I don't spend every night here, you know. More than half the week, sure, but I'm an independent woman, and I need some time alone now and then."

I follow her inside, my face instantly damp from the air. It's humid, warm, and smells of wet dirt. There are rows of tables covered in small pots of soil, green shoots just barely shrugging out of some of them. There's also a spiral staircase to a balcony area above us. Judy, the gardener, is up there, watering more seedlings. She doesn't even look down at us.

I stop for a moment, because there's something familiar about this. The layout of the tables, the staircase. Then suddenly I realize—it's like the library. Except where the library was all stone and cold, here it's all warm glass.

"What is it?" Elsie asks, turning around when she sees I've stopped.

"It's the same layout as the soap library," I say.

"Is it?" Elsie looks around. "I was only down there once but . . . I suppose so."

"She designed it that way," Judy says, coming down the stairs. Her footsteps on the metal create hollow echoes. "There was an old greenhouse, but it was too small, she said."

"Irene?" I ask.

Judy nods and steps off the last step, looking at me. Her face is even, unreadable. "So she had it torn down, and built another one. Said it should be like the library, same size and shape. She told me she didn't want to have to bother thinking of another layout."

"Was she in here a lot, then?"

"Can't you do your detecting some other time?" Elsie asks before Judy can respond. "We have rabbits to kill."

Judy walks across the room to another batch of plants without saying anything and starts to water them. I'll come back to her later, when I don't have Elsie breathing down my neck.

I follow Elsie to the far end of the room, where there's a cabinet, some shelves, and a table, none of them with plants. Gardening tools, gloves, shears, and below the table, some large bottles with skulls and crossbones on them—poisons of some kind. Pretty common in a greenhouse, but the nurse said it could have been a common poison that did it. I imagine Irene popping the cork on a different, safe-looking bottle, and inhaling, sniffing loudly and dragging all that death into her.

I don't linger on the poisons, though. I don't want to draw attention to them. Elsie opens up the cabinet without saying anything, so I don't think she noticed. Inside are a few old rifles, leaning against the side, and a shelf on top has bullets. I grab a rifle and some bullets, loading the gun as Elsie closes the cabinet.

"So anyone can get in here?"

"The greenhouse?" Elsie almost laughs. "Yes. We don't lock the greenhouse. What, you think someone knocked her over the railing with a rake?"

There's another set of doors next to us and she opens these, the cooler air blowing and drying the sweat off my face. We walk outside together.

"Everyone trusts each other here, Andy," she says, following a path to the edge of the garden. "And since you're a detective, and we both know you're going to ask—that's why I know it wasn't murder. We've got drama, sure, just like any family. But not the kind to kill over."

"You'd be surprised what people are willing to kill over," I say. "We're out here about to take out some innocent creatures for digging up some carrots."

Elsie laughs. "They're *my* carrots. And besides, rabbits aren't family."

"How about the people at the Ruby? They your family too?"

"Of course. Though they're also my employees."

"How'd you start the club, anyway?" I ask, genuinely curious. "You came out of the blue."

"Here," Elsie says as we come up on a vegetable garden. It's huge, and loosely fenced in, but the fence has been burrowed under in several places. "If you see one, point." She lowers her voice. "And I came from New York. I know that's out of the blue for some people, but there's a whole other coastline on the other side of the country, you know. I was married to a club owner there. Watched him do it, thought it was pretty easy, so when we divorced and I came here, I used what he'd paid me to go away to set up the Ruby."

"Husband?" I ask, surprised.

"Like the rabbits, I enjoy life on both sides of the fence, Andy." She turns and smiles at me. Her lips are bright red. "Surely that's not shocking." She turns back to the horizon. At the wall are the redwoods, reaching up like headstones, but in front of them are some woods, if you can call them that. Small clumps of different trees, a suggestion of something wild. "I see them at the tree line a lot," she says. I wonder how they got past the wall. Dig under it? A gap? This place isn't nearly as inaccessible as it pretends to be.

I turn my gaze away from her and to the trees, watching for movement in silence for a few minutes, but we don't see anything.

"So how'd you meet Margo?" I ask.

"Fundraiser for your former employer. Policeman's ball. I donated, of course, because that's how you keep them out of your hair. Henry gave because it looks good. So we were all at the party—I was even wearing a dress. The moment I saw her, I knew we'd get together. She's just my type: cold on the outside, hot on the inside, and probably more trouble than I should be courting."

"Trouble?" I ask.

"The setup. We can't go out together in public without bringing down an entire soap empire and destroying her stability. I could probably take care of her, but . . . truth is I like this place. I like coming out here to the country where everyone acts like we're a happy normal family, like Henry and Margo are siblings, not spouses. It's like an ideal queer little world. It's different from my more bohemian family back in the city. No cooks or butlers there, but more dances and parties. I do sometimes wish I could show Margo more of that, and she knows it, but it's her call. She decides how much risk to take, and I can go off and party without her when I want."

"Sounds nice."

"It's not bad. Way better than my marriage was." She smirks, then suddenly raises her gun, points, and fires. The sound cracks in my ear, makes my blood rush like startled horses. If she were going to kill me, this would be an easy way. A stupid way, though. Whoever murdered Irene was smart: poison, waiting. They wouldn't just shoot me in the backyard. I hope, anyway.

I look over to where she's fired and I spot the rabbit she was aiming at just as it ducks out of sight.

"Damn," she says. "Missed. We should get closer."

"No, just give it a second," I say. My mouth tastes metallic. "If we get close now, they'll just hide. Let them think they're safe." The air smells like flowers and gunpowder and a faint breeze creeps up my jacket sleeves, giving me goose bumps.

"Speaking of thinking they're safe . . . how are you doing? With people knowing about you now?"

I keep my eyes on the horizon. "Not great." I lick my lips. "I got fired, kicked out of my apartment, people I worked with won't speak to me, and today someone called me a faggot."

Elsie leans back on the fence bordering the garden and lets

out a low whistle. "Well. That doesn't sound great. What was your life like before?"

"What?"

"Before people knew. What was your life?" She pushes herself off the fence and turns to me. "No, wait, let me guess. I'm usually pretty good at this."

I shake my head a little. "Sure."

"You were excellent at your job, went to work every day, threw yourself into it." She paces a little, one hand circling in the air like she's thinking. "You wanted to make sure that's what people saw when they looked at you—the job, a cop. Not a fairy. So you worked hard, and then went home, and worked some more, maybe drank, went to sleep, got up, went to work . . . day in, day out. No friends, of course—friends mean people who know you, and then they notice things, like how you never take any girls out, how your eyes linger on that one suspect's jawline. And making sure no one noticed was how you spent most of your life."

I raise my gun to the tree line, but nothing moves.

Elsie keeps talking. "Except for those breaks you took at the clubs. But they were always quick little things. You went there for release, not companionship. Or maybe to reward yourself, another week with no one figuring it out? Maybe you even thought you were better than the people there? After all, they're the outcasts, but you were still a respected member of society. And you had a secret. No one knew. Until they did. And now you think your whole life is gone, shattered, because all you had was the job. That sound about right?"

I don't turn to look at her. I know my face is angry and I don't want to give her the satisfaction. Sure, I was married to the job. What else was there for me to be married to?

"Well, Andy," she says, turning back to the tree line and raising her gun in a mirror of me. "I hope you're not offended, but your silence tells me my guesses are right, or close to it, and that thing you called a life isn't worth mourning. Those friends you never made at the club are living more than you ever did. But if you make an effort, you can start a real life now."

I snort, but keep my eyes on the trees. "Real life as what? Something like one of these rabbits, there for people to take shots at or keep locked in a cage? I don't have the money to live like you do, Ms. Gold."

"Elsie. Call me Elsie. And neither did I, once. For a cop, you sure do scare easy." She fires at the tree line, and I realize the rabbit had poked its head up again, and she just hit it. She starts up the hill to the site of the corpse. Except it's not a corpse. It's shot, bleeding, and can't move, but it's still alive. It blinks up at us, looking confused and terrified.

"Damn," Elsie whispers. She kneels down and cradles the rabbit's head, almost tenderly, before snapping its neck. She does it easily, quickly. She's killed before. "I hate that," she says, standing up.

I swallow. I am like a rabbit. Maybe I won't be hunted and shot by a woman in a feathered hat, but I could be harassed and kept from working until I starve to death in some alley. The coroner knew, and he didn't want to help. I can't imagine anyone else will. Maybe he even told my old friends, the police, and they'll be looking for me now, happy for an excuse to arrest me, and I'll get beaten to death in a cell. I don't have her money to save myself from that. Or maybe I could have a good weekend at the Ruby with some money from this case, and then pitch myself in the sea, like I'd planned. It's better to go out on my own terms than to have someone else snap my neck. It's not pretty to watch even when it's done with some compassion.

Elsie ties the rabbit to her belt, though I'm not sure the point in holding on to it. The hit means there's probably not much good meat.

"So the Ruby is successful enough you can buy a ticket to the policeman's ball?" I ask her, not wanting to go back to the topic of me. "I mean, those aren't cheap, and all the bribes you must dole out to make sure the Ruby is never raided . . . you must be doing very well."

Elsie raises her gun again and fires farther into the trees. I look to where she shot, but see nothing, even as she starts forward at a brisk pace. She strides ahead so far conversation is impossible, but I follow until I spot something twitching back toward the garden. Without thinking I instinctively raise my gun, aim at the rabbit, and fire. I hit it between the eyes.

I head back toward the garden and stare down at the small rabbit I just killed. It just wanted to eat, so it could live, and there was a garden that was practically wide open just sitting here. At least that's what it looked like right up until the rabbit died.

I sigh and pick up the corpse. Behind me, I hear Elsie approaching and turn around. She still only has the one rabbit on her belt.

"Nice shooting," she says. "That should keep the vegetables safe for a little while."

She doesn't answer my question, like she forgot, or never heard it, which is an answer itself: she doesn't want to talk about the Ruby's finances.

I follow her back to the shed, where we hang our guns up, then head back to the main house. I hand her the rabbit when she asks. She goes in through the side door to the kitchen, but I walk back around to the front, trying to forget the dead rabbit, and letting the heady scent of flowers overwhelm me. When I get to the door, I ring the bell, and Pat opens it for me with a wink.

"You know where Pearl is?" I ask him.

"Her office. Want me to tell you how to get there, or do you remember?"

"Upstairs to the left," I say.

He nods. "Second door on the right."

"Thanks," I say, and head upstairs.

"You start that book yet?" he asks me when I'm on the landing.

"Not yet. I will."

"Enjoy," he says. I walk up the stairs and find the door to the study and knock.

"Come in," Pearl calls.

I open the door into what I thought would be a small room with a desk, but by now I should have known better. It's a large room with huge windows letting in bright streams of light. The floor has an oriental rug, and the walls are covered in bookcases, or hung with what look like framed documents. In the corner, there's a bust on a pedestal. And in the center of the room is a huge wooden desk, art deco and made of a few different types of wood. An inlaid pattern in what almost looks like letters is running along the side facing me. Behind the desk is Pearl, several papers laid out in front of her, which she sweeps into a pile when she looks up and sees me. She's changed into a bright red blouse, and a white women's suit jacket hangs on the back of her chair.

"There is no place for grief in a house which serves the muse," she says, smiling a little.

"What?" I ask.

"The quote on the side of the desk that you were looking at. It's in the Greek, so I was translating. Irene had the desk made for me as a present after our first year as a couple."

"It's impressive."

"It's gaudy, but I like it . . ." She pauses, tilts her head. "Though I suppose it's a little melancholy now. Hard not to be a house of grief." She shrugs. "Maybe without Irene, we have no muse to serve." She motions at one of the chairs in front of her desk, and I sit down.

"Who's the quote by?"

"What?" She looks at me like I've spoken in tongues. "Oh . . . Sappho." She points at the bust in the corner. "Sorry, I'm just so used to everyone knowing that if I ever quote anyone, it's probably Sappho. Do you know who she was?"

I shake my head.

"The Poetess. A poet so famous they called her the tenth muse. This is in ancient Greece. She's from the isle of Lesbos, which is where we get the word 'lesbian.' Because of her. Her poetry, especially the way she talks about other women, makes her desires and inclinations clear. Some argue to the contrary, but they're all men. I've studied her extensively, and I feel quite certain."

"Quite certain?"

"That she was romantic with women. She loved so passion-ately, too. Her poetry is like nothing else."

"How'd you come across her? I didn't expect you to be a classicist."

"Because I'm a lesbian with the last name Velez?" Pearl asks, smiling a little.

"I didn't mean to offend."

"You didn't. It's not an uncommon question. My family

came here from Mexico when I was three. We were fairly wealthy, so we could afford a nice house, nice things, and as I was my father's only child, a nice education. Notre Dame de Namur, class of 1919. I studied the classics there. Learned to love them, and Sappho let me find myself. After, I thought I'd be a teacher, but there weren't any jobs, and my father was keen to marry me off, so when I saw an ad in the paper looking for an educated young woman to work as the personal assistant to the wife of a businessman, a live-in position, I took it, just to get out of the house. The wife was Irene. From there . . . everything just fell into place." She smiles, wistful, and then looks sad, probably having just remembered that her wife is dead and I'm here to tell her something about it.

I look at her desk. There are papers having to do with soap production pushed to the side, and a few books of classical poetry, but what catches my eye the most are the photos. A framed photo of Irene, smiling in a purple dress. A photo of Henry and Cliff, at some kind of party, their arms around each other like football players in a huddle. Margo, alone, smiling through a crowd, raising a champagne glass.

"That was a Halloween party for the company," Pearl says, pointing at the one of Henry and Cliff. "When there's drinking, men can be more affectionate in public. The key is to look like you're drinking a lot, but not drink so much you actually forget the rules."

"And that's Margo at a party?"

Pearl nods and taps on a face just behind her. "And Elsie, staring at her. No one would notice it but us, of course. Serendipity, this photo."

"None of you and Irene," I say.

"She never cared much for photos, and it's harder, a photo

of just the two of us, and not all the women. We had one that I cut up, but it was awkward, just us, side by side, not even touching. I like this one of her alone better. She looked at me like that a lot."

I study Irene's expression in the photo—not interrogating, exactly, but examining, and smiling, like she liked what she was discovering.

"None of Alice, either," I say.

Pearl shakes her head. "I asked once, but she just went back to the kitchen, doling out orders for the party. We never asked her to, but she really has put herself in charge of the staff. Which I appreciate. But it means she's not around for pictures."

I nod, and lean back in my chair. "So," I say. I wait, making sure she knows that we're onto more than just her love story or her family.

She nods. I've told enough people about their dead loved ones that I can usually detach from this, be polite, but this one takes me a while to say.

"It was murder." I pause, but Pearl just takes a deep breath and nods again. "She was dead before she went over the ledge. My guess is there was poison in the shattered bottle of lavender. She sniffed it. That would have been it for her, but she stumbled over to the bannister and fell over, which obscured the real cause of death." I pause to let it sink in. "I'm sorry, Pearl."

She looks at me, her face almost blank, and then suddenly releases a long breath that turns almost into a moan, but which she cuts short. "Oh," she says. "Oh, oh, oh. I . . . I feel relieved, Mr. Mills. Because that means I'm not going crazy. But then I . . . shouldn't feel relieved. Because this is awful. I didn't know what I wanted you to discover. I . . ." She wipes at her eyes, and leans back in her chair, looking at the ceiling. "Oh. I don't . . ."

She looks back down and opens a drawer in the desk, takes out a handkerchief and covers her eyes with it like a blindfold. Like she's readying herself for a firing squad. "So," she asks, her eyes still covered, "who could it be? Could someone have broken in?"

I think of the gate that should be locked but isn't always. "Maybe, but it needed to be someone who knew her habits. Who knew where the library was, and that she would sniff the bottles. The poison was probably planted a while ago. This is a very patient murder."

"So you think it was . . . one of the family?" She drops the handkerchief, looking at me.

I nod, not meeting her eyes because I know how much it will hurt her.

"No, no. I don't believe any of my family could have done that. Couldn't it have been an accident? A mislabeled bottle?"

"I suppose anything is possible. If you want me to stop investigating, I will."

I let that hang in silence for a while. It's not what I'd choose, but I need to let her decide. I'm not police anymore. I'm not looking for justice. And this could tear what's left of her family apart.

"No," she says. "No, I need to know. Who could do this?"

"Well, that's what I'll aim to find out. Were there any fights that Irene had in the past few weeks? Anyone nasty to her, or was she nasty to anyone?"

"Well . . . yes," she sighs. "Alice. Irene and Alice bickered all the time. But Alice bickers with everyone—the staff, her daughter." She looks away, slightly guilty, but also relieved. She wants it to be Alice, I think. Or doesn't want—but she's the best option. Unless she thinks of another.

I nod.

"Alice is very useful and can be very kind, but she does keep to herself. Irene once offered to get her her own little apartment in San Rafael, find her another job. But Alice was offended by that. Said she'd never abandon her daughter. So Irene let her stay. But they bickered. Though Irene bickered with each of us, really. She was very protective, you know, and would get annoyed if she thought we were taking risks. 'Safe within the walls, unsafe without.' That's what she always said. But you need to understand, it was how she showed her love. She just always forgot to finish it. To say 'and I need you to stay safe because I love you.' It was my job to remind her to say that part."

I nod. "Anything in particular she fought about with anyone recently?"

"No . . . just the usual . . . In fact, Andy, if you don't mind, I'd like you to pursue the idea that it was someone from outside. I know we're not good at locking the gate—it drove Irene crazy. She'd go out some nights and check it was locked herself. But it was raining that night, so she didn't check, and maybe someone came in in the dark, and snuck into the house and switched the bottles."

I raise my eyebrows. "If you really insist on looking into it, I can, but there were no signs of a break-in. It's unlikely."

"I do insist." Pearl nods. "Please. Look into . . . everyone else, too, if you must. The . . . staff. Though that would hurt me almost as much as if one of the family had done it. I really can't believe it would be anyone from here. So, please consider it could have been someone from outside. Maybe a competitor."

"Who's Lamontaine Soap's biggest competitor, then?"

"Gleam," Pearl says with a frown. "The Gleam Soap Company. Owned by George Cohen. He's local. I've met him a few times. Very opportunistic. Very business savvy. I never saw him as the murdering sort, but it seems more likely than anyone in the house."

I purse my lips, not wanting to say I disagree. I've never had a client before, unless you count the victim, but that's what Pearl is. My job before was just to pursue the truth. Now I have to pursue the truth and whatever she wants. I'll look into her leads, or her guesses. At worst, it just costs me time. "All right. And have you had any guests in the past few months? If we're talking about someone from outside."

"No. We seldom allow guests here, for obvious reasons. You're the first new person to come stay with us since Margo met Elsie. That was a year ago. Before that, the last person to come live here was Cliff, and that was nearly five years back. Just a few months after Alice."

I stand up. "All right. I'll look into this outsider angle because you want me to, but I'm going to follow all the leads to the very end, Pearl. That's what you're paying me for."

"I understand."

"I'm going to look at the library again, now that I know what I know. See if I can figure out what she was doing that night, if someone knew she'd open that particular bottle—or if there are more poisoned bottles."

"Oh." Pearl brings her hand to cover her mouth in shock. "Do you think there could be more? I don't want anyone else to die."

"I'll be careful."

"Bring Alice. She was down there with Irene the most, cataloguing scents and taking notes."

"So, she'd know if Irene was going to open that bottle that night?"

Pearl shakes her head. "No one knew what Irene would do next. It was like watching a poet. She would mull for a while, scents dancing in her mind, and then she'd pluck them off the shelf to mix them. There was no pattern to it anyone could discern . . . it was like magic."

"All right. Where would I find Alice this time of day?"

"Kitchen, probably." She sits back down. "Although make sure she's careful. I don't want her—or you—inhaling any poison if the killer left more."

"I'll be careful," I say. I walk to the door, and have my hand on the knob when she speaks again.

"There's one more thing, actually, Andy," Pearl says. I turn around, and she's upright in her chair, stiffer than before.

"Yeah?"

"I wanted to say, before you begin your deeper investigation, that I was serious about my offer, to be our home security. With the gate never really locked like it should be, and there's sure to be more attention on us now that Irene has died . . . I wanted to offer you the job for real, before you investigate, so you didn't think that I would only offer it to you if you solved the case the way I want."

"There's a way you want?" I ask, walking back toward her.

"You know. I didn't want you to think the offer is dependent on what you find out. So . . . are you interested?"

I stare out the window to the side of the room. It overlooks the front of the house, but we're far enough over I don't see the fountain, just the flowers. A huge lawn of them in different colors, lavender threaded among them like bold stitching. It's a good offer. It's something to do with the rest of my life, if I want to live it. A place I could be myself. I know better than to think that I'd be eating with the family every day. I'd probably end up in the kitchen with the staff. I'd go from Andy to Mr. Mills, even, maybe.

But I could drive into town with Pat, and we could find men and go back to their place without fear of losing my job or home. Maybe we'd share a room here sometimes. Maybe, somewhere along the line, I could fall in love, like Pearl did, or Henry and Cliff. I could lean my head on a man's shoulder at breakfast, hold his hand at night. The thought of it makes it feel like my whole body was asleep and it's waking up now, pins and needles all over.

How different is it here from the rest of the world, really, if there's still murder? I take a breath. The pins and needles are gone.

I turn my gaze from the window to one of the framed pieces of paper hung around the room. It's more Sappho, I think, but this time in English:

You
Just like the red apple ripening
On the farthest peak of the branch
Missed by the gardeners—
No,
They did not miss you!
They just could not reach so
high.

"I admit, I didn't expect you to have to think so much about it," Pearl says.

"Sorry," I say. "I was thinking, and then reading . . ." I nod at the framed poem.

She comes to stand beside me, reading the poem. "It reminds

me of Irene, that one. My favorite. Well. That and one other stanza, but I don't have it framed: 'Someone, I tell you, will remember us, even in another time.' I don't need to have it framed. I have it memorized."

"It's pretty."

"I think it's more than that, when you turn it over in your mind awhile. But maybe you need to do that with my offer?"

"I think it's better I finish the case first," I say. "I just don't want to mix up the two things. I appreciate that that's what you're trying to do too, though."

"That's fine. You can decide later. Just keep it in mind. Here . . . you'd live a good life. You'd be part of the family. I'd make sure you were buried with coins for the ferryman, same as I'd do for anyone else."

"The ferryman?"

"Oh." She shakes her head. "More ancient Greek. The one who ferried the souls of the dead. You buried the dead with two coins so they would be able to pay him, and wouldn't wander on the shore of the river, fading away and forgotten."

"Two coins, huh? Cheap."

She smiles and tentatively pats me on the shoulder. "But someone else has to remember to do it for you. Think about my offer, Andy."

I finally take my eyes off the poem enough to nod at her and try a smile, too, but it doesn't fit quite right again, so I walk away. She doesn't stop me.

SEVEN

Alice is in the middle of the kitchen, like Pearl said she would be. She's in a sky-blue dress with a wide yellow belt, scolding Dot.

"That's not at all the right way to prepare mashed potatoes."

I hover by the door, because she hasn't seen me yet and I want to watch.

"Ma'am, I know there are different ways to prepare them, but Irene likes them not fully creamed."

"Well, she's dead now, so we'll do it my way. Or are you going to make me do it myself like I did last night with the soup?"

Dot shakes her head, exhausted. "Fine, but if Pearl asks me to go back to the other way, next time I'll go back to the other way."

"Good." Alice crosses her arms and gives one hard nod. "I wish you didn't have to make everything an argument, though."

"Just my way, I guess," Dot says, walking over to a large pot on the stove. I can't see her face, and her tone of voice is un-readable, but Alice chuckles, then takes a look up at the ceiling, pushing her shoulders back. She seems to sense me and looks over.

"Inspector!" she says. Dot glances over, then decides not

to get involved and goes back to her pot. "Thank you for the rabbit. Elsie hit it in most of the meat so we can't use hers, but yours was right between the eyes!" She mimes shooting something with a shotgun and then laughs. "I wouldn't have expected any less. It'll be a nice stew base." She smiles and smooths down the front of her dress. "Not that I don't appreciate the visit, but what are you doing down here?"

"Looking for you," I say.

"Me?" Alice smiles, bringing her hand to her neck. "What for?"

"I was hoping you wouldn't mind showing me around the crime scene. I want to look at some things and figure out what Irene might have been doing that night. Context. And I'm told you were the one who was with her the most when she worked."

She smiles in a way that's almost an eye roll, then walks close to me. She's wearing perfume, but it doesn't smell like flowers like everything else in the house does, more like anise and freshly cut wood. "Really, Detective? I enjoy your company, and I don't want to put you out of a job or anything, but there's no mystery here. An old woman tripped. It happens all the time, I should know." She smiles and glances down at her feet, in little red kitten heels, then back up at me. "Just this time, she didn't land well."

"I'm pretty sure it was more than that."

"Oh?" I watch her carefully, but more than a slight widening of the eyes in surprise, I can't sense anything from her. Everyone else in this house wears their feelings like Alice wears perfume, but not her. She's too polite for all that, too poised.

"I'm afraid so."

"Whom do you suspect?"

"Pearl wants me to investigate the competition, but I'll go wherever the evidence takes me."

"Of course, like any good inspector would." She nods, then looks around the kitchen. "I suppose she'll be all right without me for a little while." She turns around. "Don't forget to chop the pistachios for dessert, Dot," she says. Dot doesn't respond. Alice walks past me out into the hallway. I follow.

"So murder, then," she says as we walk toward the library. "Really? I mean I know last night I said it would be exciting, but I didn't really think . . . poor Pearl." She pauses. "Unless she did it." She leaves that statement hanging there, like a question, but I don't answer it. "Are you really like them?" she asks after a moment. We're nearly to the library and the walls are close around us. "I mean . . . I can see it with the others. Henry was raised by two women, no strong father figure around, and Cliff prances around like some vaudeville starlet, but you're a strapping policeman. Did you have a bad relationship with your mother? Or maybe you had a drug problem, or alcohol? I understand a lot of police develop those, and under the influence, you could do all sorts of things." We're at the door now, and she pulls it open and flips on the lights inside. "And then, once you've done those things, maybe you think that's who you are."

"I think it's just who I am," I tell her as levelly as I can, though every word has made me feel smaller and smaller. "If I could change it, I would."

"So you've never been with a woman?" She turns around and steps close enough I can smell her perfume again.

"I've tried," I say, momentarily remembering an awkward date at the drive-in senior year.

"Maybe it was the wrong woman."

"I'm pretty sure that wasn't it." I want the conversation to end, but I also don't want to show her she's bothering me. I think of the coroner spitting that word at me again, and almost laugh at Alice. Of course I'm sure. I've tried every way not to be what I am. It never worked.

"It's just . . . a cop. It's so masculine."

"I wanted to be a cop. The other stuff . . . never had much to do with it."

Alice sighs, then shrugs. "I hope you don't think it rude of me to pry like that. I'm just . . . curious. I can never really understand it. Where these urges come from. Why Margo has them. So when someone like you comes along . . . I just want to understand."

"Sure," I say. She says it so sweetly I think it might be the truth, and I feel a pang of sympathy for her. She's the outsider here the way we are in the greater world. If Margo had just up and disappeared, would she be like the nurse I spoke to today? Smoking against the hot brick and wishing she could see her daughter again?

"Well, here we are, Inspector. What did you want to look at?"

"Can you take me through what Irene did, when she made the soaps?"

"Oh . . . certainly. Well, sometimes she would take down one of the old soaps first, and smell it." She points at the wrapped soaps. "She never told me why she went for whatever year she was thinking of, but sometimes she'd start with that, or sometimes she'd go right to smelling everything else." She gestures at the bottles on the shelves around her, then points down at the boxes of flowers.

"Was there a pattern to it that you noticed? Did she go to particular bottles at particular times?"

"Not really. If she smelled one of the bars of soap first, she usually went for the flowers or perfume that made the base of that soap first. So if she smelled purple, she'd come over here . . ." Alice walks over to the wall of bottles. "Pull down a lavender." She takes a bottle down and unscrews it.

"Wait," I say, putting out my hand at the same time as she inhales deeply on the bottle.

"And sniff like that," she finishes. She looks at me curiously. "Sorry, did you want me to stop?"

I walk over and take the bottle and give it a sniff. Just lavender. "Be careful smelling these," I say.

"They're just perfume." She shrugs. "I used to like the pink soap—rose—before I came here. Now flowery scents bore me."

"Do you know this bottle?" I ask, pointing at the shattered bottle by the railing.

Alice walks over and kneels down, looking at the label. "Lavender . . ." she says, then stands up and walks over to a side of the shelf. "It would have been from here. These lavenders are from a new supplier, but I don't think she wanted to use them." She takes a bottle down and turns it around so I can see the brand on the back of the label. Gleam. If the competition was the one who offed Irene, this would be an easy way to do it—murder shipped right to your door.

"She was sniffing out the competition," Alice says, giggling a little.

"So she was trying to figure out their scent?"

Alice nods. "She'd just gotten them a week or so before she died. Kept trying to match them, I think? Or maybe improve on them. But there was something about them that made her curious." She takes the bottle from me and puts it back on the shelf. "Though, in fairness, she was curious about all scents, all the time."

"So she would just sniff the perfumes and flowers?" I ask. "Nothing else?"

"Oh, no," Alice says, walking down the stairs and beckoning me to follow. There, she opens one of the cupboards and takes out a hot plate and a small metal barrel. "Then she would mix them all together and add them to soap. To see how each formula worked in the actual soap. My job was to write down how much of each perfume and flower she used in the mix, and then, when I came back, she'd give me notes on it—too much lavender flower, not enough perfume. Needs a dash of pine. I never really understood."

"When you came back?" I ask.

"Oh, yes, I hated being around when she melted things down and made the soap. The fumes are terrible, you know."

I look at the hot plate and the barrel, and pull a mold out of the shelf Alice had taken them from. I turn it over in my hand.

"Did you ever sniff the bottles?" I ask, the thought suddenly occurring to me.

She nods. "Oh, sure, sometimes. I don't have Irene's nose, but she'd ask me to hand her things, and that meant take them off the shelf, open them up, and then I'd sometimes take a sniff, try to understand what she was looking for. I even would make a suggestion now and then. Well, not lately, not since I first started helping. She never took any of my suggestions so I stopped making them . . ." She frowns slightly. "But she was the genius. I don't resent her for that."

"So you'd just sniff them sometimes?"

"Yes. Or Irene would sniff it and then hand it back to me and tell me it had turned. She wanted me to learn so I could go through the scents sometimes and sniff them and throw out the bad ones. They last practically forever, but she keeps them so long . . ." She looks around the room, and I follow her gaze. So many bottles. Some have to be ancient.

"So did you do that? Go through bottles and sniff them all."

"Oh . . . not really. Maybe if she asked me to. But they all smell the same to me, so I'd just put them back on the shelf. What does this have to do with someone pushing her, though?"

"Oh." I shake my head. "No, just trying to get a sense of her, and how she worked. The more I know her, the more I can piece together that night."

She nods and seems like she believes me.

It's possible Irene wasn't the intended victim, if anyone knew when Alice would next be checking the bottles. Margo clearly doesn't love her mother, and everyone else speaks of her coolly at best. If Irene and Alice didn't get along, it could even be an accidental suicide—her setting it up for Alice, then forgetting which bottle and opening it herself.

"If that's all you need . . ." Alice says, heading toward the stairs. "I do really need to get back to the kitchen. I run the house." The staff doesn't love Alice either.

"Sure," I say, then look up at her. "What does that mean, really? Run the house?"

"Oh, the usual, choosing meals, managing the household budget to make sure we spend enough on food, and save enough to make sure we have money for when we need new towels. Just . . . making sure everything runs smoothly."

"And how'd you get so good at that?"

She turns around. She's up a few stairs already and rests her hand on a bannister and smiles at the question. "You're the first person to ever ask me that." She lets her smile grow wider. "I was never fancy. I didn't come from money like everyone else here does, and Margo's father died when she was little, overseas. I was a maid at a motel. The Butterfly. And I worked hard, and then I was in charge of all the other maids, and then they put me in charge of the cooks and gardeners, too."

"So how did you end up here?"

Her eyes narrow a little and she frowns. "The motel closed. It was small, had never been especially prosperous. I couldn't find another job—overqualified to be a maid at a bigger hotel in the city, but underqualified to do what I'd done at the Butterfly. I bounced around some other jobs—maid for a rich family, waitress—but I wasn't fresh-faced anymore, and those jobs came and went until there was nothing left. That's when I rang up Margo, and she invited me here. It all worked out perfectly."

I nod, although that doesn't exactly track with her being nearly homeless on the streets like everyone has been saying. But maybe it's just the story she tells to save face.

"So that was in Oregon?" I ask.

She tilts her head and looks at me curiously. She can tell I'm fishing for information. "Yes. Bend," she says, almost like she's daring me to do something. "Need anything else?"

"No, thank you, Alice."

"Good luck, Inspector."

She goes back up the stairs and pushes open the door, letting it clang closed and leaving me alone. She likes being useful, I realize. Like Margo, but in different ways; Margo wanting to help the company, Alice wanting to help the household.

It's unlikely that someone did all this to kill Alice. They had to know Irene could open the bottle and breathe in the poison just as easily as Alice could. Maybe someone didn't mind Alice being collateral damage, though. Or didn't know about her opening the bottles too—because they're from outside the household. I need to talk to the competition.

I spend some time poking around the library, looking at all the bottles on the shelves to see if any look tampered with, but I can't tell. There are no seals, no obvious differences in the liquids that swish around inside them. I think about opening a few up and sniffing, but decide not to risk it.

Everyone seemed to know about Irene, and how she would open the bottles and inhale deeply from them. Anyone could have come in and replaced the bottle. Emptied it out and filled it with a poison that they brought in from the shed or anywhere else. There'd be a smell, maybe, from the perfume being poured out, but if they poured it out in the garden one night, no one would notice. Lavender perfume wouldn't stand out in a patch of lavender.

And they all have motives. Pearl gained the most out of the will, Margo wanted more power in the company, and Alice argued with Irene. Henry, maybe, didn't stand to gain much for the cost of his own mother, but forty-nine percent of a company isn't nothing. Cliff and Elsie seem least likely to have a reason for wanting her dead, but Cliff is a drunk and Elsie has secrets. Well, everyone has secrets in this house. Even the staff might have had some motive. But it's about more than motive, it's about temperament, too. And among this group, I don't know which of them could be a killer yet. Or rather, after watching Elsie snap that rabbit's neck, which of them couldn't.

I want to eliminate Pearl from my list of suspects. She hired me, and I just don't think she did it. On the force, though, I never eliminated anyone without proof. Follow the evidence, know the suspects. Never eliminate without a confirmed alibi, but that's impossible here. Everyone is suspect.

I don't know anything about this Cohen, who runs Gleam, either, but the murder weapon having his company name on it is suspicious even if the method of delivering the poison seems the most complicated. Shipping her one bottle of tainted perfume, knowing she would inhale it? It's possible. I don't know what he knows about Irene, though. I don't know if they were friendly or bitter rivals. And I don't know if she was ordering the bottles direct from him—she seems to have been a little too proud for that. More likely buying them with cash, wearing sunglasses, or sending Pat to get it. Which means he would have easy access to the bottles too.

Henry would probably be the one to know, running the day-to-day of the business. I glance at my watch. If he's home the same time every day, he'll be driving back now, at the door soon. The next best person to ask about Gleam would be Margo, who has to go to all the business mingling functions and play dutiful wife.

I turn off the light and close the door behind me. I wonder what they'll do with that space now. Probably a wine cellar. That has to be what it was meant for in the first place. I head upstairs, wondering where Margo would be this time of day, but when I check the sitting room, I open the door to a very different sight.

Cliff, wearing just a pale green button-down shirt, socks, garters, and I assume underwear, though I can't see them under the length of the shirt. Kay Starr singing "St. Louis Blues" is playing on the record player, a mostly empty highball sits on the table, and Cliff is dancing to the music. He doesn't see me, and I watch him dance and move his mouth in sync with the words, like he's performing it. He swivels his hips, and rocks his shoulders. He bends at the knees and I see a flash of white briefs under the shirt. My collar feels warm, and I swallow.

He sees me staring, but instead of being embarrassed at being caught, he smiles at me. Walks toward me, still mouthing the lyrics. "I got those St. Louis Blues," Kay sings as he walks closer, close enough I can smell that the highball on the table has probably been refilled a few times. "Just as blue as I can be." Cliff pretends to cry on my shoulder, his hand suddenly on my chest, loosening my tie and then his fingers pop the top button at my collar. I take a deep breath. "Oh, my man's got a heart like a rock cast in the sea," Kay sings, and Cliff undoes another button. I'm not sure where this is leading. Part of me wants him to keep undoing buttons, to undo his buttons, to roll naked on the couch with him. But I don't need it, not like I did before. So I gently take his wrist and pull it away from the third button. If this is him trying to distract me, it'll make it clear it's not working, even if it is, a little. I've been on this side before, a beautiful murderer trying to make me fall for her so I won't turn her in. Widows who murdered their husbands and knew I was on to them, girls playing innocents or seductresses—not that it ever worked, of course. The guys on the force thought I was too good a man to fall for it. I don't want to fall for it now.

Cliff rolls his eyes when I pull his wrist away, still mouthing the lyrics, and walks away, swaying his hips. He sits on the edge of the sofa and, holding on to it, does a fan kick, his legs spread momentarily at me. Then he goes back to dancing as if

I'm not even there. I watch until the song ends and the record plays dead static. Cliff sighs and picks up his glass, sees that it's empty, and sighs again.

"What are you doing, Cliff?" I ask him.

Cliff looks over at me and smirks. "I'm just having a little fun. I'm so bored!" He flops down onto the sofa. "Henry is always working. Pearl and Margo ignore me. Even you only talk to me when I'm already undressed. Like I'm just a thing."

"I haven't seen you fully dressed in a while," I say, amused. "And I had nothing to do with that."

"Honestly, I *should* seduce you. It would serve Henry right, and it wouldn't be that hard." He sits up slightly, and crosses his legs, smirking again as my eyes follow the long stretch of his thigh.

"Trouble in paradise?" I ask, going to the record player and flipping the record.

"No," Cliff says, almost petulant.

I start the record playing. "After You've Gone" comes on. I turn the volume down and then sit down in the chair near Cliff.

He rolls onto his side, looking at me. "I really do love him. Do you have a cigarette?"

I fish my cigarettes out and offer him one. Without sitting up, he stretches a hand out. He can't quite reach, though, so I stand and give it to him. He sticks it in his mouth, and then looks at me, expectant. I take some matches from my coat and strike one, lighting it for him.

"Thanks," he says, rolling onto his back and staring at the ceiling. The smoke twists up off his cigarette, fading in the air. "When I was in the army, I used to dance every night. Just a backup dancer, not the star of the show or anything. But it was a freer time, I think. The army was more free than this house."

He laughs. "I know that sounds like nonsense. Maybe it is. Maybe I just don't appreciate what I have. But sometimes this house is like a cage, and I miss the army." He inhales on the cigarette, blows smoke out in a long gust, then turns to me. His eyelids are low, and his eyelashes catch the light. "I was popular, too. Line of boys outside my room every night. Some with roses. Things were easier then."

"I know," I say. "I had a few boyfriends when I was in the navy. Didn't call them that, of course, not sure I would now, really, but we met up most nights. And people knew. We didn't have to be so nervous about it all."

"Before the war, before I joined the army, it was awful. I'm just afraid it's going to go back to that."

"What was awful?" I ask.

Cliff shivers, and I can't tell if it's because he's half-naked. He turns back to the ceiling. "Henry doesn't get it. He wasn't in the army because of his vision. He doesn't get the sense of brotherhood. Camaraderie. We were all going to die, right? No one cared who you were screwing. As long as you weren't trying to shout about it, anyway. The night Japan surrendered, I got to be Lucky Pierre with two different sets of men." He takes a long drag on his cigarette, then turns to me, smiling. "You ever get to be the Lucky Pierre?"

I swallow, remembering. "Yes," I say. I cross my legs and fish out a cigarette for myself and light it. Cliff watches all this and laughs again, throaty, and a little sad, too.

"It was different then," I say. "But at the end of the war, it got worse. Paranoid, you remember? And it just kept getting more worse after that. Even here in an open town like San Francisco. You can live a queer life, be an artist, a female impersonator, go to the bars . . . but you can't run a business. Can't be a cop."

"We're not in San Francisco," Cliff says.

"How did it happen?" I ask him. The change was gradual, but sudden, too. One moment I could kiss a man on deck without anyone minding, the next everyone was talking about being careful and the tribunals. It had always varied ship to ship, captain to captain, but it was like the temperature had gone up so slowly no one noticed until we all had to get out or be boiled alive. "How did everyone just suddenly know to start behaving themselves again after the war ended?"

"Speak for yourself," Cliff says. "I hate behaving myself, and I never went back to it."

I feel it then, for a moment. The need to reach across, to kiss Cliff, to taste his lips, probably bitter with tobacco and sweet with gin. To peel what little clothing he's wearing off of him and taste his skin, too. To do more. Not because he's flirting. He isn't, not really, now. But because I'm suddenly so sad remembering what the outside world is like. Because I want to throw myself in the bay again.

I inhale on my cigarette and look out the window instead. He's drunk, lonely, and a suspect. And I suddenly remember the poster at the coroner's office. Missing. Clive Thorpe. I study Cliff's face. Maybe I'd just imagined it. They're similar, but sketches can be wrong. Looking at him now, I'm just not sure.

"I miss my friends," Cliff says. "From the army. From when I danced in the follies. From the clubs in the city."

"Why not go out?" I ask. "You're publicly Henry's secretary. You can live your life, can't you? You can leave the house at least, see a movie? Bette Davis has a new one out—*Payment on Demand*."

Cliff laughs, then shrugs. "It's just safer. That's what Irene always said, too. She was paranoid, but she wasn't wrong."

"Safer?"

"Irene was keen on making sure no one knew. 'Safe within the walls, unsafe without,'" he says in a voice like an old woman.

"She's gone now."

"Doesn't mean it got safer out there."

I take a drag on my cigarette, watching him. His is nearly down to the stub now, and I hope he'll ask for another, which isn't a good sign. Instead, he reaches out to the table and puts it out in the ashtray. I watch the last curl of smoke from it rise up like the outline of a face.

"What makes it unsafe?" I ask. "For you, I mean? Henry goes out. Margo, Elsie, Pearl . . . What's special about you?"

He looks up at me and smiles, his teeth almost blinding. "Want me to show you?"

I do. I let the silence hang like an answer and he inches closer, his lips parting slightly. I can feel every breath I'm taking, the air between my teeth, under my tongue. I can feel my body turning toward his. But I can't do this. This is a case. He could be a killer.

So I say something to stop it. "Does your not going outside have something to do with that missing poster I saw?" I ask, words spilling out of me like they're making distance between us. "Clive Thorpe?"

He blinks, and turns his eyes up to meet mine.

EIGHT

For a moment, it's like the music Cliff is always swaying to has stopped. His body goes tense. Then he very carefully relaxes, and sighs, theatrically. "I don't know what you mean," he says, sounding very carefree. But he was always the chorus boy, never the lead, and I can see why. He's not the best actor.

"My mistake, then," I say. "Just looked kind of like you."

"I have one of those faces, maybe," he says, sitting up. "I should go put some pants on. I've really embarrassed myself, haven't I?" He turns to me, all doe-eyed. "Don't tell anyone, please? I'm just . . . pathetic and bored. The housewife who gets drunk without her husband."

"I won't tell," I say. Outside, I can hear the crunch of gravel as a car pulls down the driveway.

"Thanks," he says, standing up. "I'll go get those pants."

I watch him walk out the door I came in through, his hips still swaying. I guess he can't help that, but it makes me bite my lip and think of following him back to his bedroom, seeing how lonely he really is. But instead I take another pull of my cigarette and stub it out in the ashtray.

I go to the window to see if the car driving in is Henry,

pulling away the shade and looking out, like I've seen so many people do here. Always peeking out, cautious, unsure what's staring back at them from outside.

It's Margo. She pulls the car up and parks it, a little crooked, before getting out, then takes a shopping bag from the trunk. The dress she went to pick up. For a "simple errand," that took a while—most of the day.

I think about going outside to talk to her, but before I can move, Elsie comes from around the corner of the house. She's still in her hunting attire, and when Margo looks up, she laughs at her. Elsie smiles and gets close, taking Margo's hand in hers and saying something. Margo frowns, holding up the shopping bag a little, but Elsie shakes her head. They chat for a moment longer before Elsie pulls away and gets in her car.

Margo watches her drive away before coming inside. I meet her at the foyer. She raises an eyebrow at me. "Snooping?" she asks.

"That's what I'm being paid for."

"Well, I think you drove Elsie off. She's not staying for dinner, but she'll be back later tonight."

"She comes and goes as she pleases."

"Yes," Margo says, her eyes daring me to question that.

"You like that setup?"

"Oh." She looks surprised at the question. "I suppose. As opposed to what?"

"Her living here full-time?"

She laughs. "Can you imagine? She'd be so bored."

"Maybe," I say.

Margo rolls her eyes. "I need to go hang this for tomorrow. If you'll excuse me." She steps around me and heads up the stairs. I glance at my watch. It's later than Henry was home yesterday. Dinner will be soon.

I don't want to be just waiting by the door for him, so I head outside, and back around the house to the greenhouse. Maybe it's empty now and I can look at the poisons.

Inside, it's still stuffy, but not empty. Judy is standing by the table without the seedlings, pulling a roll of twine and cutting it into smaller pieces. She's standing right in front of the poisons. When I come in, she looks up at me, her face hard, and then back down at her task.

"What are you doing?" I ask.

"The pea vines are growing quickly. They need to be tied to the trellis so they don't fall over as they get heavy."

"Ah," I say, walking closer. As I get near enough to see what she's doing more clearly, she stops, her hands resting on the shears she was using to cut the twine.

"Did you want something?" she asks, without looking up.

"You seemed to know Irene pretty well," I say, looking at the shears. She's scared, I realize. I take a step back and her grip loosens. "I just was wondering what you could tell me about her."

"Mmmmm." She pulls more twine out and snips it off. "She was a nice woman. We didn't really talk much. She taught me how to care for the plants by showing me, and then we worked in silence. But it wasn't a rude silence."

She goes quiet, and I get the sense that *this* is a rude silence.

"You don't like me much," I say. "Should I read something into that?"

She laughs, deep from her chest. "Me not liking you makes you suspicious?" she asks, then shakes her head. "Of course it does. You're a cop. Tell me why I should like you." She makes it clear that the cop part is what she hates by the way she spits it.

"I'm not a cop anymore," I say.

She snorts. "But you would be if you could." She pulls more twine out and cuts it, then counts the number of pieces she has before turning to look at me. "I don't know why Pearl brought you in here. You're bad people, especially for people like us."

"I am people like you."

"As if that cleans your hands?" She shakes her head. "I had a brother. Not really a brother, but we found each other young and were close. He was always kind of sickly. Got caught in a raid. The police beat him so hard his bones couldn't heal up right. He was in so much pain he just killed himself a few months later. Threw himself into the ocean."

I swallow. Just like I was planning to do. I picture him, like me, but broken on the outside, too. And people I knew had done it. People I worked with, joked with. I understand why she doesn't like me. I'm not sure I like me.

"I'm . . . sorry," I say. It sounds hollow out loud. "I never was part of that, if it helps." It's true in the sense I mean it, but still feels like a lie.

"It doesn't," she says, and turns away, walking out of the greenhouse.

"I'd make it right if I could," I say, following her. "Really, I would. I became a cop because I wanted to help . . . I like helping."

She pulls open the gate to the garden and then pulls it closed behind her before I can follow her in.

"You can't help here," she says, walking into the garden. She ignores me, tying pea vines to the trellis that's around them.

"She's really not going to talk to you," says a voice behind me. I turn, it's Dot. She's wearing an apron over a plain black dress, and her hair is pulled back in a messy bun.

"She doesn't like me."

"Your choice to be a cop," Dot says. "It comes with consequences. You don't get rid of those just because you got fired."

"I never hurt anyone for fun," I say. "And I never worked vice. I made sure I never had to . . . arrest people like us."

"So what?" Dot asks. "Unless you arrested those kinds of cops? Reported them? Stopped them? Anything?"

I don't say anything. The air still seems to smell like gunpowder from Elsie and me hunting this morning.

"What do you need?" Judy calls from the garden.

"I just wanted to ask—"

"Basil," Dot shouts over me. Judy nods and goes to another patch of the garden and plucks a few handfuls of leaves, then walks over to Dot and gives them to her. Dot takes them in both fists, missing a few leaves. I watch their hands linger on each other as the herbs are handed over. The air smells of the basil suddenly, strong and green. Then they both turn away and walk back toward where they came from.

"If you have questions, come on," Dot says, calling over her shoulder. "I need to get back fast or Alice will . . . who am I kidding, she'll yell anyway."

I catch up with Dot. "You don't seem to mind me much," I say.

"Pat says you're not so bad. Says you were in a tough spot. He feels for everyone, though. He's mother hen to every homosexual in the world. So what were your questions?"

"What it's like working here, I guess. How you got the job."

"Pat found us—me and Judy. We were a couple already, he met us at some club, I think a male impersonator was performing. Pat loves those. Loves anyone in drag. I was a waitress at a diner. Judy was a tailor. He knew I could cook because we'd had him over for dinner once, and he pitched us the job. Well, me. He said he could convince them to take on Judy, though, for odd jobs. And he did, but she liked the greenhouse and the garden, and Irene liked teaching her, and needed the help. This climate, you can grow practically anything any time of year, and Irene did. New plants constantly going into the ground. Family helps out sometimes, but once Judy was here, it was clear that's what Irene really needed her for—more gardening."

"You liked Irene, then?" I ask. We're in front of the side door that leads into the kitchen.

"Sure. She was . . . quiet. But dedicated, you know? If she weren't rich and famous I'd say she kept her head down and worked. But she was rich and famous, so . . . But she liked the quiet. Treated us nicely, paid us well. And she loved her family. Really. She was so protective, the interview with us to see if we were going to rat her out was hours. She wanted to make sure we were good people. She wanted to trust us."

I almost ask if she means that Pearl's hiring process wasn't rigorous enough, that I can't be trusted. But I don't. She'll tell me the truth and I already know it. "So she trusted you."

Dot nods, and smiles a little. "It's a good life here, honestly. I have my girl, a nice job, a great place to live. It's simple. If it weren't for Alice . . ."

"What's going on there?"

"With Alice? I don't know, you're the detective. I just think she feels left out. You know, because she's not like us? So she tries to like, make herself needed. And when I can cook a meal without her, it's like me telling her we don't need her, she doesn't have a place here."

"Sounds like you do know."

Dot shrugs. "I feel bad for her, mostly. I really need to get back in, though. Dinner is on the table at six thirty sharp."

"Sure. Thanks for talking to me."

"If it helps the family, I'm glad to do it."

She's not being nice to me, I realize, she's just helping them. She pushes the door open with her back, her hands still filled with basil, and goes into the kitchen.

I suppose I deserve it. The cops aren't good to people like us, and I was a cop. I should count myself lucky Pearl was willing to trust me at all, considering. She'd even asked me, at the bar, and I hadn't answered her: Did I ever warn anyone? Did I ever try to help people like myself? No. The people I was always focused on helping were already dead. And myself, I guess. And thinking about what Elsie said today, I wonder if those two things weren't pretty close in kind.

Why didn't I ever help? I could have told someone. A phone call from the booth outside the station to the bar. "You're getting raided tonight." It could have saved someone. Maybe Judy's friend. I think of what it would have been like to be that guy for a moment. Phone calls, heroic rescues, a secret identity. Appreciation from the boys at the bars I'd saved. I could have had all that, if I hadn't been so afraid for myself. Because someone would have noticed. Someone would have said, "Why does Andy always ask which clubs we're going to hit?"

Someone would have caught me. But then, someone did anyway.

One thing I know from the job, from being an inspector, is that you can't change the past. I can't fix it with Judy, and I deserve her coldness. I deserve more, really.

I walk around to the front door, wanting to stay out in the air, hoping it'll make my body feel less flushed.

Out front, I spot Henry's car. When I go inside, he's in the foyer, giving Pearl a kiss on the cheek.

"Ah," he says, seeing me. "Still here?"

"Be nice, Henry," Pearl says. "He's doing a good job. Today he—"

"Pearl." I shake my head. "Let's not . . ."

"Oh, Inspector, surely you don't think Henry, our son, could have—"

"Not here," I say. I want to hold on to the advantage of knowing it was murder as long as possible. I want to see everyone's faces as they're told.

"Fine. Well, Andy is doing a good job, Henry. He thinks maybe it was the competition."

"What competition?" Henry asks, narrowing his eyes at me.

"Well, your mother had some Gleam perfumes in the library," I say.

"Oh." He nods. "That. Yes. She had an odd, ah, obsession with . . ." He pauses. "It's nearly dinner. Why don't you come up with me? I like to take off my coat before we eat."

I nod and follow him upstairs to his bedroom, down the hall from mine. Inside, the walls are a pale peach color, and the window curtains are silver, but pulled aside, letting light stream in. The bed is perfectly made, but the robe Cliff was wearing earlier is tossed across it. I look at the adjoining room—Cliff's room—but the door is closed. No music from inside, either.

Henry picks the robe up and folds it down into a perfect square, then lays it carefully back down, over one of the pillows. Then he takes off his coat and opens his wardrobe. He hangs his coat up, and loosens his tie.

"So?" he asks. "Perfumes?"

"Yeah," I say. "Why did your mother have Gleam brand perfumes?"

"Ah, right." He nods, turning to the mirrors. He undoes his tie, takes it off, and then unbuttons his shirt. "You don't mind, do you?" he asks, catching my eye in the mirror.

"No," I say.

He undoes his shirt, takes it off, and gives it a brisk slap in the air before hanging it on the side of the mirror. He's wearing an undershirt, but he strips that off next. Underneath, his body is fuzzy with orange hair, but otherwise looks practically carved out of marble. I try not to let my eyes linger. "Mother was an artist. She felt, ah, knowing the competition was key to keeping ahead of them. She never used their perfumes, she merely studied them."

He takes a clean undershirt out of his wardrobe and puts it on. It's tight, brings out the definition of his shoulders and stomach muscles.

"Does that answer your question?" he asks, catching my eye in the mirror again.

"Just seems odd," I say.

"A lot of things my mother did seem odd," he says, taking the shirt he was wearing off the mirror and putting it back on, buttoning it at the collar first, then down. "I don't pretend to understand, uh, all the aspects of what she did, getting the scents just right, but it was important to her, and she's what made the company great." He finishes buttoning the shirt but doesn't tuck it back. He turns around to look at me directly. "Now. I have a question for you: How much to tell my mother that my other mother's death was an accident, and leave?"

"What?" I ask, staring him down.

"You clearly have her under some kind of, ah, spell. You've convinced her it's murder. She was so excited downstairs. You must have told her something."

"Yes." I nod. "I told her it was murder." I watch him, but he rolls his eyes and turns back to the mirror, carefully pushing the bottom of his shirt down into his pants, and then tugging it until it's neat.

"And what evidence do you have?" he asks. He's watching me in the mirror again, but he doesn't believe me. He thinks this is a scam.

"The coroner's report," I say. I sit down on his bed and he turns around, glaring at where the sheets pull a little. "I talked to a nurse, went over the report. I'm sorry to say, your mother was dead before she hit the ground."

That catches his attention. His eyes flicker from the sheet back to me. "What?"

"I believe your mother inhaled poison from one of the bottles. It caused a pulmonary edema. She stumbled to the bannister and fell over. That's why she landed on her stomach. That's why there wasn't so much blood. And it's why she never called for help. It's not that long a drop, and she walked up and down those stairs all the time, Henry. She would have survived the fall. Except she was already dead."

"Poison in a bottle?" Henry asks. "No. That, ah . . ." He pauses. "No. I don't believe you."

"There's a bottle at the top of the balcony in the library. Shattered from a drop, not from being thrown. I think that was where the poison was. She wouldn't normally drop a bottle of lavender, would she."

"No . . . but . . ."

I stand up. "Believe me or don't. But you can't pay me to lie to your mother. I'm going to follow this through." I walk away from the bed. He turns back around and puts his tie back on.

"Please," he says, his voice steady. "You're upsetting my mother. And she's already devastated . . . this . . . it's not good for her."

"It's also not good to lie to her and leave her the target for the next murder. She has fifty-one percent of the company now, right?"

That seems to give him pause. He stares at something I can't see, pressing his lips together.

"Fine," he says, finally. "I'm not convinced, but I will grant you you've made me suspicious. Keep investigating if you must. But if I feel this is being drawn out . . ."

"I promise, that's not what I'm trying to do."

"Fine, then. Let's go to dinner."

"Sure," I say. "Just . . . why'd you change your undershirt?"

"It was sweaty," he says, furrowing his brow at me as though this is the most natural thing in the world.

"Okay, but why dress for dinner? It's just your family."

"I always dress for dinner."

I nod, realizing this is just who he is. We walk downstairs to the dining room. Everyone seems to be in their spots again, minus Elsie, and I sit down in the same spot as last night.

"Interrogating my boyfriend, Inspector?" Cliff asks. He's dressed now, in a green shirt with no tie or jacket. He smirks, but I can tell he's worried I was telling Henry about his behavior earlier.

"Just questions about his mother," I say, hopefully reassuring.

"That's how I hit on him too," Cliff says, winking.

Henry frowns a little, but takes Cliff's hand as they sit down.

"Well, I hope you found something useful today," Alice says to me as Pat comes out, setting down salads in front of each of us. "Waldorf salad," Alice announces. "You took me away from the kitchen for so long Dot almost burned the meatloaf."

"I'm sure she didn't," Pearl says.

"Well, I got back in time," Alice says. I think about what Dot said, how Alice needs to be needed here, to find her place. Looking at it that way, she does seem sadder. I wonder if everyone else sees her that way too. And if she knows they do.

"I made progress today, yes," I say, interrupting the fight before it really starts. "Thank you."

"So," Margo says, swirling the wine in her glass. "You going to tell us what you found out?"

I shake my head. "Let's just eat tonight," I say.

Margo rolls her eyes and drinks more of her wine.

"Did you have a nice day?" Henry asks Cliff.

"Sure," Cliff says, smiling brightly. "It's better when you're home, though."

"I know, I've been working a lot lately. I'm sorry. There's just a lot."

"Did you look into the cost of new labels?" Margo asks.

"Damn." Henry shakes his head. "I meant to, but—"

"Don't worry," Margo says. "I actually took the liberty of stopping by a few of the local presses while I was picking up my dress today. Just three, but I got quotes from all of them and some samples of their highest-quality label work. There might be better choices out there if we look some more, but personally I like Anderson's. Nice quality, low cost. Yes, there's the initial price of the new design, but . . ." She lifts her glass of wine again. That's why she was gone so long.

"You got numbers?" Henry asks with a smile.

"Already in your office," Margo says.

"You're an angel. I will look everything over. If it works out, maybe we can launch the new labels and new scents at the same time."

"So you are doing the new scents?" Pearl asks.

"Yes, but it will be a few months late. I found a . . . well, this is silly, but he calls himself a nose. A perfume maker. Comes from Rochas. He told me how our soaps' scents had changed over the years with a fair amount of accuracy, at least based on the formulas I have. He's not going to be as good as Mother, but . . . it'll be something. And he'll work from the office. The lab there. So we don't have to worry about our flowers matching the ones we buy for the soap."

"Oh," Pearl says, looking down at her hands. "So someone else will be making the scents?"

Henry nods. "I just don't have the skill," he says. "I don't think any of us do."

"No," Pearl sighs. "I suppose not." She looks up at him and forces a smile, though her eyes are watery. "It's a good solution. I guess it just means . . . she's . . ." She shakes her head. "I'm being silly."

Henry puts his hand over hers and squeezes. "Mother?"

"We'll still keep growing the flowers here, right?"

"Of course, Mother."

She squeezes his hand back and smiles at him in a way that makes my chest ache with fullness. "Thank you." She dabs carefully at a corner of her eye. "I'm glad the soaps will keep changing, too. It was . . . important to her."

"Do you have a timeline yet?" Margo asks. "I can leak it to Margaret from *Ladies' Home Journal* tomorrow."

Henry shakes his head. "Not yet. The nose still has to move

into the lab, get set up. And I have to crunch some numbers with the suppliers. But you can tell them before the end of the year."

"Perfect," Margo says.

I stare at the two of them, Henry and Margo, real masters of this soap domain they've inherited. And what's stranger is how much Margo seems to like it. She's got a head for it. I watch as Cliff wraps his arms around Henry's arm, and leans on his shoulder. If Alice is left out because she's not queer, then Cliff is left out because he has nothing to do with the business. That might give them both motive, but it gives Margo, Henry, and Pearl one, too—they wouldn't be this in control of the business if Irene were still around. And while I don't think Pearl and Henry love the new arrangement, I think Margo does.

"Meatloaf with mashed potatoes," Alice says as Pat clears away our plates and lays down more. "Without lumps," she adds.

Pearl rolls her eyes. "No texture."

"It's more proper," Alice says.

"Proper," Pearl laughs. "It's a mashed potato."

"Well . . . I like them better this way."

Pearl cracks a smile at that. "Well, then we should have them like this," she says. "Sometimes."

Alice grins and starts eating. I stay quiet the rest of dinner as they talk about mundane things; TV, music, a movie they should all go out to see sometime soon. After dessert—no bananas—they go into the lounge and Pearl turns on the TV. Alice vanishes upstairs.

"Come watch with us, Andy," Pearl says.

I shake my head. "Thank you, but I need to poke around a little more."

Pearl shrugs. "All right, but we'll be here."

I leave them watching TV, and head to the kitchen.

There, Dot is cleaning up, and Judy and Pat are still eating at the table. A small radio is playing Georgia Gibbs's "Kiss of Fire." Judy is rocking in time to the music as she eats. They don't spot me, and Dot, hearing the music, dances over to Judy, and kisses her once on the head. Judy looks up at her and they kiss on the lips again.

Pat laughs and looks away, catching sight of me. "Oh, Andy," he says. "Come on in."

Judy turns to me and glares. I don't meet her eye. Have I apologized to her? I should apologize. But I also don't know if I should bother her. She turns to her food, and Dot goes back to the washing, and I feel bad for having interrupted their moment.

"I just wanted to ask you something, Pat."

"Well, come in," Pat says, not standing. I walk closer. "What's up? Find the murderer yet?"

"I was just curious about how you got the job," I say. "Dot told me how she and Judy were hired by you, but I don't know anything about how you came here."

"Me? Oh, I was a concierge at a hotel Irene stayed at."

"Which one?"

"The Heathman," he says. "She could tell right away that I was . . . well . . . swishy. I was never very good at hiding it. Took me aside when I got off work, asked if I might want to interview for a job. Why?"

"Where's the Heathman?"

"Portland. Oregon."

Oregon. "Huh. That near Bend?"

"No, no, not at all. Hours by car. Why?"

"So you never knew Alice or Margo when you were up there?"

"Are they from Oregon?" Pat asks. "I had no idea. Of course, I'm from here originally. Just followed a fella up to Portland. Then he married a woman. Oldest story in the world."

"I don't think it is," Judy says.

Pat laughs and swats her playfully on the wrist. "It is for me."

Judy snorts a laugh.

"So you've never heard of the Butterfly in Bend?" I ask.

"Nope," Pat says. "Why, am I a suspect?"

I grin. "Almost, for half a second there."

"Well, I'm sure it was the most exciting half a second I've ever lived."

I laugh. "Thanks, Pat. I think I'm going to head to bed."

"That an invitation?"

I grin. "Sorry, not with suspects."

"Oh." He looks disappointed. "I have more work, anyway."

I head upstairs and lock the bedroom door behind me. There's a murderer in this house, and I'm not sure who it is, or why. I wish there weren't. I wish this was a happy queer house. But it was poison, I'm sure of it, and anyone could have done it. I check the lock on my door before I slip into bed. I still need to find out more about Gleam. Margo has that fundraiser tomorrow. Maybe I can invite myself along, if the Gleam owners will be there.

I want Pearl to be right about it being an outsider. Because I like these people. I don't want to think there's a murderer right outside the bedroom I'm staying in.

It starts to rain, and I hear the floorboards outside the door creak as Henry and Cliff head to bed. I fall asleep in the dark and only wake up once, just after three in the morning, to the sound of tires outside by the fountain. I look out and see Elsie pulling in. She's just a black dot in the darkness as she gets out of her car and heads inside.

I hear creaking in the hall. She woke someone else, too.

I get back into bed and fall asleep again.

NINE

The rain is gone by morning, and the sun streaming in through the window is the sort of clean light you don't get in the city. It hasn't passed through smoke or exhaust or bad memories. It's hitting you right from the source.

I bathe and pick out more clothes from the wardrobe, this time finding a gray plaid jacket that's a little loose on the shoulders but will work, black trousers, a white shirt, and a pea-green tie. The tie is daring. I would have turned away if I'd seen someone on the street in this tie, in my old life, especially on a Wednesday morning. Now I like it. Maybe. I swallow, studying myself in the mirror. I'm not sure. But I'll risk it, at least for a little while.

I go downstairs, where breakfast is laid out, same as yesterday; Cliff in his dressing robe, head on Henry's shoulder as he reads the paper, Pearl and Margo in dressing gowns, Elsie already dressed. No one is talking, and a radio I hadn't noticed before is on the windowsill, Doris Day singing "Would I Love You" softly from it. Elsie and Pearl both mouth the lyrics during the chorus.

My dad used to do that, while we were on stakeouts. Watching for some lowlife who had faked an injury for the insurance payout, or waiting to see if a thief showed up. He'd turn on the radio and just mouth the words, never sing them. I got to know all the top songs on the radio real well. I kept doing it as a cop, too. Radio on, mouthing along to the lyrics. My partner asked why I didn't just sing, and I told him I would spare him that. Seeing Pearl and Elsie do it makes me feel at home, somehow. Like I'm lying in sunlight. But it's not my home, of course. And my dad is dead.

"Good morning," Pearl says, and the others nod at me as I sit down. Pat immediately brings me a cup of coffee and a plate of waffles and bacon.

"Thanks," I say to him. I eat quietly as the radio turns to Nat King Cole's "Too Young," and then to Phil Harris's "The Thing," which is when Elsie leans back and turns the radio off.

"Thank you," Cliff says. Elsie smirks. The silence is comfortable and then Margo stretches and gets up.

"I'd better bathe and get ready for the fundraiser," she says. "Pearl, do you mind terribly if I borrowed some brooch or earrings of Irene's? I was thinking it might be good to wear something of hers for this, in case my photo ends up in the paper. Then people will see it, and think of her."

"That's . . . a good idea," Pearl says, but she looks sad as she says it.

"Really, only if you don't mind," Margo says.

"No, no, it's a good idea. There was that brooch she always wore to these events. A bouquet of flowers in various gemstones. I'll see if I can find it when I'm done eating. When do you leave?"

Margo glances at Elsie. "Noon?" Elsie nods. "Around noon," she says to Pearl.

"Plenty of time," Pearl says. "You sure it will go with your new dress?"

"I have a white bolero jacket I can wear with the dress. I think that should make it work. It's not very gaudy, is it?"

Pearl laughs. "Did you ever see Irene wear anything gaudy?"

"Well, there is that portrait," Cliff says.

Elsie snorts, which makes Henry start laughing, but he keeps his mouth closed, only his shaking shoulders giving him away.

"It should be fine," Pearl says.

I stand, done eating. "Thank you for breakfast," I say.

"Good luck, Inspector," Pearl says.

I nod and head outside. I know Pearl wants me to look for leads outside the family, and I will, but there's something else I need to check first. I make my way back around the house to the greenhouse and push my way inside. It's empty, finally. I head over to the table with the poisons underneath and kneel down to inspect them.

There are poisons of all kinds—weed, rat, wasp, and others. But wasp is what the nurse had mentioned. I find the jar of wasp poison and turn it around, looking for a date. There isn't one, but on the back of the bottle is a label directing you to donate to the war effort, so it's old enough to be cyanide. I shake the bottle. It's not liquid, though. It's a rough powder, like salt. There's no way this could be mistaken for perfume. The label explains, though: WARNING: SODIUM CYANIDE. MIXING THIS WITH WATER WILL PRODUCE DEADLY VAPORS.

So there it is. An easy murder weapon anyone in the house could access. Some of this sodium cyanide mixed with water in a bottle, stopped up fast to keep the gas inside, and then, if someone were to open it and inhale . . . I put the bottle back.

Which of them knew enough about poison to plan that, though? Which of them noticed old wasp poison in the shed and thought they could plant some in a bottle and one day Irene would open it? There'd be so much waiting. So much chance. I wipe my hands off on my pants and leave.

I don't like that I found that. I was hoping it would be modern poison, not cyanide, or something to point away from the house, like Pearl wants. And I'll look that way. But I don't think I'm going to find anything. I think it's one of them.

I get in my car and drive back to San Rafael, making my way to the public library. It's a pretty, square white building, with big windows and redbrick stitches down the sides, like it was just in a boxing match and lost. Inside, it's quiet and I get to the old periodicals without much help. I spend the next hour or so looking at ads for Gleam. What's strange is they don't seem to make a lavender soap. Unscented and vanilla. That's all they do. Two signature scents in plain white bars that come in plain white paper, wrapped with a silver label: "Gleam! The Soap to Make You Shine!" A handsome young man holds up a bar in the ads, naked except for his smile and some suds on his shoulders, the illustration fading to white just below his navel.

Then I check public records. Gleam is local, like Lamontaine, with offices in the city, and factories down the coast. But otherwise, there's not much here. I check society pages and *Good Housekeeping*, and find the usual stuff; Rachel Cohen, the wife, giving an interview and talking about how soft her skin is, some photos of them at parties. Nothing that suggests they were feuding with Lamontaine, though. Nothing to suggest they were rivals bitter enough to kill.

I glance at my watch, time to head back if I'm going to catch

Margo. I almost asked if I could join her this morning, but I didn't want to give her time to think of a reason to say no. This fundraiser, if Rachel Cohen will be there, is a great chance to get information. I can't just go up to the Cohens' door, after all. I'm not a cop. And if they don't like the kind of questions I ask, they might call the real cops on me. And I don't want to think about how that would go.

I drive back to Lavender House, passing a familiar-looking dark car on the road. It was there, pulled to the side when I left. Long time to be birdwatching. I make a note to check for it later and pull off the road toward the house and through the gate—unlocked, again.

Elsie's and Margo's cars are still here, which means I'm not too late. And inside, they're in the lounge, arguing.

"We can't show up in the same car, you know that," Margo says. She's in a nice dress, pink silk, white lace at the collar, a white coat over it with a brooch like a bouquet of flowers on it. She's putting on diamond earrings in the mirror. Elsie is in a gray suit—surprisingly feminine for her, with a tapered coat and a peplum, but still with pants. She has on a white blouse and a black pearl necklace.

"No one will care," Elsie says. "If they even notice. Oh, hello, Andy." She spots me as Margo takes her purse from the table and looks through it.

"Where are they?" Margo practically screams into her purse.

"It's for the best," Elsie says to her. "You're not a great driver."

"I'm . . . perfectly fine," Margo says, glaring at her. "Andy, you're a detective. Know where my car keys are?"

I glance at Elsie, her hands in her pockets, the small smile on her face. "I have a guess," I say.

"Rat," Elsie says to me, taking her hand out of her pocket, holding a set of car keys.

"You're terrible," Margo says, snatching them. As she does so, Elsie grabs her around the back with her other hand and pulls her in, dipping her slightly as they kiss. Margo is smiling the whole time. This is like how Cliff leans his head on Henry's shoulder. For them, it's the bickering, the flirting, that brings them closer. It's funny how many ways there are to show you're in love, and yet outside Lavender House, we never get to experience any of them.

"It's for your own good," Elsie says when they part. "You almost hit that cat last time."

"You going to that fundraiser you mentioned at breakfast?" I ask. "I have some questions for Margo. Maybe I can drive you while I ask them?"

Margo turns and glares at me now. "I can drive myself perfectly well, thank you."

"She can't," Elsie says.

Margo sighs and holds out the keys to me. "Fine. It will look good if I have a driver, anyway."

"I'm the driver now?" I ask with a smile. "Seems like a demotion."

Elsie laughs. "You volunteered."

"You can't be the detective, can you?" Margo says, heading for the door, where she puts on her coat. "People would ask why we had one."

"Just say it's the fashionable thing now," Elsie says. "Private investigators. All the rage. Like your wide belts."

Margo smirks.

"Where is this party, anyway?" I ask.

"The Palace Hotel," Margo says. "It's not a party, it's a cocktail luncheon and fundraiser. For war widows and orphans."

I look at Elsie, who is opening the front door. "Why are you going?"

"I like widows," Elsie says with a grin.

Margo sighs, but I can see her trying to hide her grin. Out front, Elsie gives Margo a quick peck on the cheek before she gets into her car, a gold Jaguar. Margo walks toward the white Lincoln Continental and opens the door to the back seat. Elsie is already speeding away, but I hear her laughing.

"I'm not going to sit up front if I'm being driven," Margo says, sitting down in the car and closing the door. I get behind the wheel and start the engine.

"You know the way?" Margo asks.

"Sure. But I'm going to talk to you while I drive."

"Certainly," she says as I pull out of the driveway and start toward San Francisco. "About what?"

"Gleam," I say.

"The soap? We don't use it."

I look at her in the rearview, she's gazing out the window, her chin resting on her hand, a little bored-looking, or maybe sad.

"You know George Cohen, though?"

"We've met at social functions, yes. I think his wife will be there today."

"Really?" I ask. "That's convenient."

"Why? Why do you care about the Cohens?"

"Pearl wants me to investigate the possibility of an outsider, maybe competition, murdering Irene."

I watch her roll her eyes in the mirror. "You have to ascertain it's actually a murder first, don't you?"

I don't say anything. Slowly, she turns to face me, her eyes meeting mine in the rearview mirror, and she looks a little shocked and a little sad. "Really? Are you sure?"

"Near about," I say.

"Poor Pearl." The line of her mouth turns hard. "Unless . . ." She shakes her head. "So you want to interrogate the Cohens? Won't that be a bit suspicious?"

"I can do it with some finesse, believe it or not."

"Well, you can't do it there. What would you even ask Rachel? She barely knows the business."

"She might know more than she lets on. Wives of businessmen often do."

She raises an eyebrow. "I'm not sure if that was a compliment or an accusation."

I don't say anything and this time both her eyebrows rise.

"Really? Me? Please. What do I have to gain?"

"You went to three printers yesterday to prove your label idea would work. You like that power."

She shrugs. "I like helping. Proving I'm useful. Who wouldn't? Doesn't make me a murderer."

"And you always go to events like this?"

"I . . . yes." She looks thrown by the question. "I represent Lamontaine, it's good for me to be in public at events like this, get my photo in the paper, so the ladies at home reading it think to themselves that our soap makes them more like . . . us."

"Us being the upper class."

She sighs and looks out the window. "I suppose."

"Do you like the parties?" I ask.

She doesn't turn to look at me in the mirror, but I see her jaw clench.

"You like being the Lamontaine wife? These people around

you, all good society folks. You didn't come from money, your mother was a hotel maid."

"She told you that? It's so odd, that she's proud of it. Being a maid. But no, I didn't come from money. And . . . yes, I like the parties. To a point."

"And before, did Irene come to the parties?"

She turns to look at me. "Yes. Sometimes. She hated them, but she came, represented the company, said all the right things. Brought me along until I could go by myself and say all the right things too."

"But then it was her face in the papers, right?"

"Yes. Her face in the papers, in the corner of all the ads, and now Henry wants to put her face on the soap! Can you imagine? The face of an old dead woman on something you use to wash yourself."

"Better a young pretty woman," I say, making it sound like I agree with her. "Better labels with her face."

"Yes," she says, then pauses, and looks at me. "Ah, I see it now. I'm the new face of the business, am I? The Lamontaine wife? I killed her out of . . . jealousy? Vanity? You really don't think much of women, Inspector."

"I'm just thinking about you, Margo. You said you had no motive, but I pinned one on you pretty quick. Did Irene like your ideas before? Would she have gone for labels?"

She glares at me in the mirror. Outside, the trees roll by like marching soldiers. "No. She was controlling. Henry listens to me more, and that helps all of us. Because I'm good at this."

"And you're going to be the face of the company."

She raises her chin. Sunlight through the trees catches her, makes half her face shine. "Yes. I should be the next face of Lamontaine. Henry is a man, he won't appeal in the same way.

I'm young, I'm pretty, that's why they chose me to marry him. I look like the perfect wife. This is my job. Irene found me especially for it—and then wouldn't get out of the way and let me do it. So yes, I was angry about that sometimes. But that's not a motive, and you know it. Inheriting the company—that's the motive. Henry has motive. Pearl has a motive." She pauses, and looks down at her nails, which are pale pink, as if checking them for dirt. "And Pearl's not exactly the wifely type," she says, her voice low. "Always trying to micromanage the company, even when Irene was alive. It wasn't even really hers. It was Irene's and Henry's. But now it's hers, I guess. She gets to offer her little suggestions like they're not orders, instead of just managing the house like a wife should do. That was really my mother, doing all the things in the background Pearl should have done. But instead she would lie around reading Latin or some nonsense. She never went to the parties to be the face, the wife."

"How would she explain that?"

"She was supposed to be Irene's secretary, same as Cliff. He always used to come out to these things, charm the women, and a few of the men too, I'll bet. Pearl never bothers, though. She's too good for all *this*. Even though *this* is what keeps us all above suspicion. That's why it should be my face on the soap. To keep us safe."

"So you think Pearl did it?"

"Maybe." She turns to look out the window again. "If she did, I'll bet Henry and I are next." She says it calmly, almost like it would be a relief. I don't think she believes it, and neither do I. Pearl would never hurt Henry. "Sometimes, I wish I could leave that place behind forever. Go live with Elsie above the club."

"Why don't you?"

Margo laughs. "My mother has a hard enough time with her current living situation. You think she'd ever accept anything from Elsie?"

"You could leave her behind. Let her fend for herself."

Margo sighs. "Don't think I haven't considered it."

"And?"

She shrugs.

I don't say anything, and we drive in silence for a while. I think about Alice sniffing the bottles too. The trees part and it's water on one side of us, sparkling like money in the noon sun. We roll over the bridge, and it echoes under the car.

"You know what your mother did to help Irene?" I ask.

"Took notes, I think. I don't know the details, I was hardly ever in the library. She didn't need to help, you know. She just insisted on it. Said if she was going to be staying with us, she'd do her share. Which I guess meant tormenting Irene all day."

"Tormenting?"

"Mother knows exactly how to be impolite while being polite. I'm sure you've noticed. Imagine that day in, day out from someone taking notes for you."

"So that's all she did? Take notes?"

"I think so." Margo shakes her head. "You should really ask her. Or do you already find her too taxing to spend time with?"

"She's not so bad."

"Sounds like you haven't spent time with her at all, then."

I nod. The only one who seems to have known Alice might inhale the bottle was Alice. So she probably wasn't the intended target. Though that doesn't mean Margo didn't do it. She sounds as annoyed with Irene as she does with her own mother.

In the mirror, Margo smooths out her jacket, and adjusts the brooch Pearl gave her. It's not just her mother who keeps her from running off with Elsie. She likes the high life. Being the society wife. She likes the money and the style. And she must have been so frustrated not to be able to show how good she was at it, with Irene always in the way.

Outside, the buildings around us seem cool in the daylight. The neon lights aren't on yet. San Francisco is just a breezy city by the bay in the daylight. It doesn't glow until the sun is down.

"How did you grow up?" I ask. "Did you stay at the hotel?"

"No, we had a little apartment down the street. I was a maid after school, all through high school. Saved all my money. When I graduated, I used it all to come here. A bus ticket and a few months' rent on a dirty little apartment. I was eighteen. I found a job as a maid, but it was different than in Oregon. Big-city hotels are less tidy, and guests are sometimes rough." She rubs her upper arm. "I was at it two years and nearly about to give up and move back home when I met Pearl in a bar one night."

I must look surprised, because she laughs.

"Yes, I went to the bars. I used to have a men's bicycle jacket in my bag, and I'd put it on once I got to the bar. And my hair was a little shorter then, too. I made lots of friends. I first met Elsie that way, too, but briefly—she still says it didn't happen, but I remember. She said I was beautiful as a flower and she wanted to pluck me." She laughs again. "Debonair, right? But she had a reputation and I didn't want to be another notch in her bedpost. After I met Pearl and Irene and Henry and eventually moved in and . . . became part of the family, I saw her again at a fundraiser. She tells the story like she seduced me, but don't believe it. I seduced her." She smiles and digs her shoulders into the back seat of the car, proud of herself. I try not to smile with her. It's a good story. It suits them, somehow.

"From a maid to the wife of a millionaire," I say. "Not bad."

She shrugs. "Exactly why I would never screw it up with anything as silly as murder, Inspector. I have a good life, even if it is a little stifling from time to time. But that's part of the job. A woman has to work to feel useful, you know?"

"Sure," I say.

I notice that the black Hudson Commodore that's been tailing us awhile keeps following us as we go through the city. I try a wrong turn, and it follows. On the highway, it wasn't too strange, but now it's looking definitely suspicious.

"So can I come in with you?" I ask. "I can say I'm your assistant."

Margo chuckles. "You can say you're my bodyguard. No one would believe assistant. We can say Henry is feeling protective because of his mother's death. People will understand that."

"Fine," I say. "Long as I can talk to Mrs. Cohen."

"Please do," Margo says. "She's a chatterbox, I'd be glad to have her talking your ear off instead of mine."

I drive a few blocks, taking a few experimental turns to see if the black Commodore keeps on my tail, and it does. We're being followed, but is it me, or Margo, and who would follow either of us? Someone from the force after me? Someone who killed Irene and wants to go for Margo next? I slow down, but the car always stays far enough behind us I can't see the driver. When I finally park in front of the hotel, it speeds by before I can get a plate number or make out anything in the driver's seat besides a blur.

TEN

The mayor's wife has rented out the entire restaurant in the Palace Hotel. It's decadent and beautiful, with a curved glass ceiling and chandeliers hanging off it like incense burners in a church dedicated to the elite of San Francisco society. The room is all gold and glass, delicate curves like a jewelry box, and the people inside are the jewels. Every woman is in a lovely dress, all of them brightly colored without being gaudy, fashionable without trying too hard, beautiful without having personality.

I'd been to a few of these as an inspector. I was supposed to put in an appearance now and then at police charity functions, smile for photographers, shake hands with wealthy women who cooed and asked me how many men I'd killed. But all those events feel like cheap kids' parties compared to this one. There's an orchestra somewhere I can't see, playing faintly, and waiters going around with platters covered in sandwiches no bigger than my thumb that no one is eating, and trays of champagne, which everyone is drinking. I follow Margo in, watching her shake off the hardness she wears at home and become that Margo I first met, with the smile and the poise.

Except this time it's not for me. It's for everyone. She shows her invitation to the doorman and explains I'm her bodyguard, which they don't even blink at. She air-kisses half a dozen women within ten minutes, and she laughs nervously when Elsie approaches and kisses her hand, before turning away and going to talk to another of the women in beautiful dresses, her expression scandalized, but amused, I assume at Elsie. It's quite a routine.

I stay as out of sight as much as I can. If this is a fundraiser hosted by the mayor's wife, it's possible some of my old colleagues will be here, but I don't spot anyone, and I have to risk it if I want to talk to Rachel Cohen. I'd have preferred George, but if Rachel is the chatterbox Margo says she is, hopefully she'll know enough to help me cross George Cohen off my list or keep looking at him.

Margo glides from person to person, sometimes posing for a newspaper photographer whose camera goes off with the loud sound of a vacuum being turned off. On the other side of the room, Elsie is surrounded by men, all of them trying to light her cigarette, as she tells what is probably a bawdy story, judging by the laughter. No one else seems to notice the way they look at each other across the room from time to time. Just one glance, which the other always instinctively returns. I wonder if it feels like they're here together, or if those glances hurt like shards of glass pressed into their palms.

"Oh, Rachel," Margo says to a redhead in a blue velvet dress that swings like a bell, "I was just talking to my new bodyguard, Andy, about you. He said he just had to meet you. He's been using Gleam his whole life."

I smile, turning to her, and extend my hand, which she shakes with a smile.

"And you hired him?" Rachel asks Margo. "How very daring."

"This way he has to use Lamontaine now," Margo says with a wink.

Rachel laughs and swats at Margo's arm. "Clever! Let's see if I can't undo the damage, though. Andy, what did you like most about Gleam?"

I smile, and glance at Margo, who is clearly amused by the position she's put me in. "It got everything clean," I say.

"Everything? Oh, my," Rachel says, reaching out and squeezing my upper arm. "Aren't you forthcoming."

I look down, pretending to blush. "I just meant . . ."

"Relax," she interrupts, "I'm just teasing. You still use Gleam at home?"

I glance at Margo, who raises an eyebrow.

"I'd rather not say," I reply.

Rachel laughs and links her arm in mine and leads me away from Margo. "Oh, don't worry about her, I know she has the perfect wife thing down, but she's a pussycat. Barely knows the business. I doubt Irene would have ever taught her, anyway."

More of Margo's façade. The face of the business, the wife—if she's wide-eyed and innocent about the business, no one will ask her for anything. But I do wonder how eager Irene was to pass on her knowledge to anyone besides Henry. Pearl knows a lot, of course, and Henry is the heir apparent. It must have been hard for Margo to prove herself to Irene. She probably wouldn't let Margo suggest things at breakfast the way Henry does.

"Did you know Irene?" I ask, taking advantage of the segue she's provided. "I just started working for them, and it's odd not knowing much about this . . . ghost in their lives."

"Oh, sure, I saw her sometimes. And my husband, he knew her well enough. She was a hard-ass, no getting around it.

That's what I mean when I say she didn't teach Margo much. Very private. Very fussy, too, with all the scents and the constant changing of the soaps . . ." She shakes her head. "Oy, it was a lot. We keep things simple at Gleam. Scentless or vanilla. All those perfumes mess with the actual cleaning power of the soap, you know."

"But you make perfumes," I say.

"Oh, sure," she says, waving at the air. "But that's a different part of the business. Those we ship to large industrial cleaning places, construction, laundromats and stuff, to make sure the chemical smell is covered. That's not soap."

"I saw some of the Gleam perfumes in the scent library Irene used," I say, low, conspiratorial.

She stops mid-stride and turns to me, her eyes wide. "Are you joking? Please tell me you're not joking. If you're not joking, I'm going to tell George, it'll make his year."

"I'm not . . ." I say. "Why would it make his year?"

"Oh, Irene always acted like she was too good for us. Her soap was so much fancier, smelled better, she did these custom mixed perfumes and used real flowers. Fresh as flowers, psssh." She shakes her head. "And sure, people loved it, but you know what? It was putting them out of business. All her formulating and reformulating the scents. The constant changing of ingredients, suppliers, instructions! It meant they took on huge costs almost every year. George always says, or said I guess now, that he didn't mind her being such a snob about the flowers, because it meant he was making more money, even if we have a slightly smaller share of the market. But if he finds out she was using his perfumes, he will be laughing about it for months. Enough to make him stop worrying about Henry, maybe, for a little bit."

We've stopped in a corner and she's leaning against a column, smiling at me.

"Worrying about Henry?"

"Oh, yeah, now that he's in charge, all that scent making, all those costs, they're kaput. It'll be a real, sensible business now, and George's worried they might start to really come for us. You wouldn't know anything about that, would you?"

I shake my head. "Sorry, I only started there yesterday."

"That new? Well, if you hear anything, and want to let me know anything about it, I'd be happy to give you a little bonus, you know?"

"I don't know if—"

"Relax," she says, taking my arm again, and now leading me back toward Margo. "Just if you want to. I'm in the phone book. Rachel M. Cohen. The only M, if you can believe it."

"Hey, Rach," Elsie says, suddenly in front of us, "who's the arm candy?"

"Bodyguard for Margo Lamontaine. I'm just bending his ear a little."

"Oh." Elsie smiles. "The competition? Remind me which one she is again?"

Rachel grins and nods in Margo's direction, and Elsie takes the moment to look over. Margo looks back. I wonder why Elsie is showing me how good she is at lying right now. Is this to show me she's loyal?

"You're the club owner," I say. "Elsie Gold."

Elsie bows a little and waves her cigarette. "I am. And you?"

"Andy," I say, extending my hand, which she shakes. "Didn't know you were involved in charity."

"Sure, I like to give back."

"And honestly, it's nice to have another Jew at these things,"

Rachel says. "Especially because she's even more scandalous than I am. But you give enough money, you get invited places. Tit for tat. And what's the point in making money if you don't use it to get invitations to nice parties and to meet fun people?"

"I guess that's true," I say.

"If I don't show up at these things, people stop talking about me," Elsie says. "And that would be mortifying."

Rachel laughs, swatting at Elsie's arm. "You're terrible. But I should bring poor Andy back to his lady now."

"Oh, it can wait," Elsie says, a slight edge in her voice. I look over at Margo again. She's talking to the mayor's wife, an older woman with a wide nose and a bright smile. But behind her are her own bodyguards—provided by SFPD.

I feel my heartbeat speed up seeing them. One of them is Jim. Jim who told me the wrong raid that night. Jim who burst into the restroom shouting "What's going on in here" and found me on my knees, pulling my pants back up, belt open, the buckle dragging on the tile floor, making it shriek. Jim who spat at me the moment he saw my face and then smiled as he pulled me up, not giving me time to refasten my belt, and hauled me out to the car. Jim who said to me from the driver's seat, "I'm not going to give you a beating, because you've been a good cop," then took the man I'd been with around the corner of the alley and brought him back, his lip cut, his face turning purple. I'd tried to apologize to him, and Jim had turned around and yelled, "Quiet, fairies," so loudly I hadn't said anything else for the rest of the trip. I'd just stared at my hand-cuffed wrists in my lap.

I look away, but not quickly enough. He's spotted me.

"I should, um . . . find the men's room." I say, my voice catching, before walking quickly for the door.

I'm just outside when I feel his hands on the back of my collar. He throws me facedown into the pavement, the sidewalk rising up like the ocean. I catch myself, but the concrete tears into my palms. The hotel doormen stare, then quickly look away when Jim flashes his badge.

I flip onto my back to find Jim over me, staring. Behind him, his partner, Sammy, is looming, cracking his knuckles like some dime-store thug.

"What the fuck are you doing here, Mills?" Jim asks. "This is a classy party, not some pervert prowling ground."

"Maybe he thought the orphans would actually be there," Sammy says.

"Yeah? You looking for kids to diddle, Mills?" Jim asks. I try backing away, but I'm on the curb. People have started to gather around us, staring. Jim bends down and lifts me up by the collar. He was too stupid to make the force on his brains, but he's a big guy, and he can nearly pull me into the air. "Let's go somewhere more private," he says, putting me down on my feet and giving me a shove so hard I stumble forward, but don't fall down again.

Before I can run, they're both on either side of me, marching me like a prisoner around the corner, and around the other corner. Even a fancy place like the Palace has an alley out back with a dumpster to throw the trash. That's where they take me before shoving me down again. I don't catch myself as well this time, and my head knocks on the concrete.

"I was just working," I say. The first time I've said anything, I realize. "Bodyguard gig." I turn around again, sit up, but don't stand. They'll just throw me down again.

Jim laughs. "Bodyguard? Nah. Not in my town. Not for you."

He kicks me in the stomach, hard. I feel the pain blossom out from my side, like the way a burn takes over all the skin around it. My breath catches and I cough. They laugh again.

"Stand up," Jim says.

"What?" I ask, panting.

"Stand up."

I slowly get to my feet, but I don't look at him.

"The thing I couldn't figure out with you is that we didn't spot you. You seemed like a cop's cop. Quiet. Strong. A tough guy. But fairies, they're all weak. Usually one good knock to the face and they fall down. So how many knocks does it take to topple a tough queer, Mills? I've been wondering that awhile. You got any guesses, Sammy?"

Sammy walks behind me, grabs my shoulders, and pins my arms to my side. "I think there's only one way to find out."

The first punch lands on my cheek and turns my vision white. The next is on my chin, and turns everything darker.

"Two!" Jim says, faking sounding impressed. "Wow. That's already twice what a normal fag can take."

He spits at me, and it hits me just below the eye. I can feel it creep down my face. I try to pull away, and get one arm free from Sammy, pushing him off me, and then swinging at Jim. But I'm too slow, and he catches the punch, wrenching my arm back from me and using his free fist to knock me square in the nose. The world spins around me, and I fall down.

"Three!" Jim says. "So now I know. Three. Now how many kicks until he passes out, you think, Sammy?"

"Usually it's just a few," Sammy says. "But there is variety. Highest I've seen is six, I think."

I turn onto my side. My lip is bleeding, and I feel like I might vomit.

"Oh, he can do better than that!" Jim says, and kicks me once in the stomach, hard enough I gag and spit up a little of breakfast. "Aw, gross. I thought you people were supposed to be prissy and clean. You just keep surprising me, Mills! Anyway, that was one."

"Two," Sammy says. "You gave him one before, too."

"Right. Two. Well, here's three."

"And four."

They take their time, kicking me in the leg, stomach, chest, counting each one out. I hear the click of a rib cracking. I wonder if it'll stab my heart. I remember Elsie's rabbit, suddenly. The way she cradled it on its side before she snapped its neck.

I lose count at eleven.

ELEVEN

I try opening my eyes, but they feel sticky, crusted over, so I lift an arm to rub them. Every movement hurts. I feel wind on my face. I'm sitting up, but moving. A car.

I blink my eyes open. My mouth tastes like bile, rubber, and metal.

"Still alive, then?" Elsie says. I turn my head, which causes the world to spin and my face to throb. She's driving. We're in her Jaguar. Out the window it's still San Francisco. The sun is still beating down from high above the city, so I haven't been out long. It's cold, though. Colder than it was before.

"What?" I manage to say. I feel blood run down my chin.

"I left Margo a note. She'll have to drive herself home. If she gets in an accident, though, I'm not going to forgive you."

"She really that bad"—I pause to wipe the blood off my mouth—"a driver?"

"No," Elsie says. "I just like to tease her."

"You saw them grab me?" I ask.

"Yeah. I waited until they were done and talking about whether to bring you in, and then I stepped out and told them to leave the trash where it was and come back to the party, that the mayor's wife was wondering where they were."

"Thanks."

"Why did you even come inside? That was dumb."

"Questions for Rachel Cohen," I say. My voice sounds hoarse and I'm finding new spots of pain are flaring up all over my body. I touch my chest. I think only one rib cracked, and not broken. I've been worse after scuffles with suspects, but not by much. I'll need to bandage myself up.

"Did you find anything out?"

"Yeah."

"What?"

"The murderer is definitely one of you."

Elsie lets out a long breath. "I should have just left you in that alley."

"You like me too much," I say.

She narrows her eyes without looking at me, then swings the car around a corner and into a garage. "Come on. Let's get you cleaned up and bandaged. Hopefully you don't need the hospital."

"Don't think so," I say.

She gets out of the car and comes around to my side, opening the door and helping me up, putting my arm around her shoulder. She's strong, and can get me into a nearby stairwell and up the stairs with only a few grunts. We come out in a large bar: the Ruby.

It lives up to its name: everything is red and gleaming. Walls covered in red wallpaper patterned in with darker red diamonds, like the facets on a cut gem. A red lacquer bar and matching tables and chairs. Red velvet curtains over all the windows.

There's a bartender at the bar—handsome, broad-shouldered,

with gold skin and dark hair. He has a row of alcohol bottles in front of him and he's carefully pouring water into one of them.

"Gene," Elsie calls, putting me down in one of the chairs, "ice!"

The bartender looks over, and his eyes go wide. He ducks under the bar and then runs over, holding a towel filled with ice.

"Gene, meet Andy," Elsie says, taking the towel and holding it to my face. "He's a private detective I know. Ran into some trouble."

"Um, hi," Gene says. He sounds a combination of amused and nervous.

"Sorry I'm not looking my best," I say.

Elsie laughs, then looks back at me. "And you're still bleeding. Get some bandages, Gene, please."

Gene runs off, and I take the ice from Elsie, holding it to the ache on my jaw. "Watering down the booze? Business not as good as you let on?"

Elsie sighs. "Are you always on the job?"

"Yes," I say, grinning.

"It's just part of the gig. Every bar does it."

Gene comes back with a roll of bandages and some more rags. Without saying anything, he kneels in front of me and starts dabbing at the blood on my lip. I look down at him. He's smiling, somehow.

"Nice to meet you, Gene," I say. "Not normally the position I meet people in."

Elsie laughs. "Sure it is."

He extends a hand, and I take it and shake it. "Gene Manalo," he says. "Good to meet you—whatever the position."

"Manalo," I repeat, because it sounds fun to say and I'm realizing maybe I've had a few too many blows to the head.

"It's Filipino," he says.

"You're very good-looking," I say.

He laughs.

"Oh, brother," Elsie says. "I'm going to go call the rest of them, let them know what happened. Gene, make sure he doesn't bleed all over the place. Take him up to my place if you can."

"Sure thing, boss," Gene says. He seems incredibly unfazed by all of this. I wonder how many bar fights the Ruby has. I thought it was classier than that.

Elsie walks off, and Gene keeps gently dabbing at my face. I reach up and undo a few buttons on my shirt.

"Maybe not the time for that," Gene says with a wink.

"They cracked a rib, I think," I say.

"Oh!" He grins, sheepish, embarrassed, adorable. He helps me take my shirt off, and I look down at the collage of purple and blue spreading out over me. I'm practically a watercolor painting. Gene feels up and around my body, which despite the pain, makes goosebumps rise on me. "Yeah, just feels cracked, though. I'll wrap it up for you. Boy, this one was mean. Normally when Elsie brings in folks the police have beat up, it's just a concussion, a black eye. But you . . . got a lot of it."

"Are you a doctor?"

"Almost," he says, pulling out a long string of bandages and pulling me forward to wrap my chest in them. "I was training as one, but then an ex sent the hospital I interned at some photos of me and him . . . Anyway. Can't work in medicine anymore."

"That's terrible," I say.

"It is," he says, and for a moment, his smile flickers away, but then it comes back. And it fits, too. He has no trouble with his smile. "But Elsie gave me this job, and I like tending bar, and I get to help people . . . and sometimes meet guys who are probably pretty cute under the bruises."

I laugh, which makes my chest hurt, so I wince and stop.

"So why'd you get the special treatment?" he asks, fastening the bandages tight around me.

"I used to be a cop," I say.

He looks up at me, wide-eyed. "Really? Why?"

"I wanted to be . . . I thought I could manage it. Thought it would protect me, even."

"Doesn't look like it."

"Yeah, I was stupid. Or maybe scared?"

"I get that."

"I should have done more . . . to help people. Been a doctor, like you."

"Did you solve crimes? Stop them?"

"Yeah . . . but . . ."

He presses the ice into my skin and it slips a little, the towel wet. I lift my hand up and gently take his wrist, moving it back to the bruise.

"That's something, though," he says. On the other side of the room, an elevator dings and a few men and women carrying instrument cases come out. They glance over at us, then quickly away, and walk toward the stage, where they start setting up.

"Maybe," I finally say to Gene.

"So why'd you leave?"

"They caught me in a raid."

"When?"

"A few days ago."

"Oh." He smiles at me, a little sad, then reaches out and gently wraps his arms around me, not romantically, but kindly.

A hug. I try to remember the last time I was hugged. I can't, but I wish this one didn't hurt so much. "I promise, you can have a great new life," he says softly in my ear. "Even when your dream is taken from you, you can have a great new life."

"Ow," I say.

"Sorry!" he says, immediately letting go. "Let me get you some aspirin and some ointment. Oh, and . . ." He takes the towel with ice I've been holding to my face. Most of the ice is melted. "New ice."

He walks back to the bar, and rummages under it.

"Did you help people when you were almost a doctor?" I ask.

"Sure," he calls back, still under the bar. "I like to think I still do." He stands, and looks at me, raising an eyebrow.

"Yeah, I just meant . . ." I let it fade for a moment. The thought is lost. "I meant . . . is it worth it this way? As much as it was the other way?"

"What?" he laughs, walking back to me. "I don't understand."

"You're not a doctor, but you still help people. I'm not a cop. Does helping people, even if you're not a doctor, does it feel like you're really helping? Helping as much as if you were a doctor?"

"Ah." He kneels in front of me, holding ice and ointment in one hand, and pills and a glass of water in the other. He hands me the pills and water and I throw the pills back in my mouth, letting them sit there, bitter.

"Yes," he says after a minute. "I'm really helping. Maybe more, this way. I don't know. But it's enough."

I nod and tip the water into my mouth, leaning my head back to swallow the aspirin, then rocking a little as a wave of dizziness hits me.

"Whoa," Gene says, reaching out to take my shoulders. "Let's

get you upstairs to lie down for a bit. I'll sit with you in case
you have a concussion."

"You have anything stronger than water?"

"I think the aspirin will be good for now," he says, helping
me up and draping my arm over his shoulder like Elsie did.
He walks me to the front of the club, where there's an elevator,
gold fronted, instead of red. Inside, it's small and despite my
swollen nose, I can smell him, like warm stone and lemons. He
hits the button for the top floor. There are only four floors.
The Ruby is on the second, and Elsie's apartment is on the top.

"So, you do that a lot?" I ask. The elevator is slow.

"What? Fix people up?"

"Water down the booze?"

"Ah . . . oh . . . You probably shouldn't tell anyone about
that. But yeah, lately Elsie has had us cut a few corners. Just
the past month or so. It's no big deal."

"Just the past month? What happened before that?"

"If we ran short, she just got some money from somewhere,"
he says, not realizing what he's telling me. I feel bad for a moment, interrogating him.

"Ran short?"

He's quiet, figuring out he shouldn't have said anything.
The elevator pings and the doors open.

"Just . . . sometimes, especially with the police bribes, we
didn't make quite enough every week," he says, helping me out
and hitting a light. We're in an alcove, tiled in red, but small,
with just one door in front. He fishes keys out of his pocket and
unlocks the door.

"You have keys to Elsie's place?" I ask, wondering if I'd mis-
read him.

"For emergencies, like this," he says, smiling. Maybe happy I stopped asking about the club's profits.

"Sorry," I say, "I'm nosy."

"Probably good in your line of work," he says, helping me through into an apartment. It's large, the entire floor, the same size as the club, and surprisingly sparse. The walls are painted gray, the window shades are venetian blinds. It's not the opulence I expected from Elsie. He takes me into one of the rooms, which has a bed but isn't her bedroom. It's nearly empty, with just the bed and nightstand, and a dresser. Nowhere for all her suits. He lays me down on the bed, sitting next to me, then takes the ointment he's been holding this whole time and dabs some under my eye. Then he moves to put some on my lip, but I catch his hand before he can.

"Wait," I say. "Before you do that."

"What?" he asks.

"I'm not dead," I say.

"No, you're not," he says.

"I thought they'd kill me for sure. I thought if any of the guys I used to work with saw me again, they'd kill me for sure. But I'm alive."

Gene grins like I'm crazy. "You are."

"Can I kiss you?" I ask.

He grins wider.

"Just because I'm not dead," I say. And saying that is like a gasp of air after almost drowning.

He lays me back on the bed and then gently presses his lips to mine. It stings a little where my lip is cut, but it feels good, too. The first kiss I've had since the last one, and the last one didn't end well. I lift my aching arm up and put it on the back of his head, pulling him into me, and he kisses deeper, his tongue softly licking the inside of my lips, his chest against mine, but not pressing so hard it hurts. He feels warm and tastes like gin and sugar. I can feel blood speeding inside me, my heart beating for the first time in what feels like too long. It's not just about the kiss. It's about being alive. After all that. I'm alive, and I'm kissing a handsome man and he's kissing me back. I smile as he kisses me. And the smile fits.

He kisses me a little harder and I wince at the cut on my lip and he pulls back.

"Sorry," he says. "I got carried away."

"I didn't mind," I say, laughing. "Bad timing, maybe. But thank you."

"Oh, the pleasure was all mine, I promise," he says. "Let's take care of that lip now, though." He puts some more ointment on his finger and gently dabs at the cut.

"It tingles," I say.

"That means it's working. Now close your eyes. I'll let you rest for a little bit. Elsie or I will keep an eye on you."

"I prefer you," I say, closing my eyes. I'm so tired, I realize. I'm so tired and every part of me aches.

He laughs. "All right," he says, and I feel his hand, lightly resting on my chest. I take a deep breath and feel sleep pull me down like the tide.

TWELVE

"Really?" I open my eyes to Elsie standing in the doorway. I'm lying in bed, shirtless aside from the bandages, and next to me, also lying in bed, reading a fresh copy of C. S. Lewis's *Prince Caspian*, is Gene. The radio is on in another room, the old "Mad About the Boy" single by Maxine Sullivan.

"I was watching him," Gene says. "Making sure his breathing didn't change."

"How long have I been out?"

"About four hours," Gene says.

"We're open," Elsie says. I strain my ears and I can hear it, a faint murmur of people, music coming up through the floor. "Can you get downstairs and tend the bar, Gene?"

"Sure thing, boss," he says, swinging his legs off the bed and standing. I feel cold where he was next to me.

"I need a ride back," I say, sitting up.

"You can spend the night," Elsie says. "It's already past six."

"I can go, right?" I ask Gene.

"He's beaten pretty bad, but he can move, sure. Probably you should take it easy for a while. Avoid the police."

"So stay here tonight," Elsie says.

"I don't have any clothes."

"By the looks of it, you don't need 'em," Elsie says, raising an eyebrow. Gene looks sheepish again.

"I'll get downstairs," he says, and Elsie moves to let him pass. I watch him leave, frowning a little.

"He flirt with all the patients?" I ask when I hear the front door close.

"No, actually," Elsie says, sitting down on my bed. "It was a little strange. He's always smiling and friendly—good for his tips, if nothing else—but he's not flirty. I sometimes wonder if he's even really queer."

"He is," I say.

She laughs. "Maybe it's the detective thing. Mysterious, wounded. That's a type that could get a rise out of people."

I sit up straighter, wincing at how much my body still aches. Then I carefully lower my feet onto the ground.

"You really want to go back?"

"Aren't you worried about Margo's driving? Want to check she made it back safe?"

She tilts her head, relenting. "All right. I brought your shirt up, tried to rinse the blood out, but I don't really do laundry. It's dry so you can wear it back to Lavender House. But I'm not helping you to the car. If you can't stand, you should spend the night."

She puts her hands on her hips and watches as I slowly manage to stand up. The dizziness is gone, at least. I definitely hurt, but I can walk. Elsie sighs, but walks back to the front door. I follow her.

"Your place is nice," I say. "Less opulent than I'd imagined, though."

"I'm a simple girl, despite appearances," she says as we walk out the front door and she locks it behind us. "I like nice things, but I don't like having too many of them. There are more important things than a fancy armoire I'm never going to look at."

She rings for the elevator and we get in, taking it down past the Ruby to the ground floor.

"I didn't say goodbye to Gene," I say when the doors open on a simple red-tiled lobby.

"I'll tell him when I see him next," Elsie says, taking me by the arm and leading me out of the elevator. I flinch at her hand. "Honestly, you're just as bad as he is. Cool and aloof and then one beating by the cops and you're going doe-eyed at the first guy you see." She leads me out of the lobby and around the block to the garage, where her car is still parked.

"Gene says you bring in a lot of folks who have been knocked around by the police."

"People know the Ruby is a safe space to bring people," she says, getting behind the wheel. I sit down next to her, and slowly close the door. She pulls out of the garage and starts driving us back to Lavender House.

The day has faded, and the neon lights of San Francisco are glowing around us as we drive, like the flashes of gunshots in the dark. Like fireworks.

"So is that where you're losing money?" I ask. "Take care of too many unlucky idiots like me?"

She keeps her eyes on the road. "What makes you think I'm losing money?"

"I was a pretty good inspector," I say.

"Gene say something?" She licks her lips.

"Not intentionally."

She sighs. "Fine, yes. We've had occasional financial issues. Part of it is keeping the first aid kit stocked, and part of it is that sometimes people are afraid to come out, if they hear some other place was just raided. People think it works like a fire, spreading through the city. But it's more like a game of pool, the cops lining up shots and taking them when they want, for their amusement. And the Ruby pays well to make sure we're not behind the eight ball."

I almost want to say it's not like that, that it has to do with morality laws, about proving something immoral is happening in the bar, but I shake my head. She's right. It's just a game for the cops. I never raided with them, but it was a game for me, too. Finding out which bar they were going to hit, avoiding it, still trying to have my fun. I never thought about everyone else. How they'd get caught. How many beatings like the one I got today could I have stopped, if I'd bothered to think about someone besides myself?

"Why not rent out the empty floor?" I ask. "If you need the money?"

"What?"

"I saw in the elevator, there's a floor between the Ruby and your apartment. Rent it out."

She shakes her head. "It's empty offices, mostly, but it's also the dressing rooms for some of the acts. No one wants to work next to the dressing rooms of a bunch of drag acts, which are already pretty messy and loud, much less above a club with a reputation like the Ruby's. At least, no one I trust. If I'm a little light now and then, that's the price."

"So why did your financial troubles start right around when Irene died?" I ask.

"Andy, you really are a pain in the ass."

"You understand why I'm asking, right?"

"To see if I was extorting her, we got in a fight, I pushed her? Some melodrama like that?"

"Pretty much." Outside, we pass another neon sign, this one of a giant woman's leg, bent like she's sitting on top of the building, waiting for someone.

"Yes," she sighs. "Irene lent me the money to keep us in the black now and then. Happy? Am I suspect number one now, despite nursing you back to health?"

"Lent?" I ask.

"Yes. It was an arrangement. Sure, I may have implied that I could tell the papers what I knew to make her give me the loan, but I was never going to do that. And she thought it was funny, my threat. She wasn't tightfisted, you know. She was sweet. And despite what Margo says now, they got along. Sometimes. Like a mother and daughter, you know? Fights, sure, but love too, I think." She relaxes her shoulders as she leans back a little in her seat.

"Love can be a killer too."

"I get why you look at her and think that," Elsie says, turning her eyes away from the road to look at me for a moment, "but she's no killer."

"You don't think you're a little biased?" I ask.

"No." She says it firmly, but I can't tell if she's trying to convince me or herself. "So take us both off your list. I'm close to paying the money back, now that people can see the Ruby is safe. And with Irene gone, I've had to try turning Henry into my bank, and he is much less fun, let me tell you. Tightfisted shmuck. But he has his reasons, I think." I look over at her, trying to sense if she's lying, looking for a smirk, or holding her breath, and she glances at me briefly, then laughs. "What? Something on my face?"

"You really care about the family, don't you?"

She grins. "Of course I do. I love Margo. You get that, right? I really love her?"

"I guess I wasn't sure. You act so . . . frivolous. And she's . . ."

"A stuck-up ice queen?" Elsie smirks. "That's why I love her. I like being the heat that melts ice."

"Evocative."

"I walked in on you in bed with my barman, you can handle a little dirty talk."

"I was asleep after being nearly beaten to death!" I say. "It wasn't dirty."

"You should have seen the way he watched you sleep, then."

I laugh and turn away to hide my blushing. We drive over the bridge, the low sun tinting the fog pink and gold.

"So you love her," I say after a pause. "And you love the family?"

"Family is family. You always love each other, even when you hate each other."

"And does Henry hate you right now, for trying to use him as a bank?"

"We had a little talk yesterday. He doesn't love the situation . . . but he understands. And he's keen for me to repay the loans."

I nod. "That makes sense. Turns out the company isn't doing as well as it should." I say it to see if she knows already. To see if she cares.

"Really?" Elsie turns to stare at me, eyebrows at the top of her forehead. "Irene never let on. And Pearl must know, too, right? And Henry? And they never told us? I could have helped! Ads for the soap in the club, maybe . . . No, that would draw attention. Irene would have hated that."

"Apparently all her reformulating the soap was expensive. They still had most of the market, but the take wasn't what it should be."

"Maybe that's why Irene was so nasty those last few weeks."

The road gets a little bumpier under us and the smell of San Francisco, which lingers even out here, finally turns to wood and grass. The redwoods rise up on one side of us like bars, and the ocean lies flat on the other side, like the smooth sheets of a freshly made bed.

"Nasty?" I ask.

"Her usual fussiness was at the highest setting. I saw her slap Cliff."

"Really?" I narrow my eyes, but Elsie just shrugs.

"I had just unlocked the gate, and was at the top of the hill, and I heard an engine rev, so I peeked down into the lot to see who was coming up. It was Cliff, but Irene was in the garden, and she looked over and practically jumped into the path of the car. Cliff stopped, of course, and then Irene walked over, opened his door, and pulled him out."

"Did you hear them?"

"Nah, they were just arguing in low voices. She slapped him, though, and then reached into the car and took his keys, got in, and drove the car back to the lot. I figure she just didn't want him driving drunk. He's been drunk a lot lately."

"Yeah," I say. "What did Cliff do?"

"He just walked back down to the house. I invited him to come out with me that night, that I'd drive, but he said no. Just sulked the rest of the day."

"And he never mentioned it?"

"No. Neither did Irene. It was dramatic, but it wasn't a big deal. Just Mom making sure her son-in-law doesn't hurt himself, y'know?"

"Yeah," I say, not entirely sure I agree.

"It was nasty, but like I said, Irene had been pretty nasty that week. And if she was worried about money, that would explain why." She straightens her back and readjusts her grip on the steering wheel. "Well, they should have told me. I'm a successful businesswoman."

"Who waters down her gin."

Elsie rolls her eyes. "Every bar does. A bar isn't about the alcohol. Did you go to the Black Cat to drink?"

I pause a beat, wondering if she's being sarcastic, but she waits. "No," I say.

"No. We go for companionship. Friends. Lovers. Family. We have to make these things for ourselves. You talk to your family at all? Were you close?"

I think back on my dad, and him teaching me his business when I was little. How to tell if someone was lying, how to wait for them to talk instead of filling in the blanks, how to pick locks and follow someone without them noticing.

"When I was young," I say, looking out at the water. The lighthouse at Harbor Point is out there, slowly spinning a beam into the water.

"And then what? You figured it out about yourself, right?"

"Yeah," I say. I couldn't tell him. What son wants to tell his dad he's a fairy? What son wants a slap to the face and to be kicked out of the house? So I hadn't said anything, and that one secret, the keeping it from him—the guy who could find any secret he wanted—it meant staying away from him. It meant not filling any silences, but staying silent, too. It meant peeling myself off of him until we were practically strangers, and then he was in the ground.

"And then you weren't as close," Elsie says. "It happens to all of us. You can't hide a part of yourself from people and still be their family. And if you show that part . . . well, most families tell you you're not family then, anyway."

"I still talk to my mom now and then."

"Now and then, sure," Elsie says. "But now your real family is going to be the one you make of other people like you. And that's what the bars and clubs are for. No one cares if the gin is a little light."

"I guess not."

"That's what Lavender House is too, you know."

"Better gin, though."

She laughs. "I take it back, Andy. I like you."

"I like you, too," I say, smiling. I mean it. I think back on the cops of the force, my old partner. We never talked like this. Never joked about lovers or discussed family. We just did the work, listened to the radio. Maybe it's the beating, but I feel warm, talking to Elsie. Having a friend.

"Look at us, a pair of sentimental types," she says. "We gotta keep it a secret."

"Deal," I say.

She grins. We drive the rest of the way in silence, but at the turnoff, as if waiting for us, I spot the black Commodore, parked to the side of the road. I almost tell Elsie to pull over, but my body still hurts all over. If it's the local PD or someone else with violence in mind, I wouldn't be able to hold my own, which would help no one. So I don't say anything, and Elsie keeps driving.

At the house, the gate is locked, and Elsie kindly gets out to unlock it. When we drive up to the house, the door opens before Elsie even turns the engine off, and Henry steps out, Margo just behind him. It's dark, the sky and gravel gray. The pink flowered trees that frame the house look bloody in the dark, and yellow light cuts through in squares from the windows and where the door of the house hangs open.

"Glad you made it back in one piece," Elsie says to Margo, who scowls at her.

"What did you tell them?" Henry asks me as I carefully ease out of the car. His face is stiff, as usual, but his eyes are bright, his jaw clenched. I can see little white half circles in his palms from him pressing his nails into his hands. Worried, angry, or both, I can't tell.

"What?" I ask. "Tell who?"

"The cops. Did you tell them who you were working for? Did you give them our name?"

"They didn't ask," I say.

Henry takes a deep breath, his body relaxing. Behind him, Margo nods to herself.

"Good," Henry says, pushing up his glasses. "Very good. Thank you, ah, for being discreet and not using our name to get you out of trouble."

"I know your concerns," I say. "But I really didn't even have the chance. They saw me and went right to the punching part."

"It's your own fault for coming in in the first place," Margo says. "What was even the point? Did you learn anything from Rachel?"

"I did," I say, finally standing. Light from the window flashes over my face and they both see my bruises clearly for the first time and flinch. "I learned about the business," I say, watching Henry, who now won't meet my eyes.

"Well, I suppose it's your choice," Margo says. "If you think it was . . . worth it." She turns away and walks back to the house, Henry hurrying past her to get inside. "We were waiting on you for dinner. I didn't realize how bad . . . You should clean yourself up. I'll have Mr. Kelly dig up some bandages for you."

"Thanks," I say. "A bath would be nice. But you should eat without me."

I follow them inside, Margo holding the door open for me, but looking me up and down like I'm trash, then smiling as Elsie comes in behind me, kissing her on the cheek. Pearl and Cliff are in the sitting room, and rush up to me when they see how beaten I am, something I realize I haven't even seen myself yet.

"Oh, no," Pearl says. "Let's call a doctor."

"No, no, it's all right," I say. "I already saw one. I'm just going to take a bath."

"Are you sure?" Pearl asks. Behind her, Cliff has poured himself a drink, his hands shaking. Henry goes over to him and holds him close until the shaking stops.

"I'll be all right," I tell her. I slowly walk up the stairs, turning briefly to see Pearl still watching me, her hands tightly clasped in front of her. By the time I get to my room, Pat is already there, the bathtub running, an array of bandages and creams laid out in the bathroom.

He looks up at me, sees me, and looks a little sad. "A bad one," he says. "A large redheaded cop with bad breath once gave me one like that. My left hip still aches when it's going to rain."

"Thanks," I say, nodding at the bath.

"Need me to help you undress?" he asks, then looks horrified at himself. "I don't think I've ever asked that without lewd intent before."

"Maybe my shirt," I say, unbuttoning it.

He pulls it off me, and sees the bandages and nods. "Gene's work?"

"Yeah."

"He's a nice boy. I'll have this shirt cleaned properly. Need any help with your pants?" He grins at me, wiggles his eyebrows.

"I think I'll manage," I say.

"Then I'll leave you to it," he says and turns to go.

"Pat, wait a sec," I say, and he stops. Suddenly, I'm not sure what to say, but I know I need to apologize somehow.

"You don't need to say it, Andy. You're not one of them, anymore."

Him saying that gives me enough of a jolt to go over and give him a weak hug. "Thanks. And I'm sorry that I was ever part of what did this to you. And that I didn't warn you when I could have."

He hugs me back gently, then pecks me on the forehead. "That time is in your past. But I appreciate the apology, Andy. Now wash off. You smell like someone threw you in a dumpster." I laugh, and turn away so he doesn't see how relieved I am to be forgiven.

He turns to leave and I strip down, aside from the bandages, and go to look at myself in the mirror.

It's as bad as I thought. I have no idea why Gene agreed to kiss me. There's a cut under my left eye, and my nose and jaw are purple. My nose is swollen, but somehow not as swollen as it feels. There's a cut on my lip and dried blood just below it.

The circles under my eyes are dark too, like I've been punched there as well.

To everyone in the house, I'm probably their worst night-mares come to life. Except Pat, who's lived it. I was found out. I paid for it. But I didn't die. I try smiling. It hurts like hell, but it fits perfectly. For the first time since Jim dragged me off the floor of the bathroom in the Cat, I don't want to pitch myself in the bay. But I do want to wash myself.

I get into the bath, which is warm, but not too hot, and relax into the water. It immediately makes me feel better. I splash my face, and the water turns a little pink in places, but I don't mind. I can feel the scum of the alley, and my sweat and blood, all rinsing away. I feel more like myself than ever. I grab one of the bars of soap still wrapped in blue like my eyes, and un-wrap it, dipping it in the water and then running it up and down my body, scrubbing away anything the water missed, my chest throbbing with pain with every motion. The perfume fills the bathroom, different than just the flowers outside, but something deeper, and darker, and then . . . sour. I shake my head, not understanding Irene's formulas, and not needing to. I scrub the back of my neck, but when I rub the soap over my left shoulder, it hurts enough I almost cry out. I look at my skin. There's a cut there I hadn't seen before. Maybe the soap made it sting?

The cut turns redder, welling up with blood. It's fresh. I rinse it off and go to put more soap on it, but stop. A single small gray curve sticks out of the soap. Almost like the flower petals scattered in it, but not quite right. I touch it, it's sharp. It's what scratched me just now.

I push into the bar of soap with my thumbs, but it's firm, so I hit it against the rim of the bathtub. It crumbles a little, and

I put it in the water and then push it away, bit by bit, revealing whatever the curve is a part of. The soap gives way like crumbling plaster, showing a small furred barb I don't recognize. I pull more and more away until half the bar of soap is gone. I almost drop it when I realize what I'm holding. Curled up in the soap, perfectly placed so it wouldn't stick out of the bar, is a small dead rat.

THIRTEEN

I throw the bar across the room, and it hits the wall and slides around the tile floor, like the rat is driving it at the Indianapolis 500. I rinse myself with the water, but the rat was in that, too, so instead I stand up, shaking a little as my body protests, and pull the drain. Then I turn on the shower, and reach for another bar of soap. I unwrap it and crack it open on the wall. Just soap, all the way through. Grateful, I wash myself off and get out. I dry myself, trying not to look at the rat soap still on the floor.

A blade could have done the job just as easy—done more damage, even. But a rat is a message. Someone wants to scare me off, not kill me. Make it clear I shouldn't rat anyone out. But what have I done recently to earn it? Or did they place it before I even arrived, and I only found it now? Anyone in the house could have done it. There are molds and ingredients in the library, they all seem to know the basics of making the soap. Any of them could have found a dead rat. It would have been easy to carefully curl the rat into the mold and pour the soap around it, wait for it to harden, and then wrap the soap and slip it in my room while I was out.

Which of them would think like that, though? Which could handle a dead rat with such ease? Cliff seems unlikely, but he was in the army, so he might be able to do it. Henry is cold enough it wouldn't bother him. Elsie had no problem killing a rabbit. Alice and Margo were maids, they've probably handled worse. Pearl is the only one who I think probably wouldn't have the stomach for it. And I was already pretty sure she wasn't the killer. I think of Judy for a moment, or Dot. They have good reasons for not liking me. This could be a little prank from them, if they've picked up soapmaking from working here.

This tells me nothing, really. Except that someone wants me gone. And that I need to remember how easy it is to get into my room, how nothing in this house is really safe.

I bandage all my wounds, including the new one from the rat's claw, and then slowly change into fresh clothes. I don't know if it's because of or in spite of the rat, but I feel more energized now. And eager to end this. I could confront them all at dinner, but no one would confess. It would just look like whoever it was had gotten to me.

Instead I open the window and toss the rat soap out. I don't want it around me anymore. I don't even want to think about it. I just want to solve the case as much as the person who sent me the rat wants me to give up.

Then I slowly, achingly, dress, only wincing a few dozen times as I move my muscles, and head downstairs. Everyone is already sitting in the same spots as last night. They're already done with their appetizers, and they each have a glass of wine, several of which are nearly empty. I think Cliff's is only full because it's his second.

As I walk in, everyone looks up at me, and I see them frown or flinch at my wounds, maybe out of disgust or pity, or both.

Alice, seeing me for the first time, stands up, her chair scooting back from the table.

"What happened?" she asks.

"Just ran into some of my old colleagues," I say, sitting down. Alice comes around the table and takes my face in her hands, examining me.

"More like their fists ran into you," Elsie says.

I laugh, and Alice lets go of my face. "You shouldn't joke," she says, walking back to her chair and sitting down. "Has a doctor examined you?"

"Thoroughly," Elsie says.

"Cracked rib, a lot of bruises, some cuts," I say, glad I have a cover for the rat-claw scratch on my shoulder, if anyone spots it. "It'll all heal. Maybe I'll have a scar."

"Scars *are* sexy," Cliff says. Henry smirks, shaking his head.

"Still," Pearl says, glaring at them. "We should have you in bed. We should be bringing you dinner. You can't just be walking around. Aren't you in pain?"

"I could use some aspirin," I say, grinning. My own mother hasn't taken care of me in years, since I joined up to get away from the doting, the questions of who I was seeing, the setups, the lies. But Alice and Pearl are mothers who know, and it's nice when Pearl frowns at me, worried, across the table. Maybe I should take her offer, move in, become part of the family. I've had my real family, then the army, then the police force. Families where it never worked out. But maybe it could, here. Even with the murder and rats in my soap, it's kind of beautiful.

"You heard him, get some aspirin, please," Pearl says to Pat, who darts out of the room. "You know anything you need, Andy, we can get it for you. I just feel so terrible this happened."

"If you hadn't hired him, it wouldn't have," Alice says to her, glaring.

"Really, Alice?" Pearl asks. "This happens to people like us every day. The police raid our clubs just to do this to us."

"Yes, but this is because he was working your nonsense case. He walked into the lion's den for you, and what are you offering him? Aspirin and soap?" She leans back and folds her arms.

"I walked in by my own choice," I say, before it grows even more tense. "I did it to investigate what I believe was a murder."

The table goes quiet. Some of them I've told already, but I look to the others. Alice stares down at her plate, naked aside from some crumbs. Cliff reaches out to take a glass of wine, which he drinks nearly half of in one sip.

"You believe?" Alice asks, leaning forward, excited now. "But what's your proof?"

"I have evidence," I say. "But I don't want to disclose it right now."

"Why not?" Cliff asks.

"Isn't it obvious?" Margo asks, sipping her own wine. "He thinks one of us did it."

The room goes quiet and Pat comes out and hands me two aspirin, which I take with the wine in front of me.

"I think, maybe, the rabbit stew now," Alice says to him, and he nods and leaves again.

"Is that true?" Pearl asks me. "I thought you were going to look into George Cohen."

"I did," I say. "I don't think it was him."

"Well, we have other competitors," Pearl says. "The Manhattan Soap Company, Lux, Palmolive."

I shake my head. "Any of those local?"

Pearl doesn't answer.

"I'm just going to follow the evidence," I tell her.

"And meanwhile, we're eating dinner with a murderer," Alice says, sounding a little delighted. I swallow. I'm glad someone is happy about it.

"Mother," Margo says in warning.

Pat comes out and places bowls down in front of each of us, and I watch them all. They're all still suspects, even if I feel like I have a handle on who's innocent—I could always be wrong.

"The stew is rabbit from the garden," Alice says, after the last bowl has been set down. "Andy killed it himself."

"I don't feel so well," Cliff says. "You'll have to excuse me." He gets up before anyone can say anything, and rushes out of the dining room.

Henry sighs and stands, putting down his napkin. "I'll go check on him," he says, following Cliff out.

"And I should probably get back to the club, actually," Elsie says, standing. "No offense, Alice, the shrimp puffs were great, but I'm just gonna grab a sandwich back home for the main course. It's past nine and I want to check out the band I hired for tonight. Plus I have a message for my bartender I have to deliver tonight." She turns to me and winks. "So my apologies, everyone. I'll ring you tomorrow, darling," she says, leaning over and kissing Margo, whose mouth rises up to meet her. I glance over at Alice, who is focused on her silverware.

"All right," Margo says, and watches her leave. Then she turns to Pearl, glaring. "This is all your fault, you know. You brought in a detective with accusations of murder and now the entire family is falling apart. And you." She turns to me, still glaring. "Murder accusations at the dinner table? Really?"

"You were the one making accusations," I say.

"No, I was merely interpreting what you were saying. Making sure everyone understood exactly how far you're willing to go to milk Pearl for a bigger payday."

I feel my jaw tighten and I try to stay calm. "I'm just following the evidence," I repeat.

"To a pile of money," Margo says. Her shoulders fall and her face changes, loosening, she looks down then back up and her eyes aren't bitter anymore. They're begging. "Please, can't you take it back, Andy? Say it was a mistake. That she just fell? Things were much simpler when we all thought she just fell." Her eyes are wide and a little watery. Her cheeks are flushed. "I'm pleading with you, Andy. Say it was a mistake. We'll pay you however much you want." I look over at Pearl, and Margo's eyes follow me. Pearl is still, a little pale, a little sad, but she's not begging with Margo.

I look down at my stew. A chunk of meat bobs on the surface, then falls under, drowning. "I'm sorry, Margo. I didn't want to do this either. But the truth is the truth."

"The family will be fine, Margo," Pearl says. "Just let Andy do his job."

I look up, but now Margo has her head in her hands. She sits up, downs the rest of her wine in one swallow, and stands. "I'm going to get to bed early, I think. Good night." She walks out of the room slowly, her heels loud on the wooden floor.

"Well . . ." Alice says, sighing. "I should go tell the cook to save what she can of dinner for something else. At least the stew will keep, might even be better tomorrow . . ." She stands and leaves the room. I look down at my stew. I'm hungry, but I don't want to eat it.

"I'll have the cook make you something simple and bring it to your room," Pearl says. "I'm sorry everybody left like that."

"I'm sorry my investigation is what caused it," I tell her.

"It's not your fault. We've all been cracking at the seams for weeks, you just pulled a little."

"Well, I feel bad about it."

"Don't."

"Cliff especially seemed upset," I say carefully.

Pearl is quiet for a moment, then lifts her wineglass. "Of course. He's a very sensitive boy," she says, and sips. "He's been broken up since Irene died. Drinking more. That makes sense, though. She was his only mother. He's an orphan, you know. We're his first family."

"Is he? He didn't mention."

"No, he doesn't talk about it. That's how you know when he really feels close to someone, when he opens up. None of that flirting or dancing around he does with you. That's just how he is. He was a dancer in the follies, after all. He's used to being overly friendly for tips." She sips her wine again and stares at me. She finishes her glass of wine and then stands up, slowly. "I need to know who did this. But, Andy"—she looks down at me—"I'm sorry. I'm going to hate you a little for being the one who figures it out. You know that, right? I'd hate anyone who told me one of my family killed my wife."

I nod. "I know," I say. "I hate it too, if it makes you feel better."

She smiles, a little sad, then goes to the window and looks out at the night. "A little," she says. "When you find out who it was, you tell me, and only me. You understand?" She turns around and I nod. "I don't know what I'll do yet. Maybe . . . maybe I can forgive them. They're my family, after all. I love my family."

She looks out the window a few minutes more in silence. Pat starts to clear away the untouched bowls of stew.

"Good night," Pearl says, suddenly, and walks out of the room without looking at me. I'm alone at the table. Pat comes out from the kitchen and smiles down at me.

"Rough day," he says. "Dot is making you a cold sandwich. That all right?"

"That would be wonderful," I say.

"You need to be fed to heal faster. I'll bring you some milk, too."

"I'm not a kid."

"Tonight you are," he says, winking at me, and then leaves. He's back a minute later with a sandwich and glass of milk.

"Thank you," I say, biting into it. He starts to clean up the rest of the table. "Do you think I should have lied?" I ask him between bites. "Told them it was an accident?"

"No," Pat says. "The whole point of this place is truth, right? Be free, be honest, be yourself. You did what they needed you to do."

"I didn't mean to ruin dinner," I say.

"They know that. And you didn't, really. I think it's your face."

I laugh.

"I mean, the beating. It's violence, written across you. Makes them feel unsafe."

"Maybe," I say.

"When I got beaten, I wore it well," Pat says. "I have a scar, too. Want to see?" He stands straight and undoes the button on his collar, loosening his tie and bending his neck so I can see a short, but wide scar across his collarbone. "One of them kicked me into a broken bottle. I lost a lot of blood, was in the hospital for a while."

I shake my head. "I guess I was lucky."

"Not really. I only had a black eye on my face. Much sexier than your purple nose."

I grin. "What, I'm not sexy anymore?"

"Maybe if we get some ice for the swelling," he says, with a grin. He's starting to button his shirt back up when Alice comes in from the kitchen, holding her own plate and sandwich. She looks at Pat and frowns and he quickly finishes buttoning, grabs the final glasses, and leaves. Alice sits down opposite me, eating her own sandwich.

"I think I owe you an apology," she says. "I was a little rude yesterday, wasn't I? When I was showing you the library."

"It's a murder scene, anyone would get upset," I say.

"It's not that," she says. She takes a bite, chews, and swallows. "Well, maybe a little. But also, right now it's hard for me. Everyone is always a little aloof to me. I understand that, I'm not one of . . . you. But since Irene died, it's felt more accusatory. Like *I* should be the one ashamed for who I am."

"Do you think we should be ashamed for who we are?" I ask her.

She takes another bite and chews, tilting her head, thinking. "I don't love it," she says after swallowing. "How could I? What mother would want this life for her child? Margo should be married to a man who loves her, and she should have children by now. Why would I want this for her? A pretend marriage, no children. When Irene and Pearl call us a family, I always have to keep myself from laughing, honestly. Does that sound cruel?" Her voice is soft, almost apologetic.

"A little," I say. "This isn't a bad life, and it *is* a family, of a sort. Better than a lot of others."

"Is it the one you wished for, as a child? Or would you fix yourself if you could? Find a nice woman, settle down? You never would have been fired. You wouldn't have been beaten today. Wouldn't all that be better than these"—she gestures around the room—"empty perversions? It's not a family. It's a fun-house mirror of a family."

I take a sip of my milk. "Then why stay here? I know Irene offered to buy you an apartment, let you leave."

"Oh, no, they need me too much here," Alice says. "The normal one. Someone to remind them what a family is supposed to look like. And I could never leave Margo. I love her. She and I are a real family. I'm her mother." We both eat in silence for a minute. "I heard Irene call herself Margo's mother once. They didn't think I heard, but I did. I was . . . very hurt by that. I almost did leave."

She's quiet for a moment, and folds her hands in front of her face, staring at them, thinking about something. She looks like a painting, I think. A widow, mourning. Outside the dining room door I see some movement as someone approaches us, but Alice doesn't seem to notice.

"Irene may have housed us and taken care of us," Alice says quietly, like a prayer, "but I'm Margo's mother. I'm the one who takes care of her."

"But you didn't always, did you?" Margo asks. She's in the doorway, wearing a long white satin dressing gown.

I watch Alice slowly turn to look at her, an expression playing on her lips, maybe something like pride, before she raises her eyebrows.

"I was hungry, so I came down to see if there was anything to eat. Pat!" she calls out, and he appears, as though he were listening behind the door. "Could Dot make me a sandwich too? Tell her I'm sorry. It's been a hard day for us."

Pat nods and leaves.

"What do you mean I don't take care of you?" Alice asks, her voice nearly a pout.

"I take care of myself, Mother. Always have. You weren't around much when I was growing up."

"Oh, please, Margo, I was a widowed mother with a very busy job. I bought you food, clothes, put you to bed at night, didn't I?"

Margo sits down next to me, pulling the chair out so she can cross her legs and lean back. "My mother worked at a hotel, you know."

"I did." I nod.

"A maid. Very busy. Especially nights."

"Margo," Alice hisses.

"You're a detective, you know what I mean, don't you, Andy?"

I look down at my plate. The sandwich is nearly gone. I don't want to get involved in this.

"She sold herself. To guests. So after she put me to bed at night, she went around the hotel, used her key to let herself into their rooms, and then . . . well. And she thinks we're the perverts."

"Margo, I never did anything like that," Alice says, standing up, her voice growing louder with every word. "I'm horrified you could say that. And offended. And shocked you would even think of it. I just flirted for tips sometimes." She turns to me, her voice softer now. "That's a normal thing for a woman to do, isn't it? A widowed mother? I used everything I could to provide for my child." She turns back to Margo. "For you! I flirted for you. And endured their grabby little hands sometimes, yes, but never . . . never what you're suggesting, you terrible child."

Margo smirks, then puts her elbows on the table and leans

forward, toward Alice. "Tell me, Mother. How'd you meet my father?"

I feel my eyes go wide. Alice goes white in the face and her mouth hangs open. Even Margo looks a little ashamed of what she just said, but she's trying to hide it, sticking her chin out, staring at her mother.

"You . . ." Alice says, her voice a whisper. Then she turns and leaves. I can hear her footsteps when she's out of the room, speeding up to a run until they fade away.

"Maybe that was a little mean of me," Margo says. I don't answer. Pat reappears with a fresh sandwich for Margo. Margo stares out at it, then looks up at me. "It's just difficult, you know? How can you love a mother who says she loves you but hates who you are? She thinks I'm broken, you know. That's what she called me when I told her the situation I was in. Broken." In the dim light of the room, with only her white robe on, she looks a little broken, but not how she means it. "Oh, and when she met Elsie . . . She doesn't understand Elsie at all. She doesn't understand love—our kind of love—at all. And she doesn't want to." She sighs and takes a bite of the sandwich. I finish mine and drink some of the milk. It's quiet, and I can feel Margo relaxing next to me. I want to ask about her father, but it can wait.

"Sorry," she says when she's eaten half the sandwich. "I get lonely when Elsie is away, sometimes. I know she likes the nights off—says she loves coming back to me. And I love that too. But that doesn't make it less lonely. And then I get mean. I like Henry well enough, and Cliff is like an annoying little brother, but they have their own little world. So did Pearl and Irene. So . . . I resent the loneliness, I think. Just a little."

"We all do," I say. I take a cigarette out and offer her one and she accepts and I light them both. Sucking on mine makes my ribs scream, though, so I exhale quickly and hold it, letting it burn down.

"We were all sort of awful tonight, weren't we? And you didn't complain at all. You were beaten nearly to death, and I said you were breaking our family up and you were very calm. I admire that."

"It's only because I'm not part of the family," I say. "I can observe. But a thing observed is changed by the observation. Someone . . . said that once." I try my cigarette again, but the pain makes me cough up broken smoke. "Everyone has been through a lot, and is still going through a lot. And you all know it's not over yet, either. You don't need to apologize." I lean back and cross my legs. "Not to me, anyway."

Margo nods. "I'll apologize to my mother in the morning. She's probably tucked away in her room, reading her mysteries, forgetting the world. I don't want to interrupt that for her."

"Do you really not know who your father is?" I ask.

"Oh, no," she laughs. "I know. Just something to get under her skin. Something to hurt her. It was cruel. But she made me that way, right?" She shrugs. She takes a few more bites of her sandwich, then looks up at me. "It's strange to have you watch me eat, Andy. Tell me something. We're always talking about ourselves in front of you, but you don't say a thing. Are you close with your mother?"

I trace the moisture forming on the glass of milk with my finger, making a spiral pattern in it. "Not really," I say. "My dad died, and then she got sort of obsessed with me getting married, having kids. Then I joined up, got stationed here, and stayed, after. But we talk on the phone every other month or so." I think of the sound of a dial tone.

Margo nods. "You never told her?"

"No." I shake my head, wipe the spiral off the milk, and then bring the glass to my lips and drink. "No."

"Did you ever want to?" she asks, wiping her mouth with the side of her hand, the most unladylike thing I've ever seen her do. It makes me like her more.

"I . . ." I think about her question. "I don't know if I've ever asked myself that."

"What do you think she would say?"

"I can't imagine anything good," I say, and drink some more milk. "We never talked about queers, growing up. I never knew they existed. Even when I was one, I was so confused, until there was this boy, junior year of high school. And I caught him making eyes at me in the showers after a game of baseball. And I stared right back and I realized: 'Oh, it's not just me,' and I sort of understood that there were more of us, but it was secret. That it was dirty."

"You and the boy get closer?"

"Oh, no." I shake my head. "No, I didn't touch a man until later."

"How much later?"

I smirk. "You want to know about my sex life?"

"I want you to tell me something funny, so . . . yes."

"The more I get to know you, the more I see how you and Elsie work," I say.

"How we work?" She raises an eyebrow.

"I thought it was like oil and vinegar, you two being together," I say. "You're the vinegar."

"Thanks," she says, not smiling. "Maybe I liked it better when you didn't talk."

"But she says you're more like fire and ice. And you are. But you're both funny."

"You think I'm funny?" She smiles, and for a moment, she looks the way she's always trying to look—sweet, innocent. She's genuinely flattered. Her smile fits her.

"I do."

She seems to realize what she's doing and puts the smile away, lifts her eyebrows, chilly again. "Maybe it's just Elsie rubbing off on me."

"Maybe," I say, finishing my milk.

"So your mother never caught on?"

"If she has, she hasn't said anything. I guess she could have, that's why she pushes for the wife and kids so much."

"That's how it used to be with my mother, too, before I told her. I wonder which is worse? Not being able to tell them, or telling them and knowing that they hate you, at least just a little, for the rest of your life?"

"I don't know." I look back at my glass and trace another spiral on it, but the condensation is gone and it doesn't leave a mark.

"I think I'll go to bed, for real this time. You should too. Give those bruises some rest."

"Yeah," I say. "Good night, Margo."

She stands up and drifts over to the door. "Good night, Andy," she says, without looking back.

I sit alone for a few more minutes, my body still aching, and too hot, like I was too close to the fireplace. Eventually, Pat comes out and clears away the plates.

"Need a hand up to your room?" he asks me. I nod. He leaves everything on the table and without saying anything, takes my arm and drapes it around his shoulder and helps me up the stairs to my room.

"Thanks," I say.

"There's a buzzer, you know, right here," he says, pointing at a switch by the bed. "Ring it if you need anything. Promise?"

"I'll be fine," I say.

"Promise?"

I relent. "I promise," I say, shaking my head, but smiling.

"Good. Good night."

"Good night," I say, and he leaves. Slowly, I manage to peel my clothes off, shut off the light, and get into bed. Sleep comes easily after that, but my dreams are made of fists and feet and Jim's voice over them, counting: eleven, twelve, thirteen . . .

FOURTEEN

The first thing I do when I get up is look around for a telephone. There isn't one in my room, so I get dressed, wincing as I pull on a pale green shirt, and go downstairs. The call I have to make has to be private, so the one in the sitting room won't do. Breakfast is just finishing up and I can hear people in the dining room, so they might be able to hear me too.

Instead, I creep out the front door, and around the side, to where Elsie and I came in with the rabbits. Dot is in here, slicing up fruit, and Pat is waiting for her to finish by the door. He looks up at me curiously when I come in.

"Out for a morning stroll?"

"I was wondering if there was a phone somewhere in the house that had some privacy."

"Oh." He raises an eyebrow and I can see him debating whether or not to ask why.

"For the case."

"Right. Well, there's Irene's old office."

"That's not Pearl's now?"

Pat laughs. "No, no. Pearl has her own office. Irene had an office too. Hardly ever used it, though, aside from storing paperwork there. Mostly she was just in the library. I suppose Henry sometimes used the office to talk to her. Like a meeting room."

"What about?"

Pat shrugs. "The business, I guess? It's on the second floor, but when you go up the main stairs, turn around, walk away from Pearl's office. It's right above the main door. I'd show you, but I'm guessing you don't want to walk through the dining room right now?" he asks, nodding toward the only door out.

"There's no other way up?"

He shakes his head. "You'll have to go back outside."

"A morning walk," I say. "For fresh air."

"Sounds like it would be good for you," Pat says with a wink. I turn around just as the cook hands Pat a bowl of fruit, and leave the way I came in.

As I'm walking back to the front of the house I hear voices, and stop. I peek around the corner. In front of the house are Henry and Cliff, holding hands, though Cliff is pulling away.

"Are you sure you're okay?" Henry asks. "You've been drinking so much, and you haven't been out in ages. You're not yourself."

"I'm fine," Cliff says, not meeting Henry's eyes. "Just go to work. Go to work and leave me like you always do."

"I always come back, too," Henry says, pulling Cliff closer and wrapping his arms around Cliff's waist. "Why are you so upset?"

"I'm not," Cliff says, and twists away, turning toward me and spotting me eavesdropping. Immediately he smiles and turns back to Henry. "I love you," he says loudly. Henry looks confused then glances toward me as I walk closer to them, not trying to hide.

"I love you too," he says to Cliff, then smiles at me. "Good morning, Inspector. Going for a walk? In your state? That's not dangerous?"

"Nah." I wave him off. "It's good for me. You about to leave for work? I was hoping we could talk. I had a few questions about the business."

"Well, that certainly sounds ominous, Inspector, but business is going well, thank you. I've made some real improvements, despite Mother's passing."

"If this is going to be another interrogation, I'm getting a drink," Cliff says, pulling from Henry and stalking back into the house. Henry watches him go and frowns, then turns back to me and turns the frown into a glare.

"I do hope you can finish up this investigation and get out of our hair," he says.

"So your mother dying lets you turn the business profitable again? I ask because the quicker I can get to the point the quicker I can finish up and leave like you want."

He rolls his eyes and then turns away. "Yes. But I would much prefer my mother over some business successes, I assure you. I'm not a monster."

I let that hang in the air, watching him. His eyes are a little red around the edges, and his jaw is set. I think I believe him. "What was it like, being raised so free and easy?" I ask.

Henry sighs. "I couldn't tell you. I can't, ah, compare it. But I think about it a lot. Cliff asked me that once too. And Margo. Like my life was charmed. And I suppose in many ways it was. But it was also lessons in the way to behave, how to hold my wrists, my waist, how to walk, how to be the perfect man to the outside world."

"When not to do your Bette Davis impression?" I ask.

He looks shocked for moment, and then blushes, violently,

from his neck up to his ears. "I . . . Cliff told you about that?" he says, taking his glasses off and rubbing them on his shirt—a way to look down.

"Yeah. He said it's better than his."

"Oh," he says, his color returning to normal. He puts his glasses back on. "Well, it is. It definitely is. But have you seen his? It's a low bar." He smiles slightly, and I feel like I've passed a little test, gotten in better with him.

"Can I see it?" I ask.

He starts turning pink again, and looks away. "Ah, well, I really should get to work. But just . . ." He looks back at me, and straightens his spine, then arches an eyebrow, lifts his chin, and says, "Fasten your seat belts, it's going to be a bumpy night," in what I have to admit is a pretty good impression.

I clap. "That's good!" I say, smiling.

"I like doing impressions of the divas," he says with a shy shrug. "But . . . that's exactly the sort of thing I can't do outside here. Not even as a party trick!" he adds, like it's part of an old argument with Irene or Pearl, from when he was kid. "Just because we know what we are, and we know what the world is, doesn't mean we can change anything about either of them. That's what Mother—ah, Pearl—always says. So in that way it was . . . more difficult. I never felt ashamed of who I was, but I felt a lot angrier at the world outside this place." He pauses, pushes his glasses up. "But not angry enough to kill anyone, if that's what you're about ask. Certainly not my mother, who wasn't the enemy in all this."

"I wasn't about to accuse you of murder," I say, shaking my head.

"No? Then why ask? You're here to do a job, not get friendly with anyone, right?" His eyes flit toward the door, where Cliff just went inside. "I know some things may seem . . . more open here. Even, unappreciated. But there's been a lot of work to do, so I don't have time to appreciate what I have here right now. It doesn't mean I don't love all of it. I do. I love my life very much."

"I don't have eyes on your boyfriend, Henry."

"No?" He raises his chin, not believing me.

"No," I assure him. "He's a good-looking guy, don't get me wrong, but I'm not the person who does that. I did just kiss a bartender at the Ruby, and I liked that a lot, so maybe that'll be something, or maybe he just felt sorry for me because I'd gotten my face beaten to a pulp. Probably that one."

Henry tries not to laugh but he smiles a little.

"I let Cliff flirt with me, though. We both seem to like that. But I can stop if you want."

"No," Henry sighs. "It's fun for him, and I don't mind it, not really. I'm not . . . worried, you know. I don't worry you'll steal him away."

"No?" I ask. "You sort of sound like it."

"I've been working a lot. There's so much to do since Mother died, and I'm . . . a little overwhelmed, frankly. But I don't want anyone to see that at work, and sometimes home feels like work, or maybe it's just easier to think of it that way . . ." He sighs. "That's too much to say to a detective, I know. I must sound pathetic."

"Your mom died and you have to handle everything now—business, family, it's a lot. Plus throwing yourself into work helps you deal with grief," I say, and put my hand on his shoulder. "That's normal, Henry. I've seen that story play out a hundred different times, different ways."

"Really?" He looks relieved. "Still. I wish I didn't have to be at work so much. I wish I could leave it at the office. And then Cliff is here, and you're here . . ."

". . . Flirting with your boyfriend." I nod, dropping my hand. "You're jealous."

"A little." I try not to smile, but I feel like I'm seeing Henry now. Not the man of the house, not the cold businessman. I've seen guys like him, after a murder of someone they love, who just turn back into kids, and they feel it happening and know they can't, so they throw themselves into work. Into drugs. Into something, just so they don't feel so helpless.

"Why not invite him by the office more?" I ask. "Spend some time with him, even if it's not romantic."

"I do . . . but I don't make a big deal of it when he says no." Henry shuffles his feet a little. "It's so much work right now. Fixing everything. And it would be so boring for him."

"I think the house is boring for him too. Do you know what he does all day?"

"Listens to records, he says. Reads sometimes. He loves *Life*, when I remember to pick up a copy." He sighs. "And he drinks."

"And do you know when the last time he left the house was?"

"Well, he came with us for Mother's funeral. Wore sunglasses the whole time to hide how he'd been crying."

"And aside from that? When did he last leave the house?"

He looks confused by the question, but then thinks about it. I can see him counting off days, weeks, more.

"It was . . . weeks before Mother's death, actually, I think. Can that be right?"

I nod. "Sounds about right to me."

He sighs, looks at his feet. "I didn't notice."

"It's not your fault," I say.

"I should have noticed, asked him. Do you know what's wrong? Is he just broken up over Mother's death?"

I let my tongue roll inside my mouth, not sure of the answer. I could tell him about the posters, about Clive, but Cliff denied it, and I'm not sure. It could be why he hasn't left the house in over a month—afraid of getting spotted, someone calling the number on the poster. But he's a grown man. Who could be looking for him?

"Did anything happen a few weeks before she died?" I ask.

He shakes his head, then strokes his beard. The air is chilly, and I put my hands in my pockets.

"There was one thing . . . but I thought he was excited about it."

"What?"

Henry licks his lips and looks toward his car, embarrassed maybe. "Mother—that is, Irene—wanted us to adopt a baby."

"You and Cliff?"

He laughs. "Me and Margo. For appearances. Though Cliff would have been a father to the child too, of course. I thought Cliff was excited about it. He told me he wanted a girl so he could dress her in showgirl costumes and teach her to dance."

I smile, picturing it. "So he was fine with it?"

"Yes," Henry says, still confused. "Margo was the one who wasn't exactly on board."

"Oh?"

He shrugs. "The thing with Margo is she's always torn between wanting to rise in society, to be the perfect wife, be in the society pages, have people recognize her, and wanting to run off with Elsie and . . . I don't know, cut all her hair off and dance the night away. Mother—Pearl—met her at a bar in the city, I don't remember the name, one of the ones just for women. She was terrified, apparently, but also lonely. Had a lot of admirers, and flirted, but always went home early. When I asked her why she'd marry me, she told me she wanted stability—money, a home. This would let her have that, and let her be herself. Except I don't think it came together quite as she pictured. I feel sorry for her, honestly."

I nod. "So she didn't want to have a kid?"

"Not at first. But Mother—Irene—she told her that Margo would be a mother, like she was to me, and to Margo and Cliff. That it was really a joyful thing. She turned her around on it, Margo always relented with Irene eventually. She loved her. Loves Pearl, too, though you might not believe it. It's because she resents them a bit, too, for having what she'll never have because of the deal she made with us."

I nod. "You're pretty forthcoming about everyone," I say.

"I don't believe any of us could have done it, so I don't think anything should be hidden. Margo, Pearl, Cliff—they're all good people. They're not murderers."

"What about the staff?"

"What? Why? I can't imagine it. They have no reason."

"And Alice?"

Henry looks surprised, like he'd forgotten about her, but tries to cover it by pushing up his glasses. "Don't be ridiculous. We took her in, and besides that she's just too . . . tidy for murder. Now, do you have anything else you want to ask, or can I go to work? I'm already late."

"Just one thing, actually," I say, remembering something. "I want to follow you."

"Follow me?"

"Yeah," I say, heading for my own car. "Just drive to work, like you normally do. I'll handle it."

Henry frowns, then looks at his watch and shrugs. "All right," he says, getting in his car.

We both start our engines and I let him take the lead, following just a short distance behind. We're on the highway maybe five minutes before the black Commodore shows up, tailing Henry. He doesn't seem to notice me, but then my car hasn't been used much lately. Henry keeps driving as normal, so I speed up and pull between them, skidding my car to a halt across both lanes and blocking the Commodore. There's a screech as he stops, and I get out of the car, staring at him. I can see the driver through the windshield—a man, maybe fifty, with a thin face. He sees me, frowns, and tries to back away, but ignoring the pain in my ribs, I run up and yank his door open before he can pull around me.

"What gives, buddy?" he asks, trying to slam his door closed.

"Why are you tailing the Lamontaines?" I ask.

"What's it to you?" he asks, taking his foot off the gas.

"I'm security," I say, opening the back door of his car and getting in behind him, but leaving the door open. "You're not subtle. They spotted you ages ago and brought me on to handle it. So this is me handling it. Why are you tailing them?"

The man sighs and turns around. He's balding, with dark circles under his eyes. He fishes in his coat pocket and for a moment I wonder if he's going to shoot me, but instead he takes out his wallet and hands me a card: Ralph Stockwell, Private Investigator, office in San Francisco. I pocket the card. I've dealt with men like him before; not just PIs, who are a mixed bag from stand-up to shady, but types like this one—the shadiest kind.

I can smell it on him like the stale gin on his breath. Probably operates out of a ramshackle office that reeks of liquor and most of his business is trailing cheating husbands, then offering to make it go away for a bigger payday when he catches them.

"So who hired you to tail them?" I ask.

"I got a tip," he says, and opens the glove compartment. He takes out a piece of paper and hands it to me—"Missing: Clive Thorpe." The same one I saw at the coroner's. It looks a lot like Cliff. "I tried getting in, even opened the gate once before that hellion with the bob spotted me and got a gun. I'm just looking for this kid. You know him? He working for the Lamontaines? I'll give you a cut of what I'm being paid."

I shake my head. "Don't know him," I say. "But he's clearly not a kid. Who looks for a grown man?"

The guy narrows his eyes at me, not believing, then shrugs. "His family wants him home. They say it doesn't matter if he wants to come home, as long as I bring him back to Kentucky. All expenses paid and a nice reward. You sure he's not there? I could make it worth your while."

I swallow. "That's a dirty business." I try not to show anything else. So it is Cliff. And he's wrapped up in something bad.

"Well la-dee-dah for you, mister, being some fancy house guard. That how you get those bruises? I didn't think the Lamontaines got in much trouble."

"Nah, this was from my night off," I say. I take the poster and crumple it in my fist. "That kid isn't with them. So leave them alone, stop tailing them, go look somewhere else. Your tip was phony."

He shrugs, slowly, then takes out a cigarette and lights it, meeting my eyes in the rearview mirror. "Funny little house, though, isn't it? Son, wife, dead mother, dead mother's secretary, and that club owner who just drops in now and then. Kinda queer, if you ask me."

I know I should nod, make some sort of explanation up, talk about rich people being eccentric, but my throat feels tight, and I just want to punch the back of this guy's head.

"Well, if I wasted all this time, and Clive ain't with them, maybe I could sell some of what I saw to the papers." He smirks, takes a drag on his cigarette, and blows the smoke out between his lips, a thin line like a lizard's tail. "Unless they want to pay me more than the papers would, of course."

I feel my hands clenching into fists.

"How'd a fella like you end up working for them, anyway? You don't seem like the type."

"I'll mention your thoughts to them," I say. "Have a number?"

"Oh, nothing big, just what was worth my time. A few grand. Maybe five."

I can feel my tongue run over my teeth. It would be easy to bash his head into the steering wheel. A car passes us on the highway, honking at how we've blocked the road.

"I'll bring it to them," I say.

"Thanks." He smiles. "Now get the fuck outta my car."

I get out and slam the door. He reverses then speeds around me, headed toward the city. I get back into my car and un-crumple the missing poster, smoothing it out on the dashboard and studying it. It's got to be Cliff. Except Cliff said he was an orphan, and this guy's family is looking for him. I fold the poster back up and stick it in my pocket, then start the engine and swing the car around, headed back to Lavender House. I still have a phone call to make, and now I have some questions for Cliff, or Clive, or whatever his name is.

When I pull my car in next to the fountain, no one comes out to greet me, and inside, the house is quiet. I don't see any-one in the dining room, so I head upstairs and find my way to Irene's old office. The door isn't locked, but I can tell no one has been inside for a while. It has the stale smell of unused spaces. It's smaller than Pearl's office, but it's got a big curve of windows that look out directly on the fountain and the flowers spreading out beyond it. There are only a few bookshelves, to ei-ther side of the windows, and a desk in the center. The walls are painted dark purple, and there's a brown circular carpet under the desk, which is in the center of the room. It's very plain, no Greek writing at all. The chair behind it is large, though, and comfortable when I sit down in it. I pull the phone over, but before I dial, I look up and see the painting on the wall oppo-site the windows. It's large, maybe done by the same person who did the one downstairs, but it's a family portrait. Irene, Pearl, Henry, Margo, Cliff, and Elsie. All of them, sitting in pairs—not their public relationships, but the real ones. Pearl and Irene stand behind Henry, who sits on a loveseat with his arm around Cliff, who leans into him. On the floor, in front of them, Margo sits, her dress spread out around her like a puddle, Elsie lying in her lap, face up, her body stretching out of the frame. Pearl and Irene are holding hands and looking at each other, lovingly. Henry looks out of the portrait, but his head is tilted ever so slightly toward Cliff, whose eyes are closed as he leans into Henry's chest. Margo is tilted staring down at Elsie, who stares back up at her. They share a smile, like one of them just told a joke.

Each of them is wearing purple. Elsie is in a lavender suit with a white shirt. Henry is in a midnight-purple suit with matching tie and white shirt. Margo's dress is a vibrant violet with darker purple flowers all over it. Cliff wears a lavender shirt, unbuttoned at the collar, and white pants. And behind them, Pearl and Irene are in matching plum dresses, Irene with a pearl necklace and Pearl with an amethyst brooch in the shape of a sprig of lavender. Behind them is nothing—just white. No Alice. Maybe she wasn't there that day. Or maybe she didn't want to be part of the "fun-house mirror" family portrait.

Irene's expression stands out. It's not like her portrait downstairs—aloof, commanding. Here, she looks gentle, like she doesn't mind being painted, or somehow didn't know it was happening. She's staring at Pearl, but her free hand rests on the back of the sofa in a way that seems to encompass the entire family. Here, she's no witch. Here, she's the mother to a bunch of children.

It's a shocking portrait. I can't imagine who they could have trusted to paint it. I stand up and go over to look for a signature, and then I find it. P. Kelly. I grin. Pat's got talent. But I don't think he painted the one downstairs. He just did this in a similar style, maybe.

Around the portrait are hung framed newspaper clippings. Margo cutting the ribbon on a new soap store. Henry and Margo smiling at a fundraiser where they were honored. Cliff and Henry in an office, Henry sitting at the desk and Cliff right behind him, hands behind his back, beaming. There's even one of Pearl from the thirties, an interview with her in a women's journal about being a secretary to Irene. She's in a posed photo for that, sitting at a desk, her legs askew, smiling at the camera, ignoring the typewriter in front of her. Like an ad for stockings.

I go back to the desk, and pull the phone over. I pick it up and it rings in my ear. No one is on the line. I dial the operator and ask for the police department in Bend, Oregon. She connects me and it rings a few times before someone picks up.

"Bend Police," says a young male voice.

I swallow. I know this should work, but I'm suddenly nervous about it. "Hi, this is Andy Mills, SFPD. We have a case down here, and Bend keeps coming up. A hotel there called the Butterfly. I was wondering if you knew anything about it?"

"Butterfly . . ." He pauses. I hold my breath. There's no reason my old colleagues would have told people in Bend, Oregon, about me, but policemen are a bunch of gossips, so it's possible they know. "Sorry, Mills, doesn't ring a bell."

"Well, it would have closed a while ago, I think," I say, trying not to sound too relieved.

"Yeah? Let me get one of the old-timers, then. Hold on."

He puts the phone down and through the receiver I can hear the distant murmurs of the police station. Police stations all sound the same; the same sorts of laughter, the same occasional silences, the same moments of anxiety when the boss walks through. It's so familiar it's almost soothing. And then my face starts to throb.

"The Butterfly," says a new voice on the line. "Haven't thought about that place in years. I'm Detective Stuart. You're SFPD?"

"Yep. Mills. The name of the place just keeps coming up in a robbery case. What do you remember about it?"

"Oh, it was a swanky little hotel, nice part of town. But then two guests died. A young couple. It was quite the scandal. Whole place shut down. Probably about fifteen years ago."

"Huh." I keep my voice calm, curious. "How'd the couple die?"

"Poison." I can hear him grinning as he says the word, excited to talk about a big case. My heart kicks up a notch. "But it was an accidental poisoning. Rat poison in the kitchen made its way into a meal. The chef was horrified and didn't even know the couple, so we didn't charge him, though we shut the place down. Said they could get it back up and running after health and safety came through, but the loss of business was too much. They never reopened."

"You remember the chef's name?"

"No . . . big guy, though. Blond. Really seemed confused. Didn't even remember making the meal. It was room service central, though. He went through plenty of meals every night."

"But only one couple died?"

"Only ones who asked for peppers in their omelets. It was the peppers that were contaminated. Someone had left them in a crate on the floor. No one with access to the kitchen had any motive, the couple were just visiting, didn't know anyone. Tragic, but not murder, ya know?"

"Yeah, that's sad," I say, though I suspect no one just left them on the floor. "You ever interview anyone named Alice? She was the head of housekeeping, I think. Or her daughter, Margo?"

"No . . . neither of those ring a bell, sorry. I can dig up the file, if you really need me to. She in some kind of trouble?"

"Nah, don't bother, then," I say. "It's probably nothing, just . . . curious, you know?"

"Yeah, gotta follow those instincts. That's what separates the men from the boys. Anything else I can do for you?"

"No. I'll call back if it gets more interesting, though."

"Yeah, let me know. Been a while since I thought about that place. It was a nice little hotel."

"Thanks," I say, and hang up. So that's two places where Alice had managed the staff and people had been poisoned, two places Margo was, too. She was teenager at the hotel, but I've seen teenagers kill. I stand up and look at the portrait again. I take out the missing poster and hold it up against Cliff's face. Yeah. Either they're twins, or they're the same.

I try his room first, knocking on the door, but there's no answer, so I head downstairs. I can hear music playing halfway down: Peggy Lee singing "Why Don't You Do Right?" I follow the melody to the sitting room, where Cliff is dancing again, this time just in his open robe and a pair of briefs, a martini glass sloshing in his hand. He smiles when he sees me.

"I knew you'd want another show," he says, his words slurring. He steps toward me.

"Cliff, it's not even noon," I say, looking at the glass.

He frowns. "Spoilsport. Fun ruiner." He shrugs and walks away, mouthing along to the words again. He turns to me to emphasize it when she sings "get out of here."

I sigh, and unfold the poster in my hand, and then hold it up for him to see.

He turns around and spots it. His eyes go wide, and he teeters. I rush forward to catch him, but he wobbles the other way and falls back into one of the side tables, knocking it over.

"Are you okay?" I ask, kneeling down next to him.

"No," he says, getting up onto his knees. He's crying. The tears are running down his face in thick, sticky rivers and his skin is red. "No no no. I haven't been all right in a long time, Andy. I haven't been all right at all." He lets out a low moan. "I'm so sorry," he says, but he's not talking to me now. He's looking at the ceiling. "I did it. I killed her. I killed Irene."

FIFTEEN

Before I even have time to understand what he's saying, I hear footsteps behind me. I turn around. It's Pearl, in the doorway, looking at Cliff, prone on the ground, practically naked, me next to him, and an overturned side table.

"What is going on?" she asks, not sure if she should be worried or appalled.

"I'm so sorry, Pearl," Cliff says.

"What?" Pearl comes closer and grabs his hands, helping him up onto the sofa. "Sorry for what? What were you doing?" She directs this last one at me.

"It's not—" I start.

"I killed Irene," Cliff says again, and then throws his head into Pearl's lap, weeping. "I didn't mean to. I'm so, so sorry."

Pearl looks at me, and I stare back, shaking my head. I don't have the full story yet.

"What happened, Cliff?" I ask.

Cliff takes a deep breath, then lets it out slowly. He sits up. His face is sticky and his eyes are red, but he looks relieved. He looks at me, then Pearl, then quickly back to me.

"It started a few months ago. I'd run into town for some groceries. Chocolate. I wanted a little chocolate and there was none in the house. And I saw those posters." He nods at the poster in my hand, and I give it to Pearl, who studies it, her eyebrows rising as she does. "The next day, there was a phone call. They were asking for Clive, but I guess Pat heard them wrong and said it was for me, so I answered. It was the detective who put those up. Looking for me. I told him he had the wrong number, but I knew it was too late then. My family had hired him to find me."

"Your family?" Pearl asks. "But you're an orphan." I stare at Pearl. She's being very calm. I see her looking at Cliff like a puzzle, waiting for him to make things clearer to her. Then she'll decide, I think. And if she decides he's responsible, if he caused her all this pain . . . I step a little closer. I want to be able to stop her if she goes in for the kill suddenly, like a rattlesnake.

Cliff shakes his head and sniffs. "I only wish I was. My father is the mayor of a small city in Kentucky—Beachwood. I'm his only son. He's . . . strict. Very religious. Very small town, and he's the richest man in it. Exactly what you're thinking. Mean." He takes a deep breath and Pearl takes out a lace handkerchief and hands it to him. He nods and wipes his face. "When I was sixteen, my mother caught me and the butcher's son in the backyard, fooling around. After that, my life became a nightmare. My parents kept me locked in my room, homeschooled me, wouldn't let me leave the house. Dad used to take the belt to me every night while reading the same verse from the Bible over and over: You shalt not lie with a man as with a woman, it is an abomination. Over and over. I told them I was cured, it was a mistake, I'd never do it again, but they never believed me. For a year, I was locked in my room all day, every day. My window was nailed shut. In summer it got so hot I would pass out. It was . . . awful."

I take a deep breath. I wonder if my own father would have done something similar. Maybe, maybe not. You never can tell with people.

"So how'd you get away?" I ask.

"I didn't. I mean, I tried—knocked my mother down when she came to bring me breakfast, tried to run for it. But they caught me. After that, they made me take some pills every morning. No food otherwise. It kept me asleep. I barely remember most of it. But when I turned eighteen, Dad had an idea. He said I'd join the army, ship me overseas, make a man out of me. Or kill me. He didn't care which. So I joined up . . ." He smiles, remembering. "And then I was free."

I nod. "If only he'd known," I say.

Cliff looks at me, and nods. "It was the best joke anyone ever played, and it was played on my old man. I told them I liked to sing and dance and they put me in the USO, and I could be myself, suddenly. I was so happy."

"Didn't they write to you?" Pearl asks. "Didn't they know you were USO?"

Cliff shakes his head. "I didn't write letters home. I didn't tell them what I was doing. And when my tour was over, I didn't go home. I just took off. Vegas, L.A., dancing in the follies. I put it all behind me. I thought they could tell people I'd died. That would be good. My dad always said he'd run for governor one day, and having a dead war hero son would help. It was the best choice for everyone."

"But he didn't?" I ask.

He takes a deep slow breath. "I don't know why it didn't work. I don't know why they started looking for me."

"Sometimes," I say, "family thinks love is about possession, about making you fill a role for them. About . . . ownership more than love."

Cliff nods. "Maybe that's it. I don't know. But within six months of my being discharged, there were detectives looking for me. Not the nice-looking kind like you." He smiles weakly at me. "Mean types. That's why I moved around so much. Joined different shows. I thought when Henry asked me to move in that I'd finally be safe. That I'd have a family, and a home, and no one could find me here. But I guess someone did."

He looks down at the handkerchief he's holding in his lap.

"So what happened?" I ask. "What did Irene do? Did she want to turn you over to your family?"

"She would never," Pearl says, her voice like a stone wall with a crack in it.

"It wasn't like that," Cliff says, shaking his head. "I told her about it, because I thought if anyone could help, it was her. And she was angry, sure. Said I hadn't been honest, and I'd led wolves to the door. Said I needed to lie low for a while—not leave the house, and I shouldn't tell anyone else. I said okay. That seemed all right. I was happy she wasn't going to toss me out. But after a month of it, I got bored. Really bored. And no one even noticed I wasn't leaving, not even Henry." He pauses, his hands clenching a little. "It was like I was just part of the house, not a person, just . . . furniture. I got so angry. I just wanted to go out. I wanted to dance. I started dancing alone in my room, music turned up. Then out here. Irene saw, and never said anything, and that made me even more angry. She knew I was trapped and she didn't care. She knew I was going crazy. It was like what my parents had done to me, all over again. Sure, my room was bigger, and nicer, but I still couldn't leave. I was trapped. I hate being trapped."

"I didn't notice either," Pearl says. "Or I just thought . . . you didn't want to go out. Those parties are so boring, and you have to pretend to be someone you're not."

"I like them," Cliff says, so softly and sadly, it's like the sound of a single drop of water. "I even tried calling her bluff. I got in the car, and I was going to drive away and see if she wouldn't let me back, and if she didn't, I'd write Henry at work, tell him everything. But she took my car keys."

I nod. This is what Elsie had seen. "And she slapped you?" I ask.

"Yes . . ." Cliff says quietly, touching his face.

"You should have told me," Pearl says. "Told Henry. Told someone so we could talk to her." Her voice is rising, getting angry, but I don't know at whom. I shift my chair a little closer to them.

"I was . . . afraid," Cliff says. "Afraid you'd take her side."

Pearl tilts her head, thinking about that. She stares at his hands, then his neck, looking like she's trying to decide if she wants to take his hand and hold it or strangle him. "So what happened?" she asks. I can hear her keeping her voice steady. She wants to scream at him. Or cry. Or both.

"The night after she died, there was supposed to be a party. A spring garden party for the employees at Lamontaine. They rented out a ballroom in the city, and I helped pick out decorations, even though I never saw the ballroom. There were balloons, in pink and green, and streamers." He sighs. "It was going to be so beautiful. And there was going to be a band. A jazz band! I wanted to go so badly. I couldn't dance with Henry, of course, but Elsie likes to dance, and Pearl . . ." He seems to remember Pearl is there and hunches his shoulders, leaning away from her. "I just wanted to get out. Have fun.

So that night, I went downstairs to the library, where she was working. It was raining, so no one heard me or anything. I asked her if I could go. I told her we hadn't heard from the detective in a month, he'd probably moved on, and it was a private party, and I'd be in a car the whole time. No one would see me. It would be safe. But she said no."

Pearl leans back a little at this, her eyes widening in shock. "She said no?"

"She said if I left the house, the detective would catch me, and I'd tell everyone all about you, about us. She said she couldn't let me leave . . . maybe not ever again. I said that wasn't fair, and she said it was my own fault for not telling her the truth to begin with. I begged her, I . . ." He starts crying again. "I just wanted to be free. I told her she was cruel, cruel as my real parents. She wouldn't even look at me. She just kept smelling those bottles." He blows his nose in the handkerchief. "I told her I'd tell Henry what she was doing to me, that I'd tell him everything. She said what mattered most was protecting her family, and I was part of that family only because she allowed me to be, that Henry would do what she said. She said it would be better, really, if I just died." Pearl gasps. "And then she just went back to sniffing. Like I wasn't even there.

"I started to cry. She didn't look up. So I left. And . . ." He looks out the window, away from us. "I was drunk. I'd been drunk for weeks. Have been drunk for weeks. There was nothing else to do . . . and halfway up the stairs, I just got so angry. So angry. I was trapped just like my parents had done to me, but this time it was by a woman who I thought really loved me and who I *knew* understood what it was like to be like me, and she didn't care! She didn't care.

"I turned around, ran back down the stairs into the library.

She had my car keys. She'd taken them out of the car and put them on her key ring, and she always had that in her pocket. I had to get it back. I had to get out. She was leaning on the balcony, holding the bannister, and I just . . . I ran up to her and tried to grab her, tried to take the keys from her pocket. I didn't think about the bannister, I just wanted to get the keys back. I didn't even shove her, really, just knocked into her as I put my hand in her pocket. And . . . then she fell over. Didn't even reach out when I tried to grab her, keep her from falling. She shouldn't have fell like that." His voice is anxious, and he shakes his head, his breaths coming quickly. "I still don't know how it happened. I must have bumped into her with more force than I thought . . . It was horrible. I didn't mean to. I didn't mean to kill her." He turns to Pearl. "I really, really didn't. I didn't want her dead." He starts to cry again, and looks down into his lap, sobbing. "But she was dead. I saw how she fell. I went downstairs to check, to see if she was all right, but she wasn't breathing. I checked her pulse, too, her skin was . . ." He swallows. "So I went back upstairs, and went to bed. I told myself it was all just a terrible dream . . . but then it wasn't. And I thought if I just drank some more, stayed here longer, did everything she'd told me to do . . . I don't know. I know I can't bring her back. I'm so, so sorry."

I look up at Pearl, who's gone white. I wait a moment, but she seems to be in shock.

"Pearl?" I ask.

She blinks a few times, looking at me, then turns to Cliff. "Irene wouldn't let you leave?" Her voice is hoarse.

Cliff nods. "I'm sorry."

"And you pushed her?" The words tear out of her and I stand up. I don't know what she's going to do, but I remember the rage she says she had inside her. "You left her to die? You . . . didn't say anything?"

"It was an accident," Cliff says. "I swear, Pearl. It was an accident, and I've felt terrible every day since, I've wanted to die too, I've wanted to do anything I could . . ."

He goes quiet. Pearl keeps staring at him, saying nothing.

"Why did you stay?" I ask.

"What?" Cliff stares at me, confused.

"You were free. Irene was dead, you had the car keys. You could have left, run away."

"But . . ." He's confused. "Irene was dead. I couldn't leave. Henry needed me, Pearl needed me, the family . . . everyone was going to be so sad, and if I left too . . . I love Henry. And his mother was dead. I wasn't going to abandon him."

I nod and look at Pearl, who won't meet his eyes. She's stiff, but it's not angry anymore, it's brittle. She might collapse into dust at any moment.

"Was she holding a bottle when you pushed her?" I ask.

Now they both look confused. "What?"

"This is important." I lean forward. "What did she look like when you pushed her?"

"She . . . wasn't holding a bottle, no. And she was leaning on the bannister."

"Like she needed it to hold her up?"

"Y-yes."

"Was there a broken bottle on the floor somewhere?"

"I . . . don't remember?" Cliff says, shaking his head. "But, before I opened the door, just before, there was the sound of glass breaking. I thought I'd knocked a bottle off the shelf when I opened the door, because I opened it so hard."

"You didn't," I say. "Irene dropped the bottle."

"What are you getting at, Andy?" Pearl asks.

"He didn't kill her," I say, leaning back.

Cliff turns around, looking at me, shocked. "Yes I did. I told you, I knocked her over. It was awful. The sound she made when she landed."

"She was dead before she hit the ground," I say. I look at Pearl. "Poison. Like I said. She was already dying when Cliff knocked into her—she probably wouldn't even have fallen if she hadn't been poisoned. She was old, but I doubt an accidental shove could send her over the balcony unless she had no strength left."

"But—" Cliff starts.

"Maybe I'm wrong, maybe she would have fallen and died otherwise," I say. "I don't know. But it's not a long drop. She was healthy, already holding on to the bannister, hard to topple. And if Cliff had gone at her full push, and she'd gone over, I think more likely she would have broken some bones, but she'd be alive, scream out for help."

"I would have helped her," Cliff says immediately. "I would have done anything to undo . . ."

"She wouldn't have died?" Pearl asks, relief in her voice.

I think back to the nurse and the file. She could have died. She could have cracked her skull or spine, but right now, I know what Pearl needs to hear, too. "Probably not," I say.

"So it wasn't me?" Cliff asks.

"You still pushed her," Pearl says quickly, turning on him. "An old woman at the edge of a bannister."

"What would have happened if she were alive?" I ask before Cliff can respond. "If Irene had gone over, but only broken a leg or hip and was crying out for help?"

"I would have gone for help," Cliff says immediately. "I would have woken the whole house."

"You believe that?" I ask Pearl. She looks at Cliff and takes a breath, exhales long and slow. She nods. "So then what would have happened?"

"We would have wanted to know why," Pearl says. "And . . . Irene and Cliff would have told us . . ."

"Everything you just heard," I say. "What then?"

"Then . . ." Pearl pauses, and I can see her imagining it. The anger in her shifting from one person to the next. "I would have screamed at both of them. Irene doing that to Cliff, not telling any of us, not telling me, so I could fix it. And you." She turns to Cliff. "You didn't tell anyone either and you try to steal some keys instead? Childish!" She strikes fast, but it's just a slap, and not even a hard one. Cliff puts his hand on his cheek where she hit him, but just looks relieved, like he's finally getting the punishment he wanted. "Stupid and childish and ridiculous, both of you!"

"And then what?" I ask.

"Then we would have fixed it," Pearl says firmly. "*I* would have fixed it. We're a family, and we handle these things together . . ." She pauses, realizing what she's just said, and turns back to Cliff, her expression softening slightly for a moment. "We're a family, and what keeps us safe is everyone working together, everyone telling the truth. We're not like *them*, outside. We're special here. Acting like we're not just causes pain.

"Irene could be cold sometimes. Especially when she was scared. It was my job to make her less scared. That's how we worked. She would get frightened and lock herself away from the people she loved, and I would unlock her and get her to apologize. I . . ." She pauses, tasting the words before she says them. "I'm sorry she never told me. I would have made her apologize. You would have gone to that party. Even with what you did, we would have worked it out. You didn't kill her. So . . . I'll try to forgive you."

Cliff starts to cry again and he puts his face on her shoulder. She strokes his back. Her face is hard, but I can see her trying to take all this in, trying to forgive him. Her anger is still there, though, looking for a target. "But we're not going to tell anyone what you just told me," she says. "Right, Andy?" She levels her eyes at me. I nod. She leans back, taking each of Cliff's shoulders in her hands and staring at him until he makes eye contact and nods. "That would make things much messier, and that's not what we need now. Irene loved you, and I love you, and Henry loves you, and maybe Margo loves you too, though who can tell with that one. But you're part of this family. And you didn't kill Irene. There was just an accident. No one's fault."

Cliff nods, slowly, and I watch his whole body relax, like someone just cut his marionette wires. He falls back into the sofa, his eyes half-closed. The record has ended by now, and it's just playing static.

"Now," Pearl says, looking at me. "This detective who's looking for him?"

"I met him," I say. "He's been watching your family for weeks. He doesn't know anything for sure, but he's made some guesses and they're not far off. He says he's going to sell his story to the papers. I'll be honest, they might buy if it's a slow news day."

"Let me guess," Pearl says, folding her hands in her lap. "He won't go to the papers if we can pay him more."

I nod. "Five grand. But I should warn you, guys like this, it's never just one payment."

"I know the type," Pearl says. "Did you get his name? Where I'm supposed to leave the money?"

I fish the business card out of my jacket and hand it to her. She looks at it and purses her lips, then stands up. "I'll handle it," she says.

"Pearl," Cliff says, "I'm sorry about this, too."

Pearl smiles and pats him on the head. "Please. This is no trouble at all. Everybody has a price." She goes to the door and grabs her coat and purse, then turns back to me. "Could you help him to his room, Andy? He needs some sleep."

"Sure thing," I say. "But the case isn't over."

"I know you still have work to do," she says. "But so do I. I'll be back soon." She smiles. She looks almost happy as she leaves. I watch her get in her car and pull away from the house, then look at Cliff, on the sofa, undressed, practically asleep. I go over to the record player and turn it off, then go back to him and offer my hand.

"Come on," I say. "You've had a long . . . few months. You should get some sleep."

He sighs and pulls himself up from the sofa with my hand, then realizes his robe is hanging open and quickly ties it shut. "Have I been terrible?" he asks as we walk upstairs. He sways and I catch him a few times. "Not just for . . . what I did. But since then. Have I been terrible to you? To everyone?"

"I think everyone will forgive you," I say.

"Even you? I've been flirting something awful."

"I didn't mind," I say.

He grins. "If I were single, you know . . ." he says. "Even with those bruises."

"Oh, I know," I say, smiling and opening the door to his room. "I'm irresistible."

Cliff laughs and breaks away from me, walking over to his bed on his own. I draw the blinds as he gets into bed, then walk to the door.

"Thanks, Andy," he says. "I don't know how I can ever forgive myself for this."

I nod, closing the door. "I know I can't be the one to forgive you. But I understand why you did it. No one likes to be trapped."

"I felt like an animal," he says, just as the door clicks closed. I stand in the hallway outside his room, and take a deep breath. He felt like an animal.

Pearl's job offer flits through my head. If I did take her up on it, would I see the bars? Could I unfocus my eyes enough that it would be like I was in utopia? I think maybe everyone here did that for a while. But now they can see it all clearly. As long as the world out there stays the same, a paradise like this keeps you in as much as it keeps you safe.

I walk down the hall to my room. My shoulder aches from the cut in it and my side aches from the bruises. I sit down and go over it all in my head. Cliff may have helped Irene along, but he wasn't the murderer. Henry says he'd prefer a failing business to a dead mother, and I believe him. Elsie was borrowing money from Irene, and her death upset her finances. Pearl hired me and has had several opportunities to get rid of me, so I don't think it was her, either. The staff—if Pat did it, I'd be shocked. No motive, helped bring me in. And Judy and Dot don't care for me, but they didn't seem to mind Irene. Seemed to appreciate her. I can't think of why any of them would want her dead.

The only two left are Alice and Margo. Alice, the mother, the outsider, who didn't get along with Irene, who doesn't seem to like that her daughter is queer, but didn't seem to hate Irene enough to kill. Margo, who becomes the wife of the new head of Lamontaine, the new face, and rises higher in the high society she both hates and loves, gains power over the company. Both argued with Irene. Either could have wanted her dead. Both are connected to another poisoning. I want to talk to Alice first. She would remember the poisonings at the Butterfly. Margo was only a teenager then, if she was still around.

I head to the kitchen first, but it's just Pat, washing up breakfast dishes.

"Did you find the phone?" Pat asks when he sees me.

"Yes, thanks."

"You weren't around for breakfast. You want some toast or something?"

"I'm looking for Alice, actually."

"Oh." He shrugs, wiping a plate clean. "It's shopping day, she won't be back for a couple of hours or so. Maybe less, if she's in a good mood. She and Dot went into town to plan the menus for the new week, and they argue about it less when she's in a good mood."

"Ah," I say. "You know where they went?"

He shakes his head. "They go all around, to the supermarket, some farm stands. She's very particular about the ingredients."

"Okay, how about Margo?"

"It's almost noon, so she'll be visiting Henry at work to bring him lunch. It's a little show they put on once a week. Margo likes to look over stuff at the office, too, especially design choices, and he likes getting her opinion on everything he can't bring home. But she left just a while ago with the basket for lunch."

"Ah," I say. "Well . . . do you think you could show me Alice's room?"

"While she's out?" He raises an eyebrow.

"I am an investigator. Snooping is part of the job."

"I'll . . . tell you how to get there. I doubt the door is locked. You go upstairs from your room, then follow the hall all the way to the end. There's a small door, a few stairs up. She doesn't like anybody in there, though. She'll probably know if you disturb anything. And then she'll blame me."

"I'll be good," I say.

"Unlikely. If they come back early, though, I'll head up to the hallway outside and start singing."

I grin. "Thanks."

"I have a very lovely voice."

I pause, smiling. "I'm sure you do. You're a lovely painter."

He stops washing and wiggles his eyebrows at me. "Just a hobby."

"How did you get them all to pose like that?" I ask.

"What do you mean?" He dries a glass and places it on the counter.

"They all looked so happy."

Pat shrugs. "Well . . . they are. They were. They will be again."

"You seem pretty sure of that. I feel like all I've seen of them is their messiness." I lean back against the wall.

"No, you haven't. Think about it. You're telling me you see no love here?"

I shrug. "I guess, sure. But that portrait."

"I got them on one of their best days," he says. "You've only seen them during their worst. Their lives are good. Mine, too. Everyone's here. And like I said, they'll be happy again."

"You sound pretty sure."

"I am." He shrugs. "Call me an optimist. But life is what you make of it, honey. You got beaten yesterday and here you are about to sneak into an old woman's room. What for?"

"I'm getting paid," I say.

"You're curious. And you're using it as an excuse. I know what you were thinking the moment you were caught in that bathroom. I've thought it too. We all have, at some point. But we get good days if we stick around, Andy. Days like the day I painted that portrait." He rinses another glass in the sink, and starts to towel it dry. "It was Irene's idea. Just a year or so back. She saw me painting in the garden one night, years ago, thought it was nice, but I thought she'd forgotten about it until she told me she wanted a family portrait. A real one. So she and Margo and Pearl got everyone together and picked out clothes and I just had them stand and sit around in the parlor and . . . that's who they were. On that day. I took a photo to use when everyone got tired of posing, and I painted a lot from memory, and just knowing them. But it was that day. Them at their best."

"Sounds like a good day."

"It was."

I shrug. "I'm sorry I didn't get to see it."

"Stick around and you might," he says, and turns back to the sink and dirty dishes.

I head out of the kitchen and walk upstairs, all the way to the top. The hallway up here is creaky and narrow. There are some small empty rooms on either side. Pat's room is like this, but in the other wing. I think about what he said, and I know he's right. There are good days ahead. Good moments. I've even seen them, had them. Kissing Gene at the Ruby. Elsie driving me back. I'm alive, and I want to stay that way. Life will be hard, and messy, but if the people here can do it and still be happy from time to time, I certainly can.

At the end of the hallway is a small door and a few steps up, like Pat said. Alice's room isn't quite what I thought it would be. I pictured something cozy, with books all over the walls and a knit blanket and a worn armchair. There are books, and a bed, but it's curiously stale. Everything is white and beige. The books aren't in wild stacks, like Pat's. They're very neatly lined up. She will definitely notice if anything is out of place.

I step quietly, looking around. I'm not sure what for, exactly, it's just a hunch. Some kind of evidence of poison knowledge? I look at the books on the shelf—all mysteries. Which could be enough, but doesn't prove much. I check under her bed, and find a small trunk there, which I pull out and open. It's got a photo album in it. All photos of Margo—from baby through teenager. Margo, an infant, in a bonnet, holding a teddy bear. Margo, grinning as a toddler, with a bow in her hair. Margo in a pretty floral dress, Margo smiling all through childhood. And then Margo at about twelve or thirteen. Still smiling, but it doesn't fit right anymore. Probably when she figured it out. I wonder if Alice could feel her pulling away. I flip through to the end. So many photos. There's no doubt Alice loves her daughter. Did Margo leave without saying goodbye? How did they part, that first time? Whose heart was more broken?

At the back of the album are some papers, a small lock of baby hair tied with a pink ribbon. I leave that and flip through the papers. Margo's birth certificate. Father is Samuel Leet. I never asked about Alice's husband. She said he died, and there's no reason to doubt that. But Margo had asked her mother how they'd met. It was to get a rise out of Alice, and it had worked. If she was selling her body for extra cash at the hotel, it's possible Margo doubts Leet is her dad. Or he only married Alice after knocking her up as her john. Or she was just being cruel. I'm not sure. I put the album back and look through the rest of the trunk—baby clothes from the photos. She's kept them all these years. And at the bottom, a photo, separate from the album, of a man in uniform. "Sam" is written on the back. I shake my head. He's a real man, not some figment.

Outside in the hall, I hear Pat singing "The Lady Drinks Champagne," and chuckle to myself, then quickly put everything back and walk out into the hall. Pat grins at me, keeps on singing as he sweeps.

"She's in the kitchen?" I ask, and he nods. "Thanks," I say, and head back downstairs. I glance at my watch. I'd been going through those old photos for over an hour.

Alice and Dot are unpacking large paper bags of groceries. Or, Dot is, and Alice is telling her where to put things.

"Those go in the icebox. Those can stay on the counter, we'll use them tonight. Those we should salt and dry."

"Hi, Alice," I say. "Hi, Dot."

Dot nods at me, and continues unpacking.

"Hello, Andy," Alice says, smiling at me. She's in a green dress today, with a little white lace at the collar. "I didn't see you at breakfast this morning, but you need your rest after yesterday, so I didn't ask anyone to wake you."

"Thank you," I say. "I did need my rest."

"Are you hungry? It's past lunchtime, but I'm sure Dot could whip you something up."

Dot rolls her eyes.

"That's all right," I say. "I just wanted to ask you some questions."

"Oh," she sighs. "More of this? Can't this be over yet?"

"They're sort of personal," I say, looking at Dot.

"Ah, well, let's go up to the sitting room, then, if Cliff isn't passed out drunk in it. Dot, you can finish up here?"

Dot nods and I follow Alice back up to the sitting room. She sits down on the sofa and smooths her dress, then pats the space next to her for me. I sit down and she crosses her legs, tilting toward me. I get a hit of her perfume again, the only thing in the house that doesn't smell like flowers.

"I hope this isn't about what Margo said last night," Alice says, looking at her hands, which are clasped in her lap. "It was all lies. And very cruel of her."

"Yes and no," I say. "Margo's father was a soldier, you said?"

She tilts her head. "Yes. Sam. He was a good man. Though I admit we weren't together long before he got shipped off. We got married quickly, then, and the night before he left was the night Margo was conceived. I'm sorry if that's too personal. But after what Margo said, I just want to assure you, I'm not that kind of woman."

"I believe you," I say, and smile, trying to look reassuring, even if the date of Margo's birth doesn't line up with any wars.

"I know you do, you're a good boy," she says, patting my knee. "Is that all you wanted to know?"

"No," I say. "I wanted to ask about the couple who died at the Butterfly."

"Ah," she says, and turns away. Her hair covers her profile, but she hunches slightly, and I think she's going to be sick, but she takes a deep breath, and turns back to me, only a little paler. She pushes her hair behind her ear. "That was . . . terrible. I honestly thought I'd never have to think about it again. But I suppose you are a detective, and since that was poison, even though it was accidental, it looks suspicious."

"Especially since Irene was poisoned too."

"Poisoned?" She fluttered her eyelashes and her eyes go large. "I thought she was pushed."

I shake my head. Pearl said what Cliff did never happened, and I respect it.

"Well . . . I can see how Margo and I might look suspicious, then, but I promise, neither of us had anything to do with that terrible accident at the hotel. I always told Manny—that was the chef—I always told him his kitchen was a mess, and he needed to clean it up. But he always said it was his domain, and wouldn't let me fix it. I blame myself sometimes, that poor couple. Thank goodness they didn't have children."

"So you don't know how it happened?"

"Poison got into their food somehow." Alice shrugs, pushes her hair back behind her ear again. "Terrible, but just an accident. I didn't even know them. Or do you think I'm some kind of serial poisoner, like from one of my books?" she asks, grinning at her little joke. "Going to arrest me?"

"I'm not a policeman anymore," I say.

"Right." She nods. "Well, I would never hurt Irene. We fought, but we understood each other. We spent so much time together that we got to be . . . comrades, if not friends. If she died, it would be Margo and Pearl I would depend on to not kick me out, and they certainly don't care for me."

"You think Margo would kick you out?"

"You heard her last night. She has some real anger in her. Sometimes I think . . ." She shakes her head, looks away. "I'm sorry. Is that all you wanted to ask?"

"What were you going to say?" I ask.

She looks at me and smiles, shakes her head. "Nothing, I've just read too many mysteries. They've made me morbid."

I lean back, nodding. "Margo was there when the hotel closed?"

"She left right after. Wrote me a letter, left it on the mantel. Said she was going to find her fortune. I was sad, of course, but we kept in touch. She wrote me letters."

"Did Margo know the couple who died?"

Her smile drops, and her hands return to her lap, fingers twining around themselves. She stares at them, as though she didn't realize she was doing it. "No," she says quietly. It's a lie, and she's doing a bad job hiding it. She wants to say something.

"Alice. Tell me."

"The woman in the couple. She was younger. And she and Margo were friendly. I saw them getting a drink together at the bar once. I didn't think much of it at the time. And now I'm sure my imagination is getting the best of me. But . . . you know, when I saw them getting drinks, I didn't know . . . what I know. So thinking about it, maybe she and the woman were . . . involved?"

"Sure," I say. "Could be. She murdered them in a fit of jealousy?"

"No," Alice says, shaking her head. "No. My daughter would never do anything like that."

"I'm sure you're right," I say, standing up.

She stands and smiles at me. "I know you'll figure it out, Andy," she says, and reaches out and strokes my cheek. "I'd better get back to the kitchen. For dinner we're having that rabbit stew I *wanted* to serve last night. But, the great thing about a stew is it only gets better the longer you leave it. So I'm sure it'll be even better tonight."

"I look forward to it," I say.

She nods and walks out of the room and I head over to the

phone. I look around, but the room is empty, so I pick up the receiver and ask the operator to call the Bend police department again. When someone picks up, I ask for Detective Stuart.

"It's Mills again, SFPD," I say.

"Oh, the Butterfly poisoning, right? You wanted to know something else?"

I nod, forgetting he can't see, as I'm distracted by Margo's car pulling in in front of the fountain. "Yeah," I say after moment. "I was wondering, what was the name of the couple who died. Any chance you remember?"

"No . . . but I could dig up the file, if you don't mind waiting a few minutes?"

"I'd appreciate it," I say.

"Sure, sure . . ." he says. He puts the phone down and I can hear the police station again. The murmur of conversation.

The front door opens and Margo comes in. She glances briefly into the sitting room, sees me on the phone, raises an eyebrow, and then heads upstairs. I listen to her footsteps go up and then fade away down the hall to her room. Then the house is quiet again. My heart beating is the loudest thing I can hear.

"Still there, Mills?" Detective Stuart's voice sounds a little winded. I wonder if the files were down a flight of stairs.

"Yeah, thanks," I say.

"Their name was Leet," he says. "Sam and Elizabeth Leet."

SIXTEEN

I feel my fingers tingle, even though I'm not sure what it means.

"Leet?" I ask. "Sam Leet?"

"That's what it says here," Detective Stuart says. "You come across some relative of his or something?"

"Something," I say. "Thanks, Stuart."

"No problem, Mills."

I hang up the phone and take a deep breath. It wasn't strangers who died at the Butterfly. It was Alice's husband, Margo's father . . . and his new wife? I know it's a different case. Figuring out the Butterfly isn't going to tell me who killed Irene, just if either of them knew how to use poison, and anyone could have thought of that. The wasp poison isn't the same as the rat poison, too. But it's stuck in my gut, and I know if I can figure it out, I'll have some clue to who killed Irene. They both had reasons for wanting her dead, after all, but they both had good reasons not to. And they're both lying to me about something. Alice practically pointed at Margo just now, wrote her name in lights over her head. And Margo's been holding back.

I saw her go up to her room while I was on the phone, so I

follow her up and knock on the door I think is hers, and not Pearl's.

"Yes?" she calls through the door.

"Margo, it's Andy. I have a few questions."

There's a long pause, and I can practically picture her rolling her eyes.

"Well, you'd better come in, then."

I open the door, and it's not what I expected. I thought Margo's private space would be like her: chilly, probably white. But it's all color and warmth. A soft rose-colored wallpaper, baby-blue velvet drapes, sheets on the bed the shade of honey. Fresh flowers are everywhere, in vases around the room. On a deep blue nightstand is a pink vase filled with white daisies, and next to it, a worn-looking pulp novel with a woman slipping out of her dress on the cover. But maybe most surprising of all is Margo in the center of room, wearing a pair of denim overalls, like a farmer, tying a bandana around her hair.

"What do you want to ask?" she says, not even registering my surprise.

"About what you said last night to your mother. About your father."

"Ah." She turns away and looks at herself in a full-length mirror on the wall, checking she got all her hair under the bandana. "I was just being cruel. She brings that out in me. I'm not proud of it."

"I want to know about your father, though," I say.

She glances at me in the mirror, then turns around and walks past me out the door. "Then you'd better come along," she says. "Lunch took longer than I thought, Henry had a meeting run over, so now it's past three and I want to get this done and still have time to wash up after."

"What are you doing?" I ask.

"I'm going to go tend to the flowers," she says, turning briefly on the stairs to smile at me. "Did you think they just grew themselves?"

"I thought Judy took care of it." I follow her down and out the front door.

"Oh, she does, but it's too much work for one person. And besides, I like it."

"You like it?" I ask, trying to picture her manicured nails digging into fresh soil.

"I do," she says. We walk out of the house to the garden shed, where she grabs a pair of gloves and a basket of tools. She's about to leave but pauses and looks around for another pair of gloves, which she hands to me, practically slapping them into my chest. I wince and stumble back a step, but she doesn't seem to care. "You can help," she says.

"I'm not much for gardening."

She marches past me, heading back to the front of the house. "Andy, you've been staying in our house, Elsie rescued you from death in an alley, and you've caused plenty of drama."

"I don't think I caused it, exactly—"

"Regardless." She spins to look at me. "The least you can do is help me with the flowers."

I follow her outside to the edge of one of the fields of flowers—sunflowers. They're nearly to my shoulders, but I can see a little dirt path through them. She turns around and walks down it, and I follow. The sunflowers brush tight against me, and give me the sense that I'm wading through yellow water, that I might drown. I realize she could probably knock me out with a quick blow to the head from one of the tools in her basket, if I turn around. Slit my throat with the shears, roll my body between the stems, so I'm hidden from view.

"What you want to do is look for dead leaves, or leaves that are blocking the sun from other flowers." She stops in front of me suddenly and puts down the basket, then stands back up with a pair of shears. She leans into the flowers a little and I hear a snip, and she pulls back. "We'll take some for my room, too, I think. Or the sitting room. Irene designed it in white to show off the colors of the flowers, but I haven't been doing a good job keeping the vases stocked since she died."

"Why do you do this?" I ask.

"I like it, though I imagine you'll find that hard to believe. I like flowers, I like helping in a way that feels useful, instead of just posing for photos in the newspapers. Irene used to do most of this, actually. She taught me about the flowers, how to take care of them." She reaches out and I hear the snip of the shears again. "We bonded, talking about flowers and women's roles in society . . . nothing I expect you're interested in, but she's the one who made me understand how important my role is at those damned society functions, even if I don't enjoy them."

"I thought you did, though?"

She shrugs. "I can be complicated. I can like and hate something at the same time. Don't you?"

"Sometimes," I say.

"I imagine you liked and hated sex, since you sought it out but also tried to hide it," she says. "Maybe that's what those society functions are for me."

"They're like sex?"

"Oh, no, I love sex," she says, flashing me a grin.

"You sound like Elsie."

"Well, you told me I was funny, so now I feel like I have to perform. What did you want to ask me about, anyway? My father?" She leans forward, snipping another leaf from a nearby flower.

"Yeah. Your mother says he died overseas?"

She kneels down and snips a low leaf. "Mmm, well, if that's what she says."

"Except it's a lie," I say.

"Oh?" she asks, not turning around, not sounding surprised.

"He died at the hotel you and your mother worked at."

She freezes, then slowly stands up, and turns around. She looks sad. "Did you tell my mother that?"

"She doesn't know?"

"Oh, she knows." Her face turns dark, and as if sensing it, she turns back to the flowers.

"When we talked before, you made it sound like you left for San Francisco before the hotel closed."

She reaches out and snips another leaf. "Did I? I didn't mean to."

"Yeah, you did. You and your mother are both lying about something, Margo."

She doesn't turn to face me, but her shoulders stiffen, and she picks up the basket and strides forward. "It was years ago, Andy. It has nothing to do with Irene, can you just drop it?"

"What happened at the Butterfly? Did you or your mother kill Sam Leets for abandoning you?"

"I didn't even know the man," Margo says, putting the basket down. "I'd never met him. I had no reason to want him dead. If anything, I—" She reaches forward and snips another leaf off, stopping herself. "I didn't kill him. I'd never met him before."

"Because you thought he'd died overseas."

"My mother never even told me his name. I wasn't a Leet before I married Henry. I was a Cassidy, same as my mother. She said she changed it back after he died, because she didn't care for the name, but I eventually put it together. They were never married. It was just a story she told to explain why she was a single mother and still stay dignified. And why ruin that for her?"

I nod. "Sure, but then he turned up. And died."

"I . . ." She stops what she's doing and turns on me. Her eyes are red, like she might start crying. "Please, Andy. Just drop it."

"I can't."

She raises the shears then, like she might use them on me. I take a step back, tripping over a root. I fall, the sunflowers rising up around me like dark water, casting me in shadow. My cracked rib sends out wildfire through me and I let out a groan of pain. Margo takes a step forward, looming over me.

She reaches out her hand like she's going to hold me down. I realize I can't get up. I could try to scramble backward, but everything hurts, and I'm so tired. Her hand gets closer. But she stops. It takes me a minute to realize she's helping me up. I take it and stand. She stares up at me. Her eyes are hard, their dark green like moss on the underside of a rock. It's quiet for a minute, except for the breeze knocking the sunflower stalks together. They make hollow noises as they hit each other, like old bones.

"She killed them," Margo says eventually. "Is that what you want to know?"

"But why?" I ask. "Scorn? She doesn't seem like the type."

"Because of me," Margo says. "He . . . he came back when I was eighteen, nearly done with school. He approached me alone first, asked if I was Alice's daughter. I said yes. He said he was my father. I was shocked, of course. I thought he was dead. But Mother's stories had never added up, and it was clearly him from the one photo she kept under her bed, so eventually I relented, admitted it was him, and asked why he'd been gone my whole life."

"What did he say?"

Margo turns away from me, looking into the sunflowers, which are about the same height as her head. "He said that my mother was just a fling. He had a fiancée, but he was about to go abroad for a while, and he wanted to leave with a little . . . 'style,' he called it. Men are terrible creatures. I feel so sorry for you, Henry, and Cliff, being attracted to them. Style." She laughs, but it's a bitter sound. "One wild weekend with my mother, who did that sort of thing with guests if the money was right, and then down to San Francisco, where he shipped out. It wasn't even for a war, I don't know why my mother used that stupid lie. He'd been in the army at the very end of the Great War, and now he was going over to help with the rebuilding effort, but not as a soldier. He was going to make it rich. And he did. Came back wealthy, married his fiancée, and ignored the letters from my mother about his daughter. Until eighteen years went by, and he and his wife never managed to have a child of their own."

She reaches forward and snips another leaf. "I don't know why he told her, eventually, but he did—he already had a child. Up in Oregon. She insisted they come up and meet me, try to be part of my life. She was . . . a good woman. Elizabeth. She had red hair, and freckles, and she was so kind. We spent one night just talking at the bar in the hotel, getting to know each other."

"Did you sleep with her?"

"What?" Margo turns, horrified. "No. Why would you think that?"

"Your mother implied you'd slept with her."

Margo glares and her mouth pinches. "Did she? My father's wife? Well, I didn't. I just liked Elizabeth. She was motherly. After talking with her, they made me an offer: yes, he'd missed all my growing up, but they were wealthy now, and they had time, and they wanted to try to know me. They asked me to come down and stay with them in San Francisco. Meet fine people, live a fine life, maybe go to college. They'd take care of me. I was wary, but I said yes, as long as I could leave whenever I wanted. Elizabeth was sad I would even think I couldn't. That's when I decided to go with them. Maybe to get to know him a little, and because I liked her, and because they were offering me opportunities I'd never have any other way. A chance to be part of society instead of just the maid. A chance to get an education, and live an amazing life."

"But they died."

"I told my mother I was going to go with them. They died that night." She looks at her feet. "I knew she did it, of course I did, but I didn't turn her in. How could I? She's my mother, even if she was never really motherly to me. She was always chilly, always hated the way I held myself. Too much of a tomboy. I needed to be a real woman. Turns out all that came in handy." She laughs again, then turns back to the flowers. "But I went to San Francisco anyway. I knew I had to go, or else I'd be trapped forever."

"So . . . why did you invite your mother to stay here? Why keep in touch with her?"

She clips another leaf. "I felt sorry for her, Andy. My whole life, I felt sorry for her. How could you not? I hated her, but she'd raised me, too. Alone. So I called now and then. When she told me she was going to be put out on the street, I wired her some money to take the bus down here, and then I met with her. She was pathetic. Hadn't dyed her hair in ages, the gray was six inches long. I don't know why that's the thing I remember the most, but I do." She cuts another leaf. "And maybe it was a little bit about revenge, too. Inviting her to stay with us, I mean. It was a chance to flaunt who I was now, how I was so far from the lady she wanted me to be, and how I was also exactly what she wanted to be herself and never would—a society lady, in the papers. Everything my father had offered me, and my mother had taken away. And I got it all anyway." She cuts another leaf. "I didn't tell anyone about what she'd done, of course. Irene would never have let her stay otherwise. And besides, it wasn't like there was another man who'd left her with a child to raise on her own and then reappeared years later, flaunting his new wife, trying to take that child back, now that she'd done all the work. I don't want to say I under-stand why she did it, but over the years, I've seen it from her perspective. I didn't think she would . . ."

"But then Irene asked you to adopt," I say.

She turns around again, confused. "Yes . . . what does that have to do with it?"

"She convinced you it was a good idea?"

Margo shrugs and smiles. "Yes. A little. I was looking for-ward to it. I thought I'd be a terrible mother, because of mine, but Irene convinced me I could be good at it."

"She said you'd be a mother to this child, like she was to you."

"Yes." Margo nods. "And she was. She was like the mother

I'd never really had, but . . ." She trails off, her eyes widening. "No, we were alone when she said that."

I shake my head. "Alice heard."

Margo starts to fall, and I go to catch her, but she waves me off, and instead lowers herself to her knees in the dirt. "I knew it," she said. "When Irene died, part of me just *knew*, but I told myself I was wrong, that there was no reason she would. She depended on Irene for her charity. I told myself they were friends." She leans back, sitting in the dirt, and looks up at me. She's crying, and the shadows of sunflowers cover her face like falling leaves. "But I knew."

"She killed Irene."

A breeze blows through the sunflowers, making their yellow heads sway. The leaves rustle, and the ones Margo has cut off take to the sky for a moment.

"Alice wasn't a good mother, and she's always been a selfish one. She killed my own father for trying to be in my life. And then she saw that Irene was like my real mother . . ."

"She emptied one of the perfume bottles, then filled it with wasp poison and some water, and sealed it shut. All Irene had to do was open it and inhale like she always did, and it would be fatal. It was patient. She must have done it all weeks before Irene died."

"I should never have brought her here," she says softly.

I reach out my hand to help her up, and she takes it, rising to look me in the eye.

"Do you think they'll ever forgive me?" she asks.

"I think you'll find that they have endless forgiveness for their family," I say.

She leans into me, and I wonder if she's about to faint again, but then I realize she's hugging me, sobbing into my chest. I reach my arm around her and hold her, patting her on the back, trying to offer some comfort. But what comfort can I offer? Her mother killed the woman who was like a mother to her. Her mother, who could never accept who she was, but had to possess her, couldn't let her find her own family. I think of the beating I took at the hands of my old colleagues. They weren't really a family, but they thought they were. And then the people at the Black Cat, like Pat, who were a family I never managed to thank. People are always trying to claim you, without ever listening to who you are. They want you to be something else, to be the role they have for you in the family. But really, we're all better off just making our own.

Margo pulls away, her face red and sticky with tears. She takes off her gloves and wipes her face as best she can.

"Sorry," she says. "That was . . ."

"Fine," I say.

She smiles. "What are you going to do?"

"What I was paid to do," I say. "I'm going to tell Pearl who murdered her wife."

SEVENTEEN

Pearl still isn't back by the time Henry gets home from work, and I start to get worried. Margo and I stay in the field not wanting to go back to the house until we have greater numbers to confront Alice with. Alice is an old woman, but she's patient, and cunning, and has killed at least twice before, and I'm still in pain from my beating. Margo agrees and sits among the flowers, head resting on her knees, which are drawn up. I can't see her face, but she stays like that, silent. I sit across from her, watching bees as they hum between the stems. They're not bothered by us. They don't care. It's a while before Henry gets home.

I walk up to his car and open the door for him, and he looks up at me curiously.

"Let's go talk over here," I say, leading him back to the flowers, and away from the windows.

"All right," he says, confused. He follows me back and Margo meets us, standing there in an army of sunflowers. The sky is darkening overhead, going from blue to orange to pink in blurry layers, and the shadows the flowers cast are long.

"Your mother is out," I say. "I don't know when she'll be back. But I know who killed Irene. It was Alice."

He blinks a few times, and then turns to Margo, as if for confirmation.

"I'm sorry, Henry. I'm . . . really sorry," she says in a whisper.

"So what have you done about it?" he asks me.

"I wanted to make sure we were together when we confronted her, and besides, Pearl told me to let her handle whatever needed to be handled. And she's not home yet."

"We should call the police," Henry says.

"And have them poke around in our lives? Ask questions about how we figured it out?" Margo asks. "Pearl hired Andy to avoid the police."

"So we just wait for her? Where is she?"

Margo turns to me. I promised I'd stay quiet about Cliff so I'm staying quiet about the blackmailer, too. "She had to run some errands in town. I expected her back by now . . ."

"Where's Cliff?" Henry asks. "Is he safe?"

"He was taking a nap, last I saw," I say. "I can't imagine Alice would try to hurt him."

"I'm not leaving him alone in the house with a murderer. And the staff, too. Why haven't you gone in and warned them?"

I shake my head. "I don't think she's going to hurt them without a reason."

"She killed Irene because of the baby," Margo says, sniffing. "Because Irene said she was like a mother to me."

There's a pause as she looks down at her feet. I know what she's thinking. That it's her fault somehow. Henry stares at her, but doesn't reach out to touch her.

"You're just guessing," Henry says. "I'm going inside right now and I'm going to . . ."

"What?" I say. "Kill her?"

"I'll kick her out on the street."

"And then she'll tell everyone about us," Margo says. "This is why I never wanted Pearl to hire an investigator in the first place. There's no way to end this. There's no justice we can seek. Even if we did turn her over to the police, she'd just say Irene made a pass at her, and she was afraid, and she'd be free by dinner."

"But . . ." Henry says. "She killed my mother."

"I know," Margo says, wrapping her arms around him and hugging him. "I'm so sorry."

"I will figure something out," I say, feeling an anger run through my body and make my bruises throb. "You have rooms you can lock from the outside, right? Maybe I can get her into one of those."

"And then we keep her as a prisoner the rest of her life?" Margo asks. She lets go of Henry, then looks up at the sky. "Actually . . . maybe that would be all right."

"Really?" Henry asks her. "You'd do that to your mother?"

"I . . . I would. To protect us."

"All right," I say. "So where do I lure her?"

"Her room," Henry says. "We can lock that from the outside, and it'll be the easiest. The key is in Irene's office, I think."

"All right," I say. "She's probably in the kitchen now, right?" They both nod. "You go up and check on Cliff, but listen to hear us head upstairs. When we've done that, go get the key and come to her room. Whistle when you're in the hall and I'll make an excuse to come out and close the door. Then we lock her in."

We're all quiet for a moment.

"What do I do?" Margo asks.

"Just . . . act normal," I say.

"All right," she says, and bends down and cuts a few sun-flowers off. "I'll put these in a vase," she says, but she holds them in front of her like a shield.

I swallow and then lead the march back to the house.

Inside, it's quiet. I look into the dining room, where Pat is setting the table for dinner.

"Is Alice in the kitchen?" I ask him. He nods. I turn back to Henry and Margo, who stare at me, lips tight, before silently going about their tasks. I walk past Pat down into the kitchen.

The kitchen is hot, the stove and fireplace both going, but Alice seems unfazed by it, stirring a large pot, sprinkling some spices in by hand.

"Isn't that Dot's job?" I ask.

"Oh, I sent her out to grab some carrots from the garden," Alice says, turning to smile at me. "The stew got a little bitter, so we need to sweeten it up."

I smile back. It doesn't fit right, but how could it? I look her over and try to see if there were signs I could have missed before. She's so closed off, so careful.

"I was wondering if you'd let me look at your books," I say. "I could use something to read before I go to bed."

"Oh, well, of course. After dinner, I can show you my whole collection."

"Might take a while for me to choose. Have any time now?"

"No, not really," she says, stirring the pot. "Have to get dinner ready."

"I'm sure Dot can handle that."

She shakes her head. "There's too much to do. But after dinner. Which will be ready soon." She glances at her watch. "Oh, yes, we're running late."

"Pearl is still out."

"Is she?" She pauses in her stirring. "Well, that'll be okay. We'll save some for her."

I stand there, wondering how to get her up to her room, but I can tell it's not going to work unless I march her there by gunpoint.

"All right," I say. "After dinner." It can wait.

I head back upstairs to let everyone know the plan has been delayed. Henry is still in his room, and looks relieved when I tell him it'll wait until after dinner. Margo is changed back into a yellow dress, and shakes her head when I tell her.

"No, no," she says, sitting on her bed. "We need to do it now."

"Can you get her up to her room?" I ask.

"No." She sighs.

"Then just wait a little longer. Come down to dinner."

"You want me to act normal at dinner?"

"I can say you're sick," I say.

She frowns and stands up. "No. That'll make her suspicious. And Elsie will be here soon, probably. Let's . . . go down." She takes my arm and I walk her downstairs. Outside, it's dark now, so we can see the headlights of a car pull up outside. A moment later, Pearl walks in. She's surprised to see us waiting by the door, and her face, which was like steel, melts into a smile.

"Did you have any luck?" I ask.

She nods, and hangs up her coat. I don't want to ask anything else, but a moment later, another car pulls in, and even before the door opens, Alice is in the dining room.

"Dinner," she calls out to everyone. "Come on in."

Slowly, the entire family walks into the dining room, and sits down at their spots around the table. Elsie comes in from outside, and gives Margo a peck on the forehead before sitting. Henry and Cliff come from upstairs, Cliff now dressed, and rubbing his eyes.

Pat emerges and puts down bowls in front of each of us, one by one.

"It's the rabbit stew from last night," Alice says. "I'm actually glad it had a chance to marinate a little longer. Develop the flavor."

"Looks good," Henry says.

"Thank you, Mother," Margo says, which makes Elsie throw a curious glance at her.

"You know, Margo," Alice says. "I owe you an apology. I wasn't a very good mother to you. That's why you turned out the way you did."

Everyone goes silent, staring at her. Even Pat stops mid-stride, before putting a bowl down in front of Cliff. The hairs on my arm stand on end. Something is wrong.

"And what way is that?" Margo asks, her voice wavering. She's scared too, but now she's angry.

"Oh, you know . . ." Alice takes her napkin and puts it in her lap, then gestures around the table. "Like all of them." She brings a spoonful of the stew to her mouth and swallows it.

"I like the way I am, Mother. And it has nothing to do with you. You were a bad mother, I agree with you. Cold, controlling, distant. But I've found some freedom here, and some love, and I'm happy with who I am. And I'm happy I owe none of that to you. You're a bitch and a murderer."

Pearl gasps and stares at Margo. I swallow, feeling my heart speed up. This was not the plan. I'll have to improvise now.

"It's true. Andy figured it out," Margo says.

"Oh, please," Alice says. "Prove it." She coughs.

Everyone looks at me. Fine, this is how we're doing it. No going back now. "I can't prove it. But I know how it happened.

You heard Irene and Margo talking about having a baby, heard Irene say she was like a mother to Margo and Margo agreed. You told me that yourself. But you hate anyone else wanting to be part of Margo's family. When her birth father showed up at the hotel all those years ago to take Margo away, you poisoned him and his wife. This time you were more patient, replacing the perfume with homemade cyanide gas from the wasp poison, probably that night, but it still worked out how you planned. Irene opened the bottle weeks later, inhaled, and died. She fell over the balcony while she did so, which gave you the perfect alibi, but you didn't really care if anyone knew it was murder. You didn't care . . ."

I stop. I feel a chill run down my back. Alice smiles patiently at me and swallows a spoonful of the stew. Cliff raises the spoon to his lips but I put out my hand.

"Stop," I say. "Don't eat the stew. Don't eat. Elsie, go tell the staff. Don't touch the stew."

Everyone stares at me, realizing what I've said, what it means. They turn back to Alice. She bobs her head to a song only she can hear, smiling as she eats another spoonful of stew, and another and another.

The smell of the stew fills the room. Sweet fat, and spices . . . and something sour. Like the smell of the soap that scratched me.

"You put that rat in my soap, too?" I ask her.

"What?" Pearl asks, but I shake my head.

"It was hard finding one the right size," Alice says with a grin.

I reach for her spoon but she draws back.

"Stop," I tell her, but she shakes her head.

"Well, what would you do with me, anyway?" Alice asks. "Tell the police? Have them lock me up? I think not. Too many questions. But I knew you'd figure it out, Andy. You're smart. I just thought it would be nice to have one more meal together. As a family."

It's quiet for a moment. The word "family" hangs in the air like a guillotine blade.

"We're not family," Pearl says, standing. "You're a monster."

"Oh, I'm the monster?" Alice says, then laughs. "I'm the monster? Look at you. With your perverted twisted little fake family. The years I've lived here have been like a horror story. You're all monsters." She daintily takes another spoonful of the strew, slurping it loudly. My stomach roils, watching her. She dabs at her mouth with her napkin. "I'm sorry I failed you, Margo. I'm sorry you're this . . . thing . . ." She coughs. "But I don't regret what I've done." She coughs again, harder this time. Everyone at the table stands, not sure what to do.

"I'm so sorry," Margo says.

"This isn't your fault," Henry says to her. She smiles at him, but starts to cry and he hugs her. "This isn't your fault, and no one blames you."

Alice coughs, interrupting them, then laughs. "Come on, Margo, eat up. All of you, eat!" She smiles broadly. There's something between her teeth. "I worked so hard making this for all of you."

"But I brought her here," Margo says, looking away from her mother.

"We all did," Pearl says. "Not for you, but because we care about you. But that doesn't make this"—she points at Alice, who coughs again—"your fault."

Alice beams back at Pearl, as if she just paid her a compliment. But her eyes are going glassy.

"Do we help her?" Cliff asks, as Alice begins to cough more and more, and her fingers clench on the tablecloth, pulling it closer to her.

"No," Pearl says, glaring.

I shake my head. "It's too late, anyway."

EIGHTEEN

The undertaker arrives an hour later to pick up the body. Pearl had been vague on the phone, just said a woman had died suddenly. Thankfully, Elsie had warned the staff in time, none of them had eaten the stew, so they'd gotten to work, cleaning everything up, throwing out any of the food Alice had touched. Then Pearl had made a phone call, and we'd all gotten our story straight.

When the door rings, Cliff opens it. He's wearing a suit now, dark gray, with a striped yellow shirt underneath and a black tie. He nods solemnly at the undertaker.

"She's in there," he says. Henry and Margo are in the foyer up the stairs a little, Margo crying into Henry's shoulder. He has his arm wrapped around her. I don't know if the tears are fake. Maybe they're not. None of this can be easy for her.

"Darling," Henry says to Margo, "let's go upstairs. You shouldn't have to see her carted off like this." Margo sobs harder, and Henry looks at the undertaker. "Her mother," he says. "She hadn't been feeling well all day, but that wasn't uncommon . . . it just happened so fast."

The undertaker, a small, solemn man, nods. "That's how it goes sometimes."

"Do you need anything from us?" Henry asks. "My secretary, Cliff, can give you any information you need." He points at Cliff. "And our cousins were in the room when she died." He nods at Elsie and me, who are holding hands, like a couple, at the entrance to the dining room. I feel my face flush slightly, and nod at the undertaker. "I just think she should get to bed, if you don't need us," Henry finishes.

"It's fine," the undertaker says. "There's no mystery here. You don't want a doctor to look her over?"

"Darling, do you?" Henry asks Margo.

She turns to the undertaker, her eyes red. Not fake tears, then. "No," she says softly. "That's . . . no." I look at Elsie, who watches Margo and Henry go upstairs. She squeezes my hand, and I know she wants to go after them, comfort her. I squeeze back. Henry is her family too. He can be there for her until Elsie is done.

The undertaker goes into the dining room, and Elsie, Cliff, and I follow.

"It was very distressing," Elsie says in a high, girlish voice. She's borrowed one of Pearl's skirts and has taken off her jacket. Her blouse is peach and she's not wearing a tie, so she barely attracts a glance from him.

"I'm sure," he says. He goes over to Alice's body and kneels, checking her pulse, putting his ear to her chest and mouth, then testing her limbs. They flop like fishtails, like the bones have been removed. "It's a shame, but sometimes it just happens to the elderly. Could have been a heart attack, or . . . you said she was coughing?"

I nod. "All day, and then a lot as she . . ." I let it drift off.

"Pneumonia maybe. She like doctors?"

"Terrified of them," Elsie says.

The undertaker sighs. "Always see the doctor if you're feeling low. Especially if you're older," he says, standing up. "I'm going to get a bag, and you"—he looks at Cliff—"you help me carry her out.

Cliff swallows. "Of course," he says.

Elsie and I watch as they bring out a body bag and zip Alice into it. I remember the girl on the beach. Alice looks like her—peaceful. But it's a lie, I know. It's just something we tell ourselves when we look at dead bodies. That they're peaceful. Some of us don't get any peace, not really. But that's not the same as happiness. Peace comes to you, if you're lucky. Happy you grab and make with your own two hands.

The undertaker and Cliff carry the body out and Cliff tells him which church to bring the body to. He drives off, and Cliff comes back in, already taking off his tie, and makes a few calls, to make sure Alice gets a burial, a funeral. They'll all attend it, I know. Elsie goes upstairs to Margo as soon as she can, and I follow, but I open a different door.

Pearl is sitting at her desk, a drink in her hand, and another waiting for me on the other side of the desk. She pushes it toward me when I come in.

"Everything go like it was supposed to?" she asks.

I take the drink and sit down, sipping it. "You all have the acting down. I was surprised how easy it came to me."

"Why? You've been doing it your whole life."

I nod, and sip my drink, leaning back in the chair. "So you took care of the blackmailer?"

"I did."

"You know, guys like him, they're pretty sleazy. He could come back, ask for more. He could tell Cliff's family anyway."

"I had him write a letter to them saying it was all dead ends, and I mailed it myself."

"Smart. How much did he cost you?"

She leans back in her chair, takes a sip. "It was cheap, just a few coins."

I want to laugh, because five grand doesn't seem like a few coins to me, but maybe to someone rich as her it does. I sip my own drink, and stare out the window behind her. It takes me that long to figure it out, and then I shiver, and turn back toward her.

"For the ferryman?" I ask.

She nods, sips her drink. "You going to turn me in?"

I think for a moment, but only a moment. "No."

I know I should, but somehow, I can't. Pearl was defending her family from someone who wanted to harm them for who they are. Alice wanted the same. All these people, trying to hurt them. No wonder Irene built this place. It's not a house. It's a fortress. And it's constantly under assault.

"Have you thought about my offer?" Pearl asks. "We could use someone like you around here."

"I think . . . I want to sleep on it," I say, standing up.

"I understand. Good night, Andy."

"Good night, Pearl."

The next morning, I put on the clothes I came in, and go down to breakfast. Everyone is already around the table. Pearl takes one look at me, and frowns.

"You're not going to come stay with us, are you?" she asks.

I shake my head. "I don't think it would be right. The way I entered your lives . . . I don't want to be that, always around, reminding you. I want you all to be a happy family again. Even if I'm not part of it." I want my own family, I think. Something like this, but not as part of the staff, not in a cage. I don't know if it's possible . . . but I know this isn't what I want.

Henry smiles and nods. "That's very considerate of you."

"But if you ever need me for anything," I say, "I'll be around."

"What if I just want you to come for dinner?" Pearl asks.

"That too." I grin.

"Well, come on, come eat your last breakfast with us, then," Margo says, pointing at my seat. I sit down, and Pat brings me a plate of pancakes, which I eat happily, knowing I probably won't have it this good for a while.

"What do you think you'll do next?" Cliff asks, resting his chin in his hands, watching me eat. "More of this?"

"I'd like that," I say. "If anyone would hire me. But I think first I'd like to stop by the Ruby. Get checked out by the doctor, make sure I'm healing up okay."

Elsie throws her head back and laughs. "You're always welcome there. And the doctor will be glad to see you."

The others look at Elsie, not quite understanding what she means, but when I'm done eating, Henry gives me a hand-shake, and Cliff and Margo each give me a kiss on the cheek before drifting back to their lives. Pearl brings me upstairs, where she writes me a check larger than I expected.

"You should take the clothes, too," Pearl says. "You looked good in them."

"Really? You're already overpaying me."

She shrugs. "I like you, Andy. I was serious. Are you sure you won't stay and work for me?"

"I don't want to be that guy, Pearl. The one who stays, the third cousin no one likes."

"We're all family, here. What does it matter how distant?"

"It matters to me," I say.

"All right. But when you get set up, let me know where. And if you can't. If you have trouble, call me then, too. You'll be welcome here."

"Thank you, Pearl," I say. "Really. You don't know it, but you saved my life."

"Of course I know it," she says. "I knew it the moment we met."

I smile, and head for the door, but turn back once. "You should have that portrait from Irene's office put in the hall, where the one of Irene is. I like that one better."

She smiles. "I like that idea."

I go back to my room, and start packing up my toiletries and the new clothes. I even steal a few bars of soap. I'll check them for rats before use, though. When there's a knock on the door, I turn to see Pat, who immediately gives me a gentle hug, mindful of my ribs.

"I'm glad you solved it," he says. "It was pretty exciting."

"I'm just glad no one else died," I say.

"So what's next?"

"I . . ." I pause. "I don't know. A hotel, I guess. A night at the Cat again, but . . . different, this time. I'm not going to be the cop with no friends again. And then . . . I don't know."

He nods. "That's not a bad plan."

"Oh." I grab his book from the nightstand. "I'm sorry, I didn't even start it."

"Keep it, then," he says. "I'll see you at the Cat or one of the others again, right? Tonight, tomorrow. And you'll come have a drink with me and my friends?"

"Of course I will."

"Then borrow it awhile longer," he says, and gives me a kiss on the cheek before leaving, grabbing my bags before I can stop him. I follow him downstairs and out to the fountain. He's putting my bags in the trunk of my car, but Elsie is leaning against it, waiting.

"So, you weren't kidding about the free drinks, right?" I ask her.

"I wasn't. In fact, I have an idea for how you could become a real regular."

"Yeah?" I ask. I take out a cigarette and light it, smoking, waiting for her.

She fishes in her pocket and takes out a business card. "I may have gotten a little ahead of myself, but I think you'll like it. You were right—I have a whole floor above the Ruby I'm not using. Enough for a large office, and an apartment. I thought maybe I could rent them to you, in exchange for a percentage of your profits at first."

"Profits? From what?"

She hands me the card. It's got the diamond pattern of the Ruby's wallpaper, but in purple. "Amethyst Investigations," it says in large letters. There's a phone number and for an address it just says "above the Ruby."

"I figured your name would cause trouble, so I left it off. Address, too. The key will be discretion and reputation. If you're going to do work for more people like us."

I blink a few times. "You want me to be a queer detective?"

"Everything we do is criminalized. Do you know many of us are blackmailed, murdered, and we can't get justice or answers? It's a big clientele, Andy. And you'd be helping people. I'd vouch for you, help you find clients, that would make people trust you.

And being above the Ruby would keep cops out of your office, make it safe. If you don't mind sharing a hallway with a bunch of male and female impersonators and show-boys, anyway."

Pat closes the trunk to my car and walks past us back to the house. "Do it," he says as he walks by me.

I look back at the house. The trees on either side have shed all their pink flowers overnight at once, blanketing the grass and part of the gravel in petals that roll softly in the wind and make the air smell sweet. I watch one of the petals tumble over my feet, and turn back to Elsie.

"I'd get free drinks?"

"Sure. People need to see you with us to trust you."

I turn the idea over in my mind. It's been a lifetime since I was dragged out of the Cat. I've seen what a life can look like, even if the one here isn't the one I want. Maybe, though, they've shown me a door to something better. It might fail. I might fail. But at least I'll do it as myself, not the man in the plain suit I pretended to be before.

"Then, sure. Let's give it a try."

"Well, then, let me get in my car and we can drive back together, so I can show you your new home."

ACKNOWLEDGMENTS

Books are hard to write. You'd think over time, writing more and more of them, they might get easier, but they don't. *Lavender House* was hard to craft. Research, language, plotting, a mystery that hung together, making this world true but accessible. It was a lot of work. The good kind, the kind that feels great to do, and also the kind I could not have done alone.

There are many, many people to thank. Thank you to everyone listed here, and many more who prefer not to be.

First, my editor, Kristin, who not only took a chance on this book, but helped me really dig into it and draw out something more personal and more potent, even as she tried to get me to cut the dead rat scene. I'm sorry I kept the dead rat, Kristin, but all your other edits have taken this book even further than I thought it could go and made it more beautiful than I had originally imagined it. You have been such a joy to work with, to laugh with, to go through everything with, even now, during a plague! Somehow you made it all fun. You're a miracle.

My agent, Joy, who I can literally never thank enough. Over a decade of working with her means I have decades more of thanking her, because she manages to put years' worth of work into a day. She looks out for me, defends me, cajoles me, improves me. I wouldn't have the career or even the life I have today without her. Thank-yous will never be enough. And to my film agent, Lucy, who has worked tirelessly to get this book out there before it's even published, who has been putting up with me the whole time (a feat), and who I am just so constantly impressed by, who keeps teaching me, and who is always a delight to speak with. And to Susan, Megan, and Samina, all of whom have helped this book so much.

My parents, who have supported my writing from day one, and also shown me old black-and-white noirs since as long as I can remember. This book wouldn't exist without them.

The first person at Forge who read this book was Arielle, who held it up and said, "This is worth pursuing"—and not only that, but gave some edits too, and they were damn good. I'm so excited for your future in publishing.

Special note must be given to Katie, the cover designer. I have never felt so involved in the cover process, never been so heard, and definitely never had so much fun! Geeking out over fonts, teasing Kristin with dead rat ideas, and just throwing so many different design concepts out there was so much fun to do. Honestly, I kind of thought that we were having too much fun for a great cover to come out of it, but this cover is truly sensational. You took ideas that felt disparate and added new ones and wove together a vision I didn't see coming but which felt perfect the moment I saw it. I cannot thank you enough for that or for the fun.

And Colin, who I didn't get to work directly with, for making the art that is on the cover. It's so beautiful, and he had SO many good ideas. Everything I've seen him do inspires me, and the enthusiasm he had for the book, the life he gave it in his art—I wanted every cover he pitched. I want to write more books just so he can make more covers.

My publicists, Laura and SallyAnne. SallyAnne I've known for years, and she taught me how to be better at talking about my books and gave me advice I still think about all the time, and I can't say thank you enough for that. You've shaped the way I think about my writing and my audience. And Laura has been so in sync with me about everything I want this book to do. They're both amazing, and I'm so excited to see everything they're going to do to get this book out there.

The whole team at Forge has been extraordinary: Troix, Jennifer, Anthony, Alexis, Libby, Lucille, and Linda, plus probably a bunch of folks I haven't met (because plague), but who worked so hard on this book and are still working. I can't thank you all enough. I've never felt so well taken care of.

My sensitivity reader, Teri, who is and always has been one the smartest, frankest, and most loving people I know. My writing group, Laura, Jesse, Dan, Robin—we've been at this over a decade now, and I couldn't be doing this without you. My boys, Adam, Adib, Tom, Sandy, Julian, Cale, Caleb, thank you for keeping me sane while also applauding my inching slowly toward madness, as long as I do it with style. And Dahlia, who is the queen of all queer lit and my constant informant, advisor, and before-plague lunch-buddy.

Alexis, my poison master, who helped me figure out the best way to kill.

John McDougall, at Murder By The Book, for his help in understanding the field and as preemptive thanks for the millions of copies he promised to personally hand-sell.

Max Teitelbaum and his illustrious students for their Sappho knowledge.

And finally, I want to thank the people who wrote books I used for research, most especially Nan Alamilla Boyd, author of *Wide-Open Town*. I've never met her, but that book was so instrumental in helping me understand the world I was writing about and making it feel alive, and queer, and breathing. And of course, Charles Kaiser, author of *The Gay Metropolis*, which I first encountered in a queer sexualities class in college and which introduced me to an entire world of queer history I didn't know I was part of. I hope that this book can deliver that same feeling of the world opening up and queer people suddenly seeing themselves in a past they felt didn't include them. Thank you for giving that feeling to me. Likewise, Hugh Ryan, who I marched with once at Pride, author of *When Brooklyn Was Queer*, and Eric Cervini, author of *The Deviant's War*—two exciting queer historians whose outspokenness has made me feel like yes, this history is there, and yes, it needs to be talked about—have been inspiring and made me feel like there is so much of our history yet to be discovered.

I also want to give a special thank you to Malinda Lo. Her book *Last Night at the Telegraph Club* is also queer fiction set in 1950s San Francisco, and though *Lavender House* was finished before that book came out, watching her succeed with it, watching the world respond so positively to it, has been wildly encouraging, and hearing her talk about research and history has made me feel so much less crazy. Feeling like I had a friend in this particular, kind of scary space (straight people love telling queer people we didn't exist before Stonewall!) has made me feel so much better about this book, like maybe this whole thing wasn't the worst idea I've ever had, which I only tricked people into publishing.

And to Chris, for being Chris.

Turn the page for a sneak peek
at Lev AC Rosen's next novel

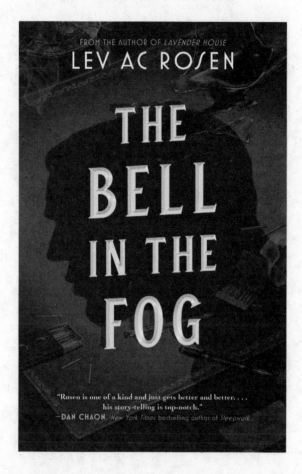

Available Fall 2023 from Forge Books

ONE

There's a crowd at the bar when I get inside, but I hang back, alone, and watch. There's a bucket swinging in my hand, rusted tin, filled with pinkish water, and my hands are dyed red. They match the walls of the Ruby, though it's so packed tonight, you can barely see the diamond wallpaper through the crowd. A constant hum of people talking over one another fills the room, pierced by a loud laugh here and there, like the church organ shrieking over the choir.

A few people stare at me—I don't know if it's the bucket or just knowing who I am, but they don't say anything. They look away, quick, back at a friend, or the stage, where the band plays "It's No Sin," the female impersonator's voice struggling to be heard.

People are dancing anyway, hands clasped, bodies close, men with men, women with women, some men with women, even. I haven't seen a mixed gay bar since the war, when women needed men to escort them in. All colors of people, too. Elsie has really gotten word out that the Ruby is the most welcoming queer bar in San Francisco.

Except maybe for me. News has trickled out about me, too—the gay PI with the office above the Ruby—but with it so has my past, and no one at a gay bar wants to get too close to a cop, even if he was kicked off the force for being caught in one. Especially not when he's holding a bucket of what looks like blood.

I push my way through the people who won't look at me, trying to be delicate, making sure the bucket doesn't spill, and make my way to the bar. Gene is pouring out drinks with steady hands that were trained for the scalpel before someone sent photos of him and a beau to his medical school. He looks gorgeous in the light. He glows. I know I should probably try talking to him more. But our kiss was months ago, and I was broken and bloody and glad to be alive. Since then, whenever I've gotten up the nerve to talk to him, he's smiled and laughed, same as he has with any other customer.

He looks down at the bucket I'm holding, and frowns.

"Need the sink?" he asks.

"If that's all right. I'm afraid I'll spill it if I try to bring it upstairs."

He moves to the left, making space for me, and I squeeze in next to him. Our shoulders touch and for a moment I think of asking him to dance, what that would be like, being out on the floor with him, shoulder to shoulder, arms around his waist. Like I belonged, I think. Like I was home.

I pour the red water out, and it sloshes loudly into the sink.

"That's not blood, is it?" a patron asks, watching. He's drunk enough to talk to me.

"Paint," I say. "Someone wrote some not-nice things on the building a few weeks back. No one else had time yet, so I washed it off."

"Aren't you supposed to be a detective?"

I shrug, not sure how to answer. The motion tilts the bucket a little harder and the last of the red water splashes back on me, hitting me in the face. The patron laughs as Gene hands me a towel.

"He is a detective," Gene says as I wipe my face off, hiding my smile. I hand the towel back to him.

"Thanks," I say, and go to wash my hands off, too. I scrub, and the paint won't shift. My hands stay stained.

"Want a drink?" Gene asks.

"No," I say. "Thanks." I stand next to him a moment longer until he reaches past me to get a bottle and I realize I'm in the way.

I leave the bucket under the sink where it belongs and retreat to an empty table away from the bar. Gene shoots me a look when I get there, but I can't read it—maybe he's confused about my not wanting a drink. I try not to order drinks. Elsie said they'd be on the house, but considering I'm not bringing in much money, like she hoped I would, I'd rather not drain her cash and her liquor. I'm supposed to be paying her a percentage of my earnings from cases, but cases aren't exactly pouring in. As a cop, they used to find me; now . . . I'm not sure how to get them. I wait in my office most nights, and sometimes someone will walk in, but most nights it's empty, so I come down here, and stand to the side, hoping that'll drum up business somehow. Tonight I at least got to make myself useful when one of the cocktail waitresses mentioned the graffiti. At least I cleaned up something.

Elsie sits down next to me. "Oh, will you just ask him out already?" she says, lighting a cigarette. She's in a blue suit turned nearly purple from all the red light bouncing off the walls. Large ruby earrings sparkle from the shadows of her bob.

"What do you mean?"

"I mean it's been months of you two making baby eyes at each other and nothing happening. If you don't do something soon, he's going to assume you're not interested in him. It's nearly October already, Andy, get to it if you want to ring in '53 with him."

"I don't . . ." I shake my head and look back at him. He's laughing at something a guy at the bar said. Maybe I've been making eyes at him, but has he really been making eyes at me, or just staring at my stare? "How would I even do that?"

"What?" Elsie blows out a smoke ring. "What do you mean?"

"I mean . . ." I don't know what I mean. Two women, one in a suit, dance past us.

She sighs. "You just go up to him and ask him if he wants to get a drink."

"He works at a bar."

"Somewhere else." Elsie shrugs.

"But—"

"Elsie, Stan is trying to sneak another number into his set."

I look up at Lee, the showgirl who's interrupted us, and check for lipstick; deep red tonight. She's in a yellow halter-neck dress that sets off her cool onyx skin, and a black wig that's tied back in a bun with a large yellow flower. She sees me staring, and winks. I've met a lot of the showgirls and -boys in passing, but Lee has been the closest to welcoming. She told me flat out that when she's got the lipstick on, to call her miss, and when it comes off, to call him sir, and if I did that, we'd be pals. Easy enough to check. I don't want to mess it up and have the friendliest face in the hallway, maybe the whole city, stop talking to me.

"Oy vey," Elsie says, looking at the stage, where Stan, the female impersonator, is readying the mic for another number. "I'll take care of it."

"Sorry, Andy," Lee says, "didn't mean to steal her away."

"It's fine," I say as Elsie stands.

"You have a fella waiting in your office, by the way. Nice shoulders."

"Sad or angry?" I ask. Those are the two types I get. Sad men, wondering if their boyfriends are cheating on them, and angry men, convinced their boyfriends are cheating on them. Cheap work, tailing men meeting other men, or going home to the wives they haven't told anyone about, but I can't be picky. I'm new at this, and I need to bring in whatever I can.

"Not sure." Lee shakes her head. "I think he came up through the garage, though." The ground floor under the club is a garage with an entrance in the alley. There's parking down there; my car, Elsie's, some others—but with it being out of the way and a

THE BELL IN THE FOG   281

bouncer in the stairwell keeping an eye out for the cops, it's an easy way up to my office without even setting foot in the club.

"Better get to work, then," Elsie says, walking away, "and ask him out." She glances meaningfully over at Gene.

"Ask who out?" Lee asks, grinning at me. "You finally find a boy you like, Andy? It better not be Stan."

"No," I say quickly. "It's . . . something else. Thanks, Lee. Sorry I won't get to hear you sing. I'll try to get down before your set is over."

"You'll hear me through the floorboards, honey," she says, walking after Elsie, her hips swaying. Gene's eyes flicker to mine for a moment as I pass the bar, or maybe I imagine it, and he's just staring at a drink as he pours it. I can talk to him later. Leaving a client waiting means they have time to reconsider and walk out. Elsie hasn't set an expiration date on this little experiment of having an in-house detective, but I must seem like a bad idea by now. I bring in enough to feed myself, sure, but her percentage is much lower than the value of renting me the space, and we both know it. How long before she decides my office and apartment were better before, as storerooms for booze?

I have to shove through the crowds, and by the time I get halfway upstairs to my office, I can hear Lee singing "How High the Moon." The floor above the club is just a hallway from one elevator to stairs, with dark purple walls, and lined with doors, most of them open. The two closest to the elevator are my office and apartment, respectively, but the other four are the dressing rooms, doors always thrown open, the hallway bustling with performers and musicians and sometimes waitresses here on break, or fans coming to leave flowers for their favorite performers. People laugh and talk as loudly as downstairs as they paint on makeup or fake mustaches, zip up dresses, button vests. At first, the chaos worried me, but it actually feels like home, the same sort of clamor as working at the police station, only now I'm not looking over my shoulder to see if they're realizing the truth about me.

Right now, the hall is filled with white feathers slowly floating down through the air and scattered on the floor like flower petals after a thunderstorm. I glance into one of the dressing rooms and see Walter trying to squeeze into a white dress that's covered in feathers. Sarah, already in a full tuxedo, is trying to pull up the zipper for him, but it's not going, and he hops up and down, hoping to make it fit, shedding feathers as he does.

"It fit last week," he says.

"You got fat this week."

In the next room, two female impersonators are peeling off their makeup, cackling at a joke I didn't hear. A male impersonator is leaning against the wall, smoking. When I nod, she nods back, which is something. They never nodded back the first few months I was here. Even if they're coming to terms with my old life, they don't love that I'm suddenly living and working next door. Clients don't love it, either. Even with a covert way up here, the way people gossip, you need to be careful.

But I'm the only queer detective in town, so some of them still risk it. Even when I'm not here, someone always tells me if a client shows up. It's still uncommon enough it's noteworthy. Not that the cases are. I'd thought I could do something here, maybe make up for who I was. But all I do is follow people, tell people who love them their secrets. I'm not helping out the way I wanted. No one even trusts me enough to ask me when they're in real trouble. Why would they?

Elsie had the door redone when I moved in, AMETHYST INVESTIGATIONS stenciled in dark purple. I don't love the name, but I get why she chose it—being affiliated with the Ruby, being another of Elsie's gems—it means I'm trustworthy, like the Ruby is. Most welcoming gay club in San Francisco, most welcoming gay PI, too. In theory anyway. Certainly not everyone is buying it, though, or I'd have more business. I wonder who's desperate or angry enough to come see me tonight.

There's a man sitting in the chair that faces my desk. His back is to me, but I can see he's blond, broad shouldered, tall. I close the door with a click and he turns around.

Oh.

The recognition hits like an anchor that's dropped too fast, crashing into the seabed, into both of us, sand flying up, fish fleeing, a heavy thud, and a scar on the ocean floor.

He looks just as shocked as I feel. Well, at least that's two of us.

"I didn't realize it would be you," he says, almost apologetically. He stands up. "I can go. I mean, I should go."

I think about letting him. He can drift out the door like smoke and I can go back to thinking of him as a sour memory. But I can't be turning down clients. And . . . I want to know. What happened.

I shake my head. "No, sit down. If you're here, there's not many other places you can go, right?"

"Sure, but—"

"James. Don't worry. I can help."

I make my face calm, professional, even smile a little, though it kills me, and I go around to my side of the desk. He looks almost the same, even though it's been seven years. He has gray creeping in at his sideburns, but is still shockingly handsome, with a square jaw and bright blue eyes that not even the dark circles can hide.

"So," he says after a moment, and I realize he's been looking at me the way I've been looking at him, finding all the changes, all the things that stayed the same. "Been a while, huh?"

I stare at him. I don't know what to say to that. He's the one who vanished. A faint whiff of him comes across the desk. Pine, the ocean. Just like he used to smell. For a moment, it's like the lines in his forehead and the grays vanish, and it's just us again, like when we were alone on base, or in the sonar cabin of the *Bell*, all our crewmates somewhere else. Just dim light, him, me, the sway of the ocean, our hands and bodies. He used to hold me tight when the ship really rocked. Kiss my earlobe.

I realize I haven't said anything, and so does he. "You look well," he says, smiling. He never could handle the silence. He always had to fill it with a grin or a joke or his mouth on mine.

"Thank you," I say. And as I get used to this—the two of us together again—I suddenly realize there's another presence.

"You ever hear from Helen?" he asks, as if sensing it, too.

I shake my head. "Not for years."

Helen had been the third of our motley crew—a member of WAVES, the navy women's auxiliary. Never went on a ship, but worked at Treasure Island, as a driver. After James vanished, though, we couldn't make the friendship work, just the two of us. The crater he left in our lives with his sudden disappearance, with us not knowing what had happened—it was so big, too terrifying to keep sidestepping. But I don't tell him all that. He doesn't get to know what he left behind.

Lee's voice comes through the floor, just like she promised, but it's muffled, the lyrics unclear. Just the sound of a voice, and music, too foggy to have any real meaning.

"Why don't we talk about why you're here," I say.

"Yeah. That's probably better than dwelling on the past."

"Sure," I say. "Better than that."

He swallows. He was barely prepared to do this, and then it was a swell of old memories that came in the door. I almost feel for him. But then I remember his bed on base, right next to mine, but empty one morning. Perfectly made. His luggage gone. His locker door hanging open, nothing inside. Not even a letter. Just emptiness waiting to be filled with fear and questions: Had they caught him? Was I next?

"I'm up for a promotion," he says finally. "Rear admiral, lower half."

"Oh," I say, trying not to look like I was just slapped across the face. "Congratulations. I didn't realize you'd stayed in the navy."

"Well, yeah," he says, tilting his head, confused. He used to do that a lot. "That's why I—" He stops himself. "After the thing with the spy, the brass noticed me."

I nod. He knew a little German from his grandmother. He'd never told anyone that—knowing German was suspicious during the war—but he overheard some supposed tourists speaking it on base, trying to get something to the mainland, and he'd reported it. He'd stumbled onto a spy, stopped a Nazi plot. But there was barely time to celebrate—the *Bell* left for Okinawa, our first real action since we'd enlisted, aside from escorting ships between San Francisco and Pearl Harbor.

We didn't get back until the end of '45. We spent our days looking for enemy subs and clearing out underwater mines around the coast—I ran the sonar, searching, and James was the captain's secretary. But we'd known each other before that. We'd come through training together. We were always together.

His eyes look the same now. He stares at me, waiting for a reaction.

"I remember," I say finally.

He nods, and takes out a cigarette case from his jacket pocket, offers me one, which I take. We tap our cigarettes on the desk almost in unison and then he takes out a lighter and brings it to his cigarette. Then, without even looking at me, without hesitating, he leans over the desk and lights mine, his fingers close to my mouth. I don't even realize how intimate it is until it's over. Old

habits, memories our bodies haven't gotten rid of, the way alco-
holics undo themselves drinking any glass put in front of them
without realizing.

"Well . . ." he says, and blows smoke out between his lips in a
long gust, "after that, I was on officer track. Worked hard. Kept
my nose clean, y'know?"

"A change for you, then?"

He laughs, but it's sad. "Yes, well. That was the point. I
mean . . . we all knew it wasn't going to last. The . . . openness.
Right? The moment we took Okinawa I knew. The rules were
going to change back as soon as we won the war." James always
knew when the party was over. When to leave the bar before the
raid, when to not go out at all. He said it felt like a thermometer,
and the mercury was fun, release, going up up up . . . you had to
leave before it hit the top. People like us, we only get our fun in
doses, like junkies. Too much and you're dead.

"Just one of your feelings?" I ask.

He nods, cigarette smoke swirling around him at the ges-
ture, like a frame around his portrait. "After we got back it was
boiling. We'd gotten away with so much. Not every homosexual,
I know. But you and me, we were lucky, Captain Teller didn't
care much as long as we were good at our jobs. Some captains
would have had us court-martialed just for the way we smiled at
each other. With the war over, guys leaving, the navy bringing
in those new shrinks to study us . . . it was time to go. No more
fun for a while." He looks at me, a little sad, and then up at the
ceiling. "Anyway, that's where I am today. Captain."

"That's fast," I say. "You must have really loved the job."

He doesn't wince at that, and I'm not sure he was supposed
to. "Well, a lot of guys left after the war, and I'd already been
to college. And I'm good at it, too. I always told you I would be
if they'd given me a chance. And now there's this rear admiral

spot. My name is being tossed around, now that Michaelson is retiring."

He pauses, takes a hit off his cigarette.

"Except?" I ask. "Someone make the captain spill about us?"

"Oh, no, I don't think . . . I mean, no one really remembers me then. I restarted. I was posted in the Atlantic until I made captain two years ago." He chuckles, low and familiar. "People call me Jim now. And with you gone . . ."

"Sure," I say, inhaling on my own cigarette. It's bitter.

"But there are some photos. More recent ones."

"I thought you said you kept your nose clean."

"I did. I do. But you know how it is, Andy. You go weeks, months, and you start to feel . . ."

"Yeah," I say, remembering how it felt at the station, the nights I was off duty and felt like I barely existed. "It doesn't feel like that if you're more open about things, for what it's worth." I decide I don't like the cigarette and twist it out in the ashtray on my desk. I haven't kissed anyone since Gene but I don't feel that ache, that loneliness like I used to. I haven't needed to shove myself against another man just to feel my own skin.

"Well . . . that must be nice," James says. He looks around my office and I follow his eyes: coatrack, desk, ashtray, pens, paper. On a shelf are some books my friend Pat lent me. I keep it discreet in here. Nothing personal. Still feels odd to have him looking around, like he might find something.

"I never got married, you know," he says, turning back to me. "I didn't want to do that to a woman, unless she was in on it. I suppose I could have asked Helen, but . . ."

"But that would have been even more trouble," I say.

"Yeah, she was always trouble." He smiles, inhales on his cigarette.

She'd recognized us from base, and come up to us one night

at a gay bar, fearless, to offer us a ride next time we were headed out—provided we escorted her in. The gay bars were more mixed then, men and women, and it suited us all to pair off, for appearances. But we got close. She was funny, flinty, wild both in a car and out of it, always going for the girls with boyfriends, husbands, diving out a back window when he came home. She'd pick us up from our hotel at the time we'd agreed, her blouse still half-buttoned from having to run.

"So the photos?" I ask, suddenly missing her more than I missed him. She didn't vanish. I let her slip away.

"Yeah, right." He nods, then puts the cigarette out. "Me and a professional. Not someone I picked up in a park or anything, not some punk looking to roll me. He's a fairy I see sometimes. Discreet. But then these photos came the other day. Not from him, I don't think. They're not signed. Tells me to leave ten grand in a locker Wednesday or else they get sent to the admirals. I'll get dishonorably discharged, maybe court-martialed." His voice is getting higher, reedier. "Andy, I don't have that kind of money. What am I supposed to do?"

"Why are you so sure it's not from the hooker?" I ask.

"Danny's a good guy. And I pay him well enough—why turn on me now?"

"He could need a payday—could be he's being blackmailed himself. Or he's moving, or just got tired of it and decided to cash out. Could be he only just got a camera."

"I don't think he—"

"What, another feeling?"

"I've never been wrong." He crosses his legs and starts rubbing his hand on his knee, like he's polishing something. His nervous tic. "Though I haven't been able to get in touch with him, either."

"Okay. You have the photos?"

"Do you really want to see them?" We lock eyes and I think about it. I don't.

"Do you know where they were taken?"

"Yeah. A hotel I use. Fake name, and he comes up later, we don't go in together. And the hotel never asks questions."

"What's the hotel?"

"It's on California, just east of Pacific Heights."

"Okay, but what's it called? I'm going to have to go there."

He looks away, won't meet my eyes. "The Belltower."

A laugh rips out of me like a knife.

"It just seemed like a good sign."

"Sure," I say. "You know what room they were taken in?"

"I always ask for the same one. High up enough there aren't other buildings out the window. Room 608."

I start jotting down notes. "And how did you meet, exactly? Did he have a madam or handler?"

"No, no, he was on his own. I met him at a bar—not a queer one. But he spotted me anyway, y'know, like we used to do with—" He stops. The past keeps pouring out of him, and he knows he's going to choke on it.

"You have a phone number, and address?"

"Just his phone number." He rattles it off, and I write that down, too.

"All right," I say.

"So you'll take the case?"

"I'll do what I can. I'm fifty bucks a day, plus expenses." It's higher than I usually charge. I'm entitled to some pettiness.

"Fine," he says. "But I need the photos—the negatives, too—by Wednesday or else . . ."

"I can't make any promises. But five days should be enough time. And if it's not, I can watch the locker, find out who's black-mailing you, get the money back."

"I don't have money like that, I can't even get it together."

He looks so sad for a moment, so scared, I feel a need to protect him. To hold him. He must be so desperate if he came here—a club where setting foot inside could get him fired if anyone saw. Then I remember that I felt the same way when he vanished, terrified that I would be next. The pity fades.

"We'll figure something out if it comes to that. But let me poke around first. Could just be Danny, desperate, and I can scare him off. All right?"

"Yeah . . . yeah." He takes a deep breath, goes to take out his cigarette case again, then stops. "You always looked out for me, Andy. I guess this is . . . just like old times."

"It's not, James."

"Maybe it could be?" he asks, standing. He takes the pen out of my hand and writes a phone number on the pad. He bends his body over the corner of the desk to write, and without the furniture between us, I can smell him clearly, feel him. Touch him if I wanted. There's a spot on his spine where if I ran my fingers, he would melt. I could take him to my room across the hall, better than the cheap motels we used. It would be easy, I think. He wants me to. The memories are like magnets, trying to snap our bodies back together.

He drops the pen. I look up at him. I think for a moment he's going to kiss me, and I don't know if I want him to or not.

"I'll be in touch," I say.

"I don't know if I'm glad or terrified that it ended up being you," he says softly.

"Only queer detective in town."

"I know. People talk about it. But I never thought . . . What did you do? After?"

"I left. I became a cop. That didn't work. Here I am."

"Do you hate me?"

He stares at me, narrowing his eyes a little, willing an answer out of me, but I don't know if he wants a yes or no. Below us, Lee is singing another song: "That Old Black Magic." The music rises up like perfume.

"Not anymore, James. It's been seven years. We don't even know each other."

It's a lie. He knows it's a lie as well as he knows me. Or some version of me. Some version of me that's already reaching up, hungry mouth first.

But that version of me isn't here, not now. We stare at each other a moment longer. Then he turns and goes.

ABOUT THE AUTHOR

Rachael Shane

LEV AC ROSEN writes books for people of all ages, most recently *Lavender House*, a Lambda Literary Award nominee. His young adult novel *Camp* was a best book of the year from *Forbes, Elle,* and *The Today Show,* among others. He lives in New York City with his husband and a very small cat.

levacrosen.com
Twitter: @LevACRosen
Instagram: @levacrosen